# The Secrets We Keep

# Also by Amy Lillard

**Kappy King Mystery Series**
*Barking Up the Wrong Tree*
*(Kappy King and the Puppy Kaper)*
*In a Pickle (Kappy King and the Pickle Kaper)*
*Pie in the Sky (Kappy King and the Pie Kaper)*
*This Little Pig (Kappy King*
*and the Pig Kaper)*

**Sunflower Café Mystery Series**
*Dairy, Dairy, Quite Contrary*
*A Murder of Aspic Proportions*
*A Murder for the Sages*

**Sugarcreek Amish Mystery Series**
*O Little Town of Sugarcreek*
*Shoo, Fly, Shoo*
*Stranger Things Have Happened*

**Other Amish Cozy Mysteries**
*Unsavory Notions*

**Main Street Book Club Series**
*Can't Judge a Book by Its Murder*
*A Murder Between the Pages*
*A Murder Like No Author*

**Other Contemporary Cozies**
*Pattern of Betrayal*

**Clover Ridge Series**
*Saving Gideon*
*Katie's Choice*
*Gabriel's Bride*

**Wells Landing Series**
*Caroline's Secret*
*Courting Emily*
*Lorie's Heart*
*Just Plain Sadie*
*Titus Returns*
*Marrying Jonah*
*The Quilting Circle*
*A Wells Landing Christmas*
*Loving Jenna*
*Romancing Nadine*
*A New Love for Charlotte*
*More Than Friendship (e-novella)*
*More Than a Promise (e-novella)*
*More Than a Marriage (e-novella)*

**Harlequin Love Inspired**
*The Amish Christmas Promise*
*The Amish Bachelor's Promise*

**Amish of Pontotoc**
*A Home for Hannah*
*A Love for Leah*
*A Family for Gracie*
*An Amish Husband for Tillie*

**Paradise Novellas**
*The Amish Christmas Sleigh*
*(A Mamm for Christmas)*
*Amish Brides (A Summer Wedding in Paradise)*

**Paradise Valley Series**
*Marry Me, Millie*
*The Amish Matchmaker*
*One More Time for Joy*
*When Hattie Finds Love*

**Stand Alone Historical Romance Novellas**
*As Good as Gold*
*No Greater Treasure*
*Not So Pretty Penny*

**Brides of Calico Falls**
*The Gingerbread Bride*
*The Wildflower Bride*

# Writing as Amie Louellen

**Cattle Creek Series**
*Loving a Lawman*
*Healing a Heart*

**Mayhem and Magnolias Series**
*Southern Hospitality*
*Southern Comfort*
*Southern Charm*

**Stand-Alone Romance**
*All You Need Is Love*
*Blame It on Texas*
*Brodie's Bride*
*Can't Buy Me Love*
*Forget Me Not, Baby*
*Love Potion Me, Baby*
*Take Me Back to Texas*
*Ten Reasons Not to Date a Cop*

# The Secrets We Keep

*A Novel*

## AMY LILLARD

NEW YORK

Books should be disposed of and recycled according to local requirements. All paper materials used are FSC compliant.

This is a work of fiction. All of the names, characters, organizations, places and events portrayed in this novel are either products of the author's imagination or are used fictitiously. Any resemblance to real or actual events, locales, or persons, living or dead, is entirely coincidental.

Copyright © 2025 by Amy Lillard

All rights reserved.

Published in the United States by Crooked Lane Books, an imprint of The Quick Brown Fox & Company LLC.

Crooked Lane Books and its logo are trademarks of The Quick Brown Fox & Company LLC.

Library of Congress Catalog-in-Publication data available upon request.

ISBN (hardcover): 979-8-89242-124-9
ISBN (paperback): 979-8-89242-245-1
ISBN (ebook): 979-8-89242-125-6

Cover design by Joceyln Martinez

Printed in the United States.

www.crookedlanebooks.com

Crooked Lane Books
34 West 27th St., 10th Floor
New York, NY 10001

First Edition: June 2025

The authorized representative in the EU for product safety and compliance is eucomply OÜ Pärnu mnt 139b-14, 11317 Tallinn, Estonia, hello@eucompliancepartner.com, +33757690241

10 9 8 7 6 5 4 3 2 1

*To Rob:*
*Simply the best.*
*Thank you. Always.*

# Prologue

The sight before her was real, crisp and tangible, yet unbelievable. Wholly unbelievable. Was it because she didn't want to imagine what her eyes were seeing was true? Or was it because she didn't want to trust what her heart knew but didn't want to acknowledge?

"Dat?" Her voice trembled with her tumbling emotions. Disbelief, the building grief, the horror of the sight before her.

Her brother, her sweet, sweet Albie, was hanging from a rafter in the barn. He swung back and forth, ever gently, horrifically. One side of his face was swollen and bruised. Murky stains dripped down the front of his homespun blue shirt. Dried blood was caked in the strands of his dark-blond hair, clumping it together in near-black tufts. His eyes were open, red and staring at nothing.

Everything else around her was exact. The sounds of the animals shifting in their stalls, the buggy horses gently chuffing, the occasional bird flying in, then fluttering back out again. The smell was the same as it had always been, the scent of hay, manure, and good Mississippi dirt. From somewhere outside, the old hateful rooster crowed that it was morning the same way he did every day. It was just him, her brother, hanging there that made it all seem like a nightmare.

It didn't *seem* like anything. She didn't have to pinch herself to prove that she was awake, that the sight before her was real. It *was* a nightmare. A nightmare she wouldn't wake from.

"This—" Her father started, then shook his head. Like her, he was overcome with choking emotions. Sadness, disbelief, grief, anger. She didn't know which one to allow herself to feel first.

"Get him down, Dat. Please get him down."

Samuel Gingerich grabbed a utility knife from the worktable in the tack room, then moved toward the vertical ladder that led to the hayloft.

She started toward him. Until that moment she hadn't realized that she had been frozen in place, stuck to the ground beneath her in shock. She wanted to grab her brother's legs, support him in some way, even as she knew it would do no good. He dangled too high in the air and those blank, staring eyes . . .

"I don't understand," her father said. Unshed tears added a thickness to the words, and it seemed that perhaps they were almost too heavy to say. His voice sounded tired and old. Worn down with the loss he had to face.

"What if he's still alive?" She said the words knowing they weren't true, knowing she was just babbling. She had been standing there locked to the ground, watching instinctively to see if her brother was still breathing, even as she knew the truth. Albie had been hanging there for a while. Somehow she knew: He had been there all night.

"Wait," she cried, rushing toward her father. "We need to call the police." She turned as if to do just that, but there was no phone in their barn like some of the fancier Amish she had heard about in Pennsylvania and Ohio. She would have to run to the nearest *Englisch* neighbor's house to use the phone.

# The Secrets We Keep

Her father paused only for a moment before continuing up the ladder. "No police," he said. His voice held the stern note of authority. He was the *vatter* and his word was final. "This is a family matter. We will deal with it as a family."

Rachel wanted to protest, wanted to go over all the possibilities they needed to consider. It was a family matter. It was a shameful family matter. Suicide. What an ugly word. One that didn't go with her beautiful Albie.

"He couldn't have done this," she said. Her words were coming out too fast, and she couldn't get in enough air to support her lungs. "Albie would have never done this." Her feet, once glued to the dirt floor of the barn, seemed unable to be still now. She paced back and forth, two steps, maybe three, before she spun around and went in the opposite direction.

Her father stopped, turned to face her, tears shining in his pale-blue eyes. "But he did," he said sadly. "He did it, and now we have to deal with it. But our way. Not the *Englisch* way."

She watched, horrified, as he continued up the ladder to the loft. Just as her brother had done some time in the night. But he wouldn't be coming down the same way.

"Mamm?"

Rachel gasped and whirled around at the sleepy voice that sounded behind her.

"Kate." She scooped her four-year-old daughter into her arms and pressed her head down. The child shouldn't see the scene in the barn. She shouldn't see her *onkle* hanging there.

Behind her, Rachel could hear her father cutting the rope that held Albie suspended in the air. But she couldn't watch. She wasn't sure, but she thought she heard a sob. Her tough, stoic father reduced to tears. But she didn't turn around to check on him. She

3

gave him the privacy she knew he would want. Besides, she had other matters to attend to.

"What's going on in the barn?" Kate asked. She had never been one to take life at face value. Ever inquisitive, she was continually asking questions about one thing or another. And Rachel knew she was sure to have a great many questions about why Albie had died and her *mamm* was so sad. "Are the puppies being borned?"

"No, *liebschdi*."

"I want to see," Kate insisted.

"Not now," Rachel said in the most soothing tone she could muster. Unfortunately, her voice broke on a sob. She needed to keep it together, if not for her own sake, then for that of her two girls. "Are you hungry?" she asked Kate, hoping to divert the girl's rapt attention from the happenings in the barn.

"*Jah*," Kate replied. She nodded to back up her announcement and, in the same motion, forced Rachel to release her head. "I'm so very hungry."

Rachel blinked back tears at those innocent words. Now was not the time for crying. She had a daughter to feed. Two of them, actually. As well as her sister and her father. "Good. Let's go make everyone some breakfast." She set Kate on the ground, and immediately her little bare feet turned to take her back into the barn.

"I'll get Dawdi," she said.

"No." Rachel caught her arm and hauled Kate back to her side. "He'll be along when he's ready."

"Okay." Kate didn't look too happy about leaving him behind. "What about the milk?"

Rachel bit back a sigh and pasted on a trembling smile. "Today the milk can wait."

# The Secrets We Keep

"It can?" Her *dawdi* liked his milk fresh, still warm from the udder.

"*Jah*. And"—she dragged out the word in an expectant manner—"today we're having something special for breakfast." Anything to distract Kate from the truth.

"What is it?"

Rachel's mind searched for an answer, but she couldn't see past the image of Albie hanging in the barn. "You'll just have to wait and see," she finally managed.

"But it's a good something special?"

"*Jah*." Rachel's voice choked, but thankfully Kate was too intrigued with the unnamed surprise to notice.

"Whoo!" Kate skipped ahead, none of the world's pressures weighing her down. "Can I wake up Amelie and tell her?"

"Of course," Rachel replied. She could use all the distractions she could get.

"Amelie! Amelie! Amelie!" Kate called as she ran into the house. The screen door slammed behind her. "Guess what?"

Rachel stopped on the porch. Her knees nearly buckled. She wanted to go back and help her *dat*. Check once more to see if maybe, please God maybe, Albie was still alive. But she pulled in a deep breath and said a small prayer that what they were doing was right. That they really didn't have any other choice. He was already gone.

But later she would look back and wonder why she had bowed once again to her father's command. Habit? Upbringing? Both always played a role in an Amish woman's decision-making, but she knew what really kept her in the kitchen that morning. It was the fact that she didn't want to fight against the truth. That her brother had indeed killed himself.

*You can't go back home to your family, back home to your childhood . . . back home to a young man's dreams of glory and of fame . . . back home to places in the country, back home to the old forms and systems of things which once seemed everlasting, but which are changing all the time—back home to the escapes of Time and Memory.*

—Thomas Wolfe,
*You Can't Go Home Again*

# Chapter One

〜

"Nathan?"

Nate Fisher had never thought he would hear that gruff yet familiar voice ever again. Only in his dreams sometimes did it come to him once more. Yet it was a voice he knew well. Almost as well as he knew his own.

"Leroy," he said in return.

On the other end of the line, his brother cleared his throat, unaccustomed to talking on the phone. "Dat's dead."

The words seemed so simple and yet not.

Nate sat back down in his worn leather chair. He had been about to go get some lunch, but now . . .

Now his legs were numb, his heart stalled. The world around him buzzed along, and yet he was . . . still.

"I'm sorry." It was the only thing he could think to say. The news had locked up his thoughts, his emotions, everything. For so long he had not allowed himself to feel anything about leaving his family behind—his father, his mother, his siblings. But now, with his brother's words, all his dammed-up emotions threatened to break free.

"He was your *vatter* too."

"Yes." Nate studied the toes of his cowboy boots and tried to think of something else to say.

Karl Fisher was indeed his father, but he hadn't spoken to him in over twelve years. Not since the night Nate had packed and left the Amish for the outside world.

The line was silent, and for a moment he thought perhaps they had been disconnected.

"Lee?" he asked.

"I'm here. I just thought you should know."

"When's the funeral?"

"Tomorrow, but—"

*You aren't welcome. Don't come home.*

Like he considered Mississippi his home. Once, but no longer.

Nate cleared his throat.

"Okay," his brother said. "That's all I needed." But there was still so much more to say. "Goodbye, Nathan."

It was left unsaid.

"Bye, Leroy."

Nate hung up the receiver and stared off at nothing, the wall, the space that happened to be ahead of him. Idly, he thumped a pencil against his desk blotter, a calendar that was normally scratched with scrawled notes and messages to himself—dates, times, and appointments. But it was clean now. Today was his third day back at work since his time off from "the incident."

Or at least that was what he had been calling it.

It had to have a name, and since no one was willing to call it what it really was . . .

He had shot someone. In the line of duty. Justifiable, but resulting in a death all the same.

"Fish?"

Nate turned as Travis eased up from the side. Travis Nelson was tall, thin, and a little dorky looking, with thick-lensed glasses

# The Secrets We Keep

perched delicately on his hooked nose. He was like a rougher version of the scarecrow from *The Wizard of Oz*, and he was the closest thing Nate had to a partner, since the detectives didn't work in set pairs. Travis was probably his best friend in Tulsa, but his father's death was something Nate didn't want to talk about yet. Not with anyone.

"I'm all right." The words were instinctive. They came without him calling them. They had become habit.

"Funny how you keep saying that." Travis allowed the sentence to trail off to nothing.

"You need something?" Nate hadn't intended for his words to come out so angry, but they were blistering.

Never one to be put off by someone else's mood, Travis held up both hands and took a step back. "Easy there, player. I just came to see if you wanted to go get something to eat."

Five minutes ago, Nate would have said yes, but five minutes ago he hadn't known his father was dead. Now he only wanted to be alone.

Nate shook his head and gestured toward the file on his desk. "I should probably stay and work on this." *This* was a robbery gone wrong on the west side, just outside the city limits where truck stops led the way to the turnpike.

And *this* could wait. A fact both he and Travis knew. Just as Travis knew Nate wasn't all right as he had claimed countless times over the last three days and before he had even returned to work from administrative leave.

Investigation was standard procedure when deadly force was used. Did the officer need to draw his weapon? Did he need to fire? Was his response excessive or in line with the situation? Nate had been given a clean bill on all accounts, but the nightmares continued. He still woke in the wee hours of the morning in a cold sweat after dreaming he had carried the young man from the crime scene all the way to the hospital, cradling him in one arm while he held the boy's guts in with the other.

"You sure?" Travis would only push so far.

"I'm sure." Nate picked up the file as if that were proof enough of the work that needed to be done. "But you can bring me back something if you don't mind."

"Of course. I'll text you from wherever we decide to go."

Nate waved away the words. "Whatever's fine." Then he opened the file and stuck his nose inside until he was certain Travis was gone. Thankfully, he had taken the other two detectives who had still been in the office with him. That left Nate by himself.

He had thought that would be a comfort, but it felt as if the walls were closing in on him.

His father was gone.

Nate could still remember the last angry words they had shared twelve long years ago. His father informing him that he was sure to go to hell if he left; Nate remaining prideful and unwilling to tell his father that more than anything he had to go for Mattie. His sister needed him. God had given him a talent for baseball, and he could use that talent to get the money she needed for medical bills and medications and doctor appointments. So many expenses. The way some of these players got paid, he might even have enough to buy her a new heart. But not if he stayed in Cedar Creek.

So he had left. That was the last time he'd spoken to his father. It was the last time he had spoken to anyone in his family except for when Mattie died four years later. And now today.

Nate dropped the file back on his desk. Keeping up the pretense of working was no longer necessary. He was alone.

## The Secrets We Keep

His father was gone. It was the only thought filling his mind.

It was over. There would never be a reconciliation. Truthfully, he had never counted on one, but as long as his father had been alive, there had been a possibility. Now that was gone too. That and the potential for something more.

Suddenly, all his feelings came surging back in a tidal wave that threatened to drown him with its intensity. It rose higher and higher until it cut off his air, all the life-giving oxygen he needed. His throat clogged, his eyes watered, and a sound unlike any he had ever made squeezed from his throat. It was too much. Everything was simply too much.

He braced his elbows on his desk and buried his face in his hands.

"Fish?"

He jerked back and looked into Travis's concerned eyes once again.

"Don't tell me you're all right," Travis said. "I've never believed it before, and I sure as hell don't now."

"My . . . my father died."

"And you're sitting here?"

Nate swallowed hard. "I thought you had gone to lunch."

Travis shook his head at himself. "I forgot my wallet." The man who could track down the smallest lead in a case and bring culprits to justice was hopeless when it came to matters other than police work. Like matching his tie to the rest of his clothes and remembering to brush his teeth. Which was why Trav carried an extra toothbrush in his car. And why he was back in the office when Nate had thought he was gone.

"Tell the captain and get out of here," Travis said. He obviously didn't expect Nate to do as he instructed, since he pulled up a chair and sat down next to him.

**Amy Lillard**

"It's not important," Nate said. "We weren't close."

"It is important. It's always important with family."

At one time it had been, but that time had passed. He had ruined it with pipe dreams and arrogance.

But now that his father was gone . . .

"Go tell the captain," Travis started once again. "Then get in your truck and head back to Missouri."

"Mississippi," Nate corrected solemnly.

"Wherever," he continued. "You need to be there for the funeral."

Nate shook his head. "I'm not welcome at the funeral."

Travis sat up as if someone had goosed him with a cattle prod. "How can you not be welcome at your own father's funeral?"

That was simply too complicated to even try to explain. "The Amish have more rules about such things than the *Englisch*."

"I keep forgetting that you were raised Amish." Trav shook his head. "Wait . . . Amish in Mississippi? Is that really a thing?"

"Yep."

"It just doesn't compute," Travis said.

Nate didn't respond. Travis didn't want to hear the history of how the Amish had made their way into the Magnolia State and Nate didn't want to recount it, but they were there and thriving. Making it just fine all these years without Nate.

"Go talk to the captain," Travis quietly intoned. "Take a long weekend. You can start again on Monday."

Start again on Monday. Was it as simple as that?

\* \* \*

Nate looked around his apartment and ticked off a mental checklist. He was only going overnight, but he felt as if he was forgetting

## The Secrets We Keep

something. Something important. The stove was off. The lamp was on for safety. Nothing out of place.

*Time to go,* he told himself. He opened the door and stepped out into the breezeway. The bed was made, the refrigerator shut, the iron off. Like he had ironed anything in the last decade. And still he felt like he was forget—

The cat!

Nate dropped his carryall in the doorway and walked back into the apartment. Okay, so truthfully, the large brindle tabby wasn't his. But the rough-looking stray with one ear had looked so angry and forlorn that Nate felt they were somehow connected. Kindred spirits, Bree had said. He hadn't taken the time to examine what it implied. He had bought a bag of cat food and that was that.

He grabbed it and headed back to the door. He poured a large amount into the bowl that sat just outside his apartment. The bowl next to it contained water, though he had seen the tabby drinking out of the fountain that sat in front of the building.

Now. Surely he was ready to go.

The funeral was in the early afternoon, so he'd still be on the road when it happened. He would drive into Cedar Creek, maybe on into Tupelo, where the motels were more plentiful. After the eight-hour drive, he would spend the night, and in the morning he would get up and head to the cemetery. He would visit the grave for a bit, and afterward he would head back home. Then, on Monday . . . he would start again.

"Going somewhere?"

Nate turned as Bree, his across-the-way neighbor, came out of her apartment. Most likely she had heard him scraping around in the breezeway that separated their front doors. She was still dressed in her pajamas, though her hair had been fixed and her makeup was under construction.

"Yeah," Nate said, not elaborating.

He and Bree had been on-again, off-again since he had moved in four years ago. Neither of them was looking for anything serious, just friends with benefits. At least that was what she had told him, but there were times when he saw something more in her eyes. And *more* was something he just couldn't give.

"You're going to attract possums with all that mess." She nodded toward the overflowing bowl. They might be in the middle of a city, the forty-seventh largest in the country, but there were still critters lurking about.

"Then will you feed Satchel while I'm gone?" He held up the bag of cat food for her to see.

"Of course." She stepped out and took the bag from him, held it open while he poured the cat food back inside. "When are you coming back?"

"Tomorrow. Probably late."

Her perfectly arched brows rose above her cinnamon-colored eyes. "Quick trip."

"Yeah."

"Everything okay?"

"Yeah."

She paused, waiting for him to elaborate, but he didn't. He wasn't about to get into a discussion about his father, their broken relationship, and all the reasons why he was missing the funeral, including but not limited to the fact that he was under the *Bann* and he wasn't allowed or invited to attend. It was simply too much to have to explain to someone who most likely wouldn't understand. Plus he really wanted to get on the road. If

# The Secrets We Keep

he left now, he would make it just in time to have supper at the Grill.

"Be careful." Bree stepped a bit closer and pressed a kiss to his cheek. He could feel her warmth through the T-shirt she wore, the softness of her. Then she moved away.

"I will," he promised, and it was one he would keep. He needed the drive, slow and steady, to help him clear his head. To brush away the cobwebs of memories that were stored in the back of his brain, those he had pushed away long ago and never brought out again. There were those and so many more, a lifetime of celebrations, dreams, and promises that would never come true.

His father was gone, and any of those dreams of reconciliation with him would never be realized now. There was a small measure of hope with his mother, but not yet. Now was the time for saying goodbye. Maybe later, in a few months, he could make his way back and see if his mother's attitude toward him had softened any with his father's passing. But he knew that was more of a pipe dream than baseball had turned out to be.

"Don't forget to feed my cat," he told Bree.

She shook the bag at him with a smile.

Nate returned it and headed for his truck.

The drive didn't take nearly long enough. It was just after five when he pulled to a stop in front of the offices of the Americana Inn. The motel had been there for as long as he could remember and, for the most part, looked as run-down as it always had. It had changed hands over the years and had been painted a rainbow of colors, but he was certain it was still the cheapest place to stay in town. It wasn't like he was going to be there long.

So much for driving into Tupelo. But now that he was here . . .

# Amy Lillard

The sun wouldn't set for a couple of hours, and it surely wouldn't be dark until well after eight. He could swing by the Grill and get a bite to eat, then head over to the cemetery. He would pay his respects—if that was what you could really call looking at the mound of dirt that covered his father's coffin—and be asleep in his room by ten.

He would be back on the road to Oklahoma first thing in the morning, he thought as he opened the glass door that led to the motel's front desk. In and out, and no one would be the wiser. It was better that way, he told himself. Better for everyone.

Room rented and belly full, Nate headed out to the cemetery. Just because he went tonight didn't mean he couldn't go again tomorrow, maybe even hang out a little before heading back. The call of his home was strong. All the emotions he had been ignoring, pushing aside for so long, were rising to the surface unbidden. He had Bree keeping an eye on things, and he *was* supposed to be getting his head together.

But if that was the case, he should just start for home now. There was no getting his head together in Mississippi. Too many ghosts lingered, spirits from days long past. The happiness of youth and the hope of a future. But none of that existed for him. Not any longer. In spite of all his wishing, it was the way it was.

He swung himself into his truck, then took off his straw Stetson and slid it between the windshield and the dash. He headed toward the edge of town where the Amish cemetery was located.

Like most, his childhood hadn't been all that bad nor all that good. It was filled with enough love from his mother, more than his fair share of discipline from his father, and plenty of direction from the church. But then, baseball . . .

# The Secrets We Keep

In those early days he liked to tell himself that he had only left because of Mattie. The youngest Fisher child had been born with a severe heart defect. There were always doctor appointments, prescription medications, special diets, herbs, other pills, and massages. His mother was willing to try everything short of voodoo to heal his sister. When Mattie was ten, it became increasingly apparent that her best chance for survival was a heart transplant.

Nate had argued with this father then. He had a plan to help Mattie. His father disagreed, disapproved. In the end, Nate had left the Amish to pursue a career in baseball and get his sister a heart. He had failed at both.

His own heart thumped heavier in his chest as he thought about that time. He turned his truck onto the red dirt gravel road. It was only May, but the heat was already in the upper eighties. It wouldn't have been so bad had the humidity not been in the nineties. But this was the South.

Nate navigated the road, missing ruts and holes gouged out by the motorized *Englisch* farm equipment and a recent rain. In a day or two, someone would come out and grade the road and smooth most of the spots back into place. In a day or two it wouldn't matter. He'd be back in Tulsa, in his apartment, doing his best to start again. Life after death.

He'd forgotten how poor the area was. Well, he remembered, but seeing it again sharpened those memories that had been worn down by time. Even the *Englisch* houses out this way were run-down and in obvious need of repair. Tires had been tossed onto tin roofs to hold the pieces in place. Others had been turned into yard planters. It was still early in the year, and those who had actually taken the time and money to plant something in the space still had flowers blooming. But he knew as well as anyone that, come June, there wouldn't be the time nor the water to keep everything alive. It just got too damned hot down here for the average person to care for such a luxury.

He passed the Levi Gingerich farm. Levi and his family had been some of the first settlers in the area. Then families like Nate's had joined. They'd even had a few groups move down from Ohio in search of more land to farm. Every mailbox was a stab of nostalgia.

There was an *Englisch* writer who had said you can never go home again. Nate understood what that meant now. He was sure the man said that because it hurt too badly to see all that you left behind. And once you were away . . .

Half a mile down Pots Road, Nate slowed his truck. There was a small place for him to pull into the cemetery itself, just a gap in the rusted barbed wire barely big enough to navigate through. There was no sign in place to tell passersby that it was there. Nothing but a narrow dirt lane with a strip of grass growing down the middle. Bitterweed, wild daisies, and other grasses grew up on the back side of the wire fence and hid the plots from view.

Nate parked on the opposite side of the road. He waited a second for the dust to settle before redonning his hat and letting himself out of his truck. He crossed over to the cemetery's entrance, his boots crunching against the gravel. Just as he got there, a horse and buggy filled the opening in the fence.

He had no excuse for why he hadn't seen it, only that it was such a natural sight to him that it didn't register that someone was already there when he arrived. Some late mourner of his father's, perhaps, or even a widow or widower come to visit the grave of their lost loved one.

**The Secrets We Keep**

Nate raised his hand in a wave but stopped before the action was complete. The very last person he had expected to see was driving the dusty black buggy.

Rachel.

Her name echoed inside his head.

She saw him too. Her face grew pale, and her mouth became a thin line. She appeared locked in time, but only for a moment. She roused herself and lifted her chin before snapping the reins over the horse's back and urging the chestnut gelding to move a bit faster.

Quick as a wink she was gone, and he was left staring at the back of her buggy.

Two pairs of hands clasped the edge of the rear window. He could see two gray prayer coverings that little girls wore and two sets of green eyes watching him as they drove away.

The rain started just after dark and brought a bit of relief to the oppressive heat. He had been away from Mississippi for years, and his body had adjusted to the lower humidity of the Sooner State. Tomorrow he would get up, check out, and head back to Oklahoma. He didn't belong here. Rachel's reaction toward him was proof enough. There had been a time, before he had decided that he could play ball and help Mattie, when he had thought he would marry Rachel.

He had only seen her for a moment this evening, but she was the same. A little older, but still as beautiful to him now as she had been then. Honey-blond hair and meadow-green eyes the same color as the two sets of eyes that had stared at him from the back of her buggy. She had daughters. Daughters who, for the brief glimpse he had gotten of them, looked very much like their mother.

21

Nate stood at the window in his motel room and gazed out over the parking lot. It was empty except for his big black Chevy. Rain pounded down, drops bouncing into puddles and wetting everything in sight. He had lived here as a farmer's son, and he remembered such rains. It might not be hurricane season, but any storm that blew in from the Gulf kept going north, drenching everything in its path. A tropical depression maybe, just up from the coast. Once the rain stopped, the humidity would rise even higher than before.

No matter; he was leaving tomorrow.

A knock sounded on the door and gave him a start. He had been too wrapped up in his thoughts and watching the rain fall that he hadn't noticed anyone approaching. No car had driven up, so it had to be the lady behind the front desk. She had questioned him as to how many occupants would be in the room. When he told her one, she seemed not to believe him. He had no idea why. She just asked him again and then once more before he signed his credit card slip and took the key card from her reluctant hand. Perhaps she had decided she needed to see his single occupancy for herself.

Then again, it was after eleven. That would take some strong suspicions, but he supposed anything was possible.

He moved away from the window, unable to see who was at the door from that angle, and peered out the peephole. It wasn't the dark-haired Indian lady with the bindi on her forehead. It was Rachel.

Yes, truly anything was possible.

His heart stuttered in his chest. Just the sight of her made him . . . well, it didn't matter what it did to him. She had married another. Nate had had his chance—*twice*—and he'd blown it both times. Now there was no going back. Yet his hand trembled as he slid the chain lock free and opened the door.

# The Secrets We Keep

There she stood. Rachel. His Rachel. Not his Rachel. Freeman Hostetler's Rachel. She had given Nate four years to come back and marry her. When he hadn't, she had found another.

The pounding of his heart and the dryness in his mouth had nothing to do with love. He was thinking about that *Englisch* author again. Those words. Nate knew he couldn't come back home. Shouldn't come back. He'd been too long in the modern world. It was so much easier to adjust to having electricity and freedoms than it was to adjust to a world without them. Being forced to confront Rachel, knowing she belonged to another and knowing they would never be . . .

"Can I . . . can I come in?"

Nate pulled himself from his thoughts and took a step back. She eased into the room, barely setting her feet inside before stopping.

She was dressed just as he remembered her—homemade blue *frack*, faded purple apron, black lace-up shoes. She had covered her white prayer *kapp* with one of the stiff black bonnets that Amish ladies wore when traveling. Raindrops sparkled on the heavily starched material.

"Sorry." She gave a small chuckle, but it ended more like a sob. "I'm dripping and getting your rug all wet."

He shrugged. "It's not my rug." It was the motel's carpet, and he supposed Bindi Lady would charge him for whatever cleanup the mess required. He didn't care. Even so, he moved toward the bathroom and grabbed one of the white bath towels hanging on the rail. He handed it to Rachel.

"*Danki.*" She smiled, and he swore the simple action took him back twelve years. To *before*.

That was how he saw it now. In befores and afters. Before he left. After he had tried to save his sister. Before he had broken Rachel's heart.

After he had broken his own.

"Why are you here?" he asked. It was a blunt question, but he was finding it difficult to watch her pat her clothes dry and not say anything at all. It was best to find out why she was standing in his motel room after twelve long years apart.

Eight if you counted when he had come home for Mattie's funeral. Then Rachel had been one of the few people who would even speak to him. Rachel and his sister Sarah. But Sarah had only cried and told him to go home. To go back to his *Englisch* life.

"I need to talk to you about something." She clutched the towel in both hands as if it were a lifeline she couldn't let go.

Nate wanted to sigh, to tell her they had nothing to talk about and push her back into the rain, but he couldn't. He simply couldn't. He was exhausted from the drive. Worn out from a trip to the cemetery to peer down at the mound of dirt that covered his father's coffin. There was no headstone yet, just freshly turned earth to honor his grave until the actual marker was made. "About what?" he finally managed to ask.

"I need your help," she said. "Perhaps you're the only one who can help me."

"How's that?"

She gestured toward the desk chair. "Can we sit?"

He wanted to tell her no. Because sitting down would mean a long conversation, and he wasn't prepared for that. He wasn't prepared to see her in his room at all, much less sitting around and chatting like the old friends they should have been. But a chasm separated them. The chasm between Amish and ex-Amish.

*You can never go home again.*

And yet that was what Rachel was to him. Home.

But he had walked away, and another had swooped in and captured her for his own.

Nate gestured toward the chair and moved to the end of the bed. He sat on the corner while she perched on the hard, vinyl-covered seat.

She smiled at him, the action trembling and a bit hesitant. "It's good to see you, Nathan."

He almost melted. He just about forgot all the years between them and the fact that she was married to another, even the fact that he was no longer part of her faith. He almost forgot it all and told her it was good to see her too. Even if it was, that wasn't the point. He wasn't sure what the point truly was, only that this wasn't it. "Why are you here, Rachel?"

The smile died on her lips, and the light in her eyes dimmed. He felt like an ass for hurting her, but her lingering would only make it harder when it came time to go. "It's Albie."

"Your brother?"

She nodded, pressed her lips together. He could see the tears rising in her eyes, a rain-drenched meadow full of sadness and something else. Remorse? Anger? Perhaps both. She twisted the towel in her lap and looked down at her fingers as she continued. "He's dead."

"Rachel," he breathed. His heart clenched in his chest. "I'm so sorry."

She looked up, and this time the tears did fall. One from each eye, leaving twin wet streaks down her cheeks as they raced toward her jawline. "*Danki*," she said again.

"What happened?"

"That's the problem." Her earlier agitation returned, and she jumped to her feet, pacing back and forth. The room was small, and the skirt of her dress brushed against his leg with her every turn. He could smell the flower scent of her hair and the whiff of detergent coming from her rain-soaked clothes. It was as intoxicating now as it had been years before.

25

"A couple of weeks ago," she started. "I went out to the barn in the morning, like I always do, and there he was. Dead. They're saying that it's a suicide, but—"

"Suicide?" The revelation was staggering. "Albie?"

She stopped pacing directly in front of him. He could reach out and touch her if he chose. "That's what I'm saying. Albie wouldn't have done that. He just wouldn't have."

Nate didn't know what all had happened while he had been gone, and twelve years was a long time for things to go sideways, but there hadn't been any suicides in their community before he left. "Has anyone else ever . . ." He didn't need to finish.

She understood what he was asking and shook her head. "No. Never. And Dat—" She stopped again, and Nate waited patiently for her to continue. "Dat's gone *ab im kopp*." Off in the head.

That Nate could understand. Albie had been a good kid when he had known him. Of course he had been a little kid six or so years old, but Albie had never given Samuel any grief. At least none that Nate had known about. "Your *dat* is grieving."

Rachel shook her head. "It's more than that." She was beginning to look a little wild around the edges. A bit desperate as she continued. "He cut Albie down. Then he sat with him in the barn for a long time. After that he burned his clothes and the rope—" She choked on that last word, but it answered another of the questions floating around in Nate's cop brain.

*How did he do it?*

He had hung himself.

Nate waited quietly for her to continue.

"It was like he was trying to wipe it all away. He is not himself now," she said. "He's not himself at all."

Nate could tell that she was worried about her father. But what daughter wouldn't be when faced with such a tragedy?

# The Secrets We Keep

Samuel Gingerich was a stoic man. Not one to show emotions or weakness. What the *Englisch* would call a man's man. And when a person kept those raging emotions in check . . . well, they could only be contained for so long. They always spilled out, sometime, somehow.

"They buried him the next day," she finally said.

*They* most likely being the bishop and Samuel, Rachel's father. "That's normal for such a . . . death." There might not have been any suicides in their little community before, but the parent community in Ethridge, Tennessee, had suffered a few. In each case, the person had been buried before sunset the next day. No viewing, no ceremony. The victim was buried outside the cemetery proper. It was their way, part of the *Ordnung* that ruled their society.

But that also meant that the police weren't called. A report wasn't filed. He was sure that to Rachel it seemed as if they were erasing his very existence. Dead. Gone. Done.

"They just—" She was beginning to inch beyond desperation. "They just buried him."

Nate stood and grasped Rachel by the arms. He wanted to shake her, but he refrained. He wanted to pull her close and rock her back and forth and promise that everything was going to be okay.

That urge was almost more than he could resist, but it wasn't appropriate. She belonged to another.

"Rachel." He stooped down so he could look into her eyes, those meadow-green orbs that took him back to better times, better days, a better life. "Rachel," he said again. "What's the real problem?"

She sucked in a deep breath, but he could tell she was close to an all-out panic attack. "He didn't kill himself," she whispered. "I know he didn't."

"But you found him hanging in the barn." That much he had gleaned from her words.

Tears drowned the meadow once more. "He didn't kill himself," she said again.

"Then how did he die?" he pressed.

She sucked in another breath, and this one seemed to help. The air shuddered toward the end, but she pulled herself together. He let go of her arms, and she took a step back. "There are these *Englisch* kids. A whole group of them. They'd been harassing Albie lately."

Unfortunately, in small communities like theirs, hassling the Amish was something of a sport. Usually it was nothing too harmful, just annoying. Letting the cows out, egging the houses, setting manure on fire in the yards. At least it had been so innocuous when he had lived there. Irritating but mild.

"That's a strong accusation," Nate said. He settled back onto the corner of the bed and waited for Rachel to return to her seat.

She remained standing. "It was them," she stressed. "I know it was. And since Dat didn't call the police, nothing is going to happen to them. They can just kill my brother and get away with it. When is it going to stop?"

"What am I supposed to do?" he asked, bringing the conversation back round to where they had started.

"You're a cop, aren't you? That's what Sarah told me."

"I am, but I don't have any jurisdiction here." And truly he was done. He was only realizing it now. He was a cop in oath and uniform, but taking the life of a seventeen-year-old kid had sucked the spark out of him. It had used up whatever store he had to correct the balance between good and evil. Before he had shot the young man and killed him, the world had been black and white. Now everything was shades of gray.

## The Secrets We Keep

"Maybe you can talk to the police here. See if they can restart an investigation or whatever it is."

He knew what she was asking. It wasn't impossible. He could go to the police with the information. For that matter, she could, but the revelation might bring down more than she had bargained for. "Your father could be charged with illegally moving a corpse." Or worse, if the police so chose.

"He was grieving," she said, throwing Nate's own words back at him. He wondered if she realized it or not. "He wasn't thinking straight. He's still not."

"Maybe you should talk to them yourself."

She shook her head. "I've tried. They don't listen to me. The leader of this group of kids, he's some politician's son."

"Untouchable," Nate said.

"Something like that," she replied. Then she waited a heartbeat more before continuing. "Please, Nathan, will you talk to them?"

He needed to cut his losses and walk away. If he could invent a time machine, he would go back a day and decide not to come to Mississippi after all. Back even further and stop himself from pulling his gun from its holster and lethally firing it. But he had no time machine, and what was one more day of his life given to Rachel Gingerich?

*Rachel Hostetler,* he corrected himself.

"Fine," he said. "I'm not sure what good it will do, but I'll talk to them tomorrow."

29

# Chapter Two

❧

*Nathan Fisher. Nathan Fisher. Nathan Fisher.*

The name continued to run around in her head as Rachel stared down into the iron skillet filled with eggs. She had kept her memories of him locked up for so long they were like a wild colt finally set free in a fresh spring field. She hadn't allowed herself to think about him in years. Well, if he had asked, that was what she would have told him. The truth was she didn't allow herself to think about him more than once or twice a week, and she managed that just fine. Mostly.

She would push him to the far back corners of her mind, then someone would say something that would take her back to the summer before he left, the summer of sunshine and happy times. When neither of them thought past the next singing, an afternoon of fishing in the creek, and joining the church come fall. Except Nathan had left a few months after joining the church, left to pursue dreams of playing baseball for money. It was a concept she hadn't been able to comprehend.

But things hadn't worked out for him the way he had planned, and he ended up working security at the baseball stadium, or so Sarah had told her. Then he hired on with the police where he lived now in Oklahoma. Sarah had told her all this and more, but some

# The Secrets We Keep

of it Rachel couldn't let herself believe. That Nathan was happy in his *Englisch* world. That he didn't miss the Amish ways or the home of his youth. How could he not? It was just one more thing she didn't understand.

Yet when she had seen him at the cemetery, she knew he was the one person who might be able to get to the truth about what had happened to her brother. God had answered her prayers and brought Nathan to help her.

She wasn't smart like the sheriff and his deputies. She had heard tales of how certain police detectives could tell things about a death that the average person wouldn't know to look for. But she didn't need special schooling to understand that Albie hadn't gotten those bruises on his face from hanging himself. Add in the fact that Albie wasn't the kind of person who would take his own life . . . well, that alone was enough to tell her that someone else had been involved. She had allowed herself to believe the ugly lie for just a little while, then she began to think about it. See it for what it was. She had seen the blood caked in his hair. And she could imagine those kids hitting him with a baseball bat, then stringing him up. When she had said as much to her father, Dat had told her she shouldn't be thinking about such things. She had no response to that.

"You were out late last night," her father said as he came into the kitchen.

Rachel turned and gave him a small smile. "Just restless." It was a partial truth. And that restlessness had left her drained and tired. But still she had been up before her *vatter*, as was her custom. She had made a pot of coffee, then gone into her sister Miri's bedroom to get her ready for the day. Now Miri sat with her wheelchair pushed up to the table, a plastic tumbler filled with milk within easy reach. Rachel was cooking breakfast, and she had her alibi all ready:

She had been unable to fall asleep, so she had gone out to the barn to check on the new litter of puppies born just a few days before.

"This restlessness wouldn't have anything to do with Nathan Fisher being back in town."

She did her best to pull her expression into one of disinterested surprise, but her face felt as if it were made of that Silly Putty stuff the girls played with. "Nathan's back? Not for good, I'm sure." She grabbed a potholder and lifted the skillet. Deftly she dished out the sunny-side-up eggs onto everyone's plates.

Miri clapped her hands in delight. *Dippy eggs* were her favorite.

"Will you call the girls?" she asked her father.

He continued to stare at her a beat longer than necessary, then turned and trudged into the living room. She breathed a small sigh of relief as she heard him holler their names up the staircase, followed by "Breakfast."

But the reprieve was brief.

Moments later her father came back into the kitchen. "They're coming."

Dat sat at the head of the table as Rachel nodded and removed the bread from the oven. He folded his hands as he waited for the girls to come down from upstairs.

Almost without thinking, she dumped the toast into the waiting basket. Then she returned the pan to the stovetop. Rachel had learned a while ago that a hot pan on the table wasn't a good idea when you had an overinquisitive child and a sister who had trouble controlling her movements.

Kate would learn in time to keep her hands to herself. It was Miri that Rachel worried about the most.

Miriam Elizabeth Gingerich had been born with a rare condition called Angelman syndrome. Unfortunately, the genetic disorder was a little less rare in very close Amish communities than it was in the rest of the population. Over the years, Rachel had heard all the doctor-speak about it. Delayed this and that, but what it meant to her was that her sister smiled more than anyone she had ever seen—including her sunny daughter—and was plagued with seizures.

After one particularly nasty fit, Miri had fallen and hit her head on a sharp corner on her way to the floor. The resulting injury had left her wheelchair dependent and in need of constant care.

Rachel's heart broke to see her sister in such a state. But she accepted that Miri's condition and the following accident were both simply part of *Gott's wille*. She couldn't say it was easy to accept, but Miri herself had adjusted well enough. She enjoyed the remaining parts of her life. Amelie, Rachel's older daughter, read to Miri every day, and the girls took her outside to "play." And then there was church. Miri seemed to enjoy church most of all.

"Something smells *gut*," Kate said as she skipped into the room.

Amelie was right behind her. "You always say that." Her words were followed with a frown.

The sisters both carried Rachel's coloring—fair skin prone to freckle and green eyes. But that was where their similarities ended. Amelie had Rachel's reddish-blond hair. She was tall and thin—willowy, Rachel thought she'd heard someone say. Even at seven, Amelie was as somber as an old barn owl.

Kate, on the other hand, was round to the point of chubby, constantly smiling, perpetually happy. Sturdy. Always ready for a new adventure. She was only four and still might lose some of her "baby fat," as they called it, but Rachel figured she took more after her father, who was a big man. Husky. Kate also had his dark, shiny hair, silky and fine, apt to escape whatever pins Rachel used to secure it.

"That's because it's true." Kate stuck out her tongue.

"Sit down," Rachel said, her tone tired but admonishing. "It's time to eat."

The girls did as she instructed and immediately lowered their heads for the silent prayer.

Rachel pressed a hand to the back of her sister's neck to help Miri, but her own thoughts weren't filled with words of praise and thanksgiving. They were all about Nathan Fisher. How had her father known that Nathan was back in town? Perhaps the same way she had.

Rachel had been more than shocked to see him at the cemetery. Then the jolt had turned immediately into an idea. He could help her. Of course he hadn't been at his father's funeral. He was under the *Bann*, after all, but he had come home. Just like when he had come back to lay his sister Mattie to rest.

*Not quite,* she told herself. But similar.

Rachel had prayed, and *Gott* had answered.

The rustling around her brought Rachel out of her thoughts. "*Aemen,*" she whispered, though she hadn't said a prayer at all.

She moved her hand from her sister's nape and started filling Miri's plate.

"Pass the jelly, please." Amelie pointed to the muscadine jelly sitting in front of her sister.

"When's Dat coming home?" Kate questioned.

Rachel bit back her sigh. It was something her youngest asked first thing in the morning, at every meal, and then again just before bed.

As usual, Rachel gave her the single answer she knew to be true. "Only Jesus knows when he'll be back."

"Next time we pray," Kate said, swinging her feet happily as she spoke, "I'm going to ask Jesus when He's bringing Dat home."

"If it's the Lord's will," Rachel's father grumbled.

## The Secrets We Keep

But Kate was nonplussed. "Then I'm going to pray that it's the Lord's will that Jesus bring him home." She seemed very satisfied with her conclusion.

"Eat your breakfast," Rachel replied, ignoring the stabbing pain in her gut.

Her *vatter* frowned but didn't add anything more to the exchange. He just scooped up a forkload of grits and looked pointedly at Rachel. She was certain she would hear about it later.

"Will you pass the jelly, please?" Amelie's voice was growing impatient. It seemed to Rachel these days that the happier Kate was, the more sullen Amelie became. And Kate was usually very happy. Rachel supposed the majority of Amelie's moodiness came from losing so many loved ones so fast. At least she hoped that was the case. Amelie understood more than Kate that her uncle was in heaven with Jesus and that it meant he was never going to be in this world with them again.

As for their father . . .

"Pass your sister the jelly," Rachel instructed.

Kate did as she was bade, stopping, of course, to add the spread to her own piece of toast and dropping a spoonful into her grits before handing the jar to Amelie.

Rachel had been happy with her life. Mostly. She loved her family. She loved her daughters. Caring for her sister was a never-ending chore, but what alternative was there?

Now Nathan. Why did his sudden appearance make her question every life decision she had ever made?

*Lord, help me, please,* she silently prayed. She didn't want to go around feeling like this. She couldn't. She wouldn't be able to bear it.

"Are you waiting for your food to get stone cold before you eat it?"

The girls giggled at their *dawdi*'s words. Miri followed their lead and laughed as well. Laughing was about the only sound she

35

could make. Laughing, along with a grunt of disapproval and a sigh of welcome. Such was her life. Nothing in between.

"Of course not." Rachel picked up her fork. "I was just making sure that everyone was settled before I started."

"You were daydreaming," Kate trilled.

"Maybe I was and maybe I wasn't," Rachel replied. "But if you want to go out and help me with the new pups, we have to eat breakfast, clean up the mess, and get Miri settled on the porch."

"I do want to help! I do," Kate exclaimed. "Can I hold one?"

Rachel shook her head. "Not until next week," she said. "They're too little to be jostled around."

"Are we really going to sell them?" Amelie asked. She had set down her toast and was staring at her plate as if it were covered in poison instead of nourishing food. Rachel knew that her oldest had fallen in love with the squirming blue heeler pups and was loath to let them go. She supposed Amelie had suffered too much loss in the last couple of years and was at her limit of acceptance for things that were out of her control. Only time and the lessons it brought would teach her that they controlled so very little. A woman's life was dictated by God, the church, and her father or husband.

"I won't jostle them," Kate promised, her voice easing into a cajoling whine.

"No," Dat said. "Stop pestering your *mamm* and eat."

Kate looked for a moment like she might possibly burst into tears, then she visibly shrugged and started in on her eggs.

It was wrong, Rachel knew, all this deflecting of emotions. It hurt to see it in her spunky Kate. But the question really was, had it always been this way and she was only now noticing it? Or was it truly something new?

* * *

# The Secrets We Keep

Nate walked into the Pontotoc County Sheriff's Office at ten the following morning. He couldn't say he wanted to be there or that he wanted to talk to anyone regarding the death of Albie Gingerich, but he had promised Rachel. He would do this, spend one more night in town, then head back to Tulsa in the morning.

"May I help you?" The woman behind the counter was compact to the point of tiny. She wore a khaki tan sheriff's uniform, her brown hair pulled back into a huge bun, and her gold wire-rimmed glasses covered half her face. Despite her size she seemed more than competent.

"My name is Nathan Fisher," Nate said. He pulled out his wallet and showed her his badge and commission card. "I work for the Tulsa County Sheriff's Office in Oklahoma. I'm in town for the day and thought I would stop by and see if I could visit with the sheriff for a minute."

The woman looked him up and down from the tips of his cowboy boots to the top of his cowboy hat. It was something of a joke among the detectives back home. Most called him Fish—just a shortened version of his last name and a nod to the name of some detective from a television show back in the seventies. Others, mostly females, called him Cowboy because he was always in a hat. It only seemed natural for him to don the Stetson after wearing a straw hat most of his life.

"I'll see if he's available." She sniffed, then punched a line on the phone. As she talked discreetly into her headpiece, Nate wandered across the small lobby to look at the framed photos displayed there. Most were of the same man, no doubt the current sheriff. He was depicted with other people—community leaders, Nate supposed. But he had been gone long enough that he didn't recognize any of the faces in the photographs.

"Detective Fisher?" a male voice intoned behind him.

Nate turned as a large man with an iron-gray flattop and black-framed glasses came toward him, one arm outstretched.

"Sheriff Walker." Nate shook the man's hand. "Call me Nate."

"Come on back," the sheriff invited, then he turned to lead the way down a green-carpeted hallway with cream-colored walls and overhead lighting.

Nate followed the man to the end of the hall and into an office that most likely stretched the length of the corridor they had just walked. There were more framed photographs on display here as well as a floor-to-ceiling bookcase that held more awards and knickknacks than books.

"So Tulsa, huh?" Sheriff Walker asked after he settled himself in the big leather chair behind the equally large oak desk. He gestured for Nate to sit in one of the uncomfortable-looking chairs in front of him.

"That's right." Nate eased down in the seat and crossed one leg over the other. Out of habit, he removed his hat and placed it on his knee.

"What brings you out to our neck of the woods?"

Nate gave a small smile. He supposed it was a bit nostalgic, but he couldn't stop that tiny curve of his lips. "I used to live here." *You can't go home again.*

Walker nodded. "I see."

"My father passed away recently."

"And you came back for the funeral." His nod had turned into an understanding bob of the head. The man was only half listening to what Nate was saying. His eyes were downcast as he fiddled with a stray paper clip.

"Not exactly," Nate returned. "I was raised Amish."

That got the sheriff's attention. Walker looked up at him with renewed interest. "Is that a fact?"

# The Secrets We Keep

"Yes. And that's what I wanted to talk to you about today."

"So this isn't a social call."

Nate shook his head. "Albert Gingerich."

"Never heard of him."

"I'm not surprised," Nate continued. "But some of your deputies have. Albie allegedly committed suicide a couple of weeks ago. His sister came in to talk to y'all about it."

The sheriff nodded. "And this is a regular kid?" He gave a small cough. "A non-Amish kid?"

"Albie is Amish. Was Amish."

"An Amish suicide?" Walker whistled under his breath.

"His sister doesn't believe he killed himself. That's why she came in."

"And you?"

"I would like to know the truth."

The sheriff stared at him a beat too long, then he turned to face the computer sitting on one end of his desk. "Let me see what I have here." He punched in the necessary information and started to scroll through the files.

"This dang thing," the sheriff griped. "Slower than molasses on Christmas morning."

Nate did his best to refrain from tapping his fingers against the brim of his hat. He didn't know the sheriff from Adam, and he was doing his utmost to not jump to hasty assumptions about the man, but he couldn't help feeling Walker was stalling on purpose. Or maybe the fact that Nate was ex-Amish was making him nervous.

No. Nervous wasn't quite the word he wanted. Cautious, maybe. Overly so.

*Tap. Tap.* He stilled his fingers. He could hear his mother's voice in his head. *Patience is a virtue.*

39

Amy Lillard

"Here we go." The sheriff hit enter on the keyboard and studied the screen. "Looks like she talked to Franklin."

"And he investigated Albie's death?"

"Well, now see, that's the problem." Walker sat back in his chair. The monstrosity squeaked with the motion. He pulled a cloth from one of the desk drawers and started cleaning his glasses. "We have no reason to believe that his death was anything other than a suicide."

For all his acting like he didn't know Albie Gingerich, Sheriff Walker was sure well versed in the case. Nate's distrust rose. "Aren't all suicides classified as suspicious deaths?"

"It's a special case," the sheriff explained. "We decided to let it stand as written."

"His sister Rachel doesn't agree," Nate said.

"His sister is grieving," the sheriff returned. "My deputies went out to the scene and talked to the father. Went over and talked to the bishop. Everything was aboveboard except for the fact that they didn't call the coroner. But that didn't seem like enough to warrant an arrest." He gave an inelegant shrug and settled his glasses back into place. Nate had the feeling that the man avoided every interaction with the Amish that he could. "The boy killed himself, and they buried him. Any evidence to the contrary is long gone."

Unfortunately, Nate had to agree with him on that one. If Samuel Gingerich had burned the clothes Albie had been wearing and the rope he had hung himself with as Rachel claimed, then what more could they go on?

"Are there any eyewitness accounts showing problems between Albie and this gang of *Englisch* boys that had been harassing him?"

4 0

# The Secrets We Keep

"English." The sheriff shook his head. "That's something I don't think I'll ever get used to saying." When Nate didn't respond, he seemed to pull himself back together. "There's never been a formal complaint against these boys, and I wouldn't call them a gang. They're just some kids who hang out together."

"And like to go around harassing others who are different from them?" The Amish had suffered persecution of one sort or another since the seventeenth century, but getting upset now wouldn't help his cause to ease Rachel's mind on the matter of her brother's death.

"It's a small town," the sheriff said. "We do our best, but there's not much for the young folks to do around here." A fact Nate knew firsthand. He might have been gone for a while, but twelve years was nothing when it came to change in a small southern town. "If there was some evidence . . ." The sheriff allowed his words to trail off. He wasn't doing anything without more to go on than an Amish woman's suspicions.

"Of course." Nate stood and put his hat back on in preparation to leave. "Thanks for talking with me today." Like it had given him any new information. But he had done what he had promised Rachel he would do. He had talked to the sheriff, and essentially, he had gotten nowhere.

He reached out to shake the sheriff's hand once more before heading for the door.

"You know that father," Walker started, "he's damned lucky we decided not to arrest him for failure to report a crime and unlawful removal of a corpse."

Nate stopped with his hand on the doorknob. "I know."

"They're not easy people to deal with," the sheriff continued. "All secretive and stuff. We do what we can and hope for the best."

# Amy Lillard

Nate grunted. That was politician speak for *I don't really want to mess with it, so I don't unless I have to.*

"You got any Amish out your way?" Walker asked.

"A couple of counties over from us."

"Well, hell, you were raised Amish. You know what I'm talking about."

"Yeah," Nate said. "I know exactly what you mean."

# Chapter Three

*You can't go home again.*

The thought circled Nate—in his mind, in his heart, around his very being—as he drove out toward his mother's house. He wouldn't stop; he just had to see it once before he left. Tomorrow he was going back to Oklahoma, though once he got there, he wasn't sure how he would make his living. One thing was certain: He couldn't be a cop anymore. Coming here had shown him that. He was spent, tired, and his heart wasn't in it now. The bad guys had turned from criminals into someone's daughter or son who had merely gotten off track. In this community, the same thing might be said of him.

What was the old bar adage? *You don't have to go home, but you can't stay here.* That was Cedar Creek.

As he drove, he noted the changes and the constants that made up this community. The hand-lettered sign advertising LOCAL HONEY was still in place at the top of the drive that led to the King farm. That meant old Ephraim was still tending bees, and by Nate's best estimate, the man had to be in his midnineties. Something to be said about clean living, he supposed. Though from the look of the black-and-white sign, it hadn't been repainted since before Nate left.

The Borntragers had a new mailbox, this one large enough to hold packages, and it was silver instead of black. Their family name and address were printed neatly on the outside in dark-red letters. Most likely paint left over from the last time the barn was touched up.

Just as he remembered, almost everyone had a shop outside their house. Each one was no bigger than a woodshed. The women all canned, everything from sauerkraut to kudzu jelly, salsa to homemade ketchup. The youngins made beaded key chains, woven potholders, and button necklaces, while the teens fashioned soaps and lotions from glycerin and goat's milk. All these wares plus fresh berries and vegetables were for sale in the shops. The Amish in Cedar Creek had made quite a cottage industry for themselves.

Most of the men either farmed or worked at the mill, though some did harness and leather work. The community also boasted a blacksmith, a buggy maker, and a man who fashioned porch swings from the trees that gave the creek its name.

Or at least it had been that way when Nate had lived there, and he saw no reason for any of that to shift in the years he had been gone. Progress and change were slow in the South, slow in a small town, and hesitant among the Amish. They saw no cause to fold to the outside world.

He let off the gas pedal as he came up to the turn for his sister's house.

Sarah Fisher had married Gideon Glick a couple of years ago. She had written Nate to tell him the news. It had been the last time he had heard from her, other than the news that their brother Jacob was marrying. That letter had been short and to the point, just a couple of lines to "let him know." Married life was an adjustment, he realized— just because he was single didn't mean he couldn't understand that. She had been busy. Or her husband didn't want her to have anything to do with her wayward brother. Most likely the latter.

## The Secrets We Keep

He didn't plan on stopping here either, but he wanted to see. Maybe he wanted to assure himself that she was doing fine without him.

The Glick property looked like so many others in the small community: white, two-story house, a barn and outbuildings with red horizontal siding, and a little red shop just across from the mailbox. The yard was efficient, no flowers to water or planters to tend to, no manicured grass to mow. The food garden was extensive, like it was for all the Amish families in the area. Work had to be given to the things that brought life, not frivolities. Sarah was outside, hanging laundry when he passed. He thought about tooting his horn to catch her attention, but he decided against it.

*You don't have to go home, but you can't stay here.*

Instead he drove the short distance to his childhood home, the home where his mother now lived with his brother Jacob and his wife Ellen. In Sarah's last letter she had mentioned that Jacob and Ellen were taking over the farm from their mother and father. That had been almost two years ago. As their custom, the *eldra* would stay in the *dawdihaus*, a kind of apartment built onto the main house where the aging parents went to live. The Amish didn't go in for nursing homes, letting the care of their "special" members or their sick or aging folks pass to someone else.

All told, there were seven Fisher children. Leroy was the oldest, followed by Lavinia, who had married Mose Esh and now lived in the parent community in Ethridge, Tennessee. Nate was next in the pecking order, then came Elias, who lived in Adamsville, a Tennessee satellite community with ties to both Ethridge and Cedar Creek. Then there was Sarah, Jacob, and Mattie.

Nate missed them all like crazy. Coming back had been heart wrenching just knowing that he couldn't stay, reliving all the mistakes he had made. As long as he was away, he could pretend that it didn't matter, that he didn't long for days past. It was just another reason why he needed to go back to Oklahoma. He couldn't say *back where he belonged*, because he wasn't sure that was where he truly belonged either. Only that he had adjusted.

*You don't have to go home, but you can't stay here.*

Nate slowed his truck and came to a complete stop. His brother's house sat close enough to the road that it could be easily seen. It looked the same as it did every night in his dreams. A field of soybeans had been planted across the hard-packed road. A large garden sat off to one side. An old oak tree grew in the middle of the front yard, shading the porch and the steps leading to it. The tree itself seemed to be the only thing that had changed. It had grown and even sprouted a new tire swing.

Nate smiled as he remembered the one they'd had when he was about twelve. Elias was ten at the time, and Nate and Leroy had convinced him to get in the swing and let them push him as hard as they could, the goal being that they push him so high he could jump onto the roof of the house and get the Frisbee that had been tossed there by accident. What happened instead was Elias missed the roof, fell, and broke his arm. Their *vatter* took down the swing that same afternoon.

Nate wondered if that Frisbee was still trapped up there on the old tin roof.

As he sat there in his truck, grinning like a fool, the front door opened and his *mamm* stepped out onto the porch. Their eyes met and locked. She had seen him in the road, and she had come out so he would know.

From this distance, Nate couldn't read her expression, but her shoulders sagged. Her chin was lifted and her arms hung loose at her sides. She looked sad. A little angry, perhaps even defiant.

# The Secrets We Keep

He shook his head at himself and that initial contact was broken. She had just lost her husband of forty-plus years. Of course she was sad.

She continued to stare at him. Now, however, her gaze appeared more menacing.

He slacked off the brake and allowed his truck to move once again. He wanted to believe she was remorseful over all the years they had lost. But he could see that she still blamed him.

No matter. He had blamed himself for years; most times he still did. He had set out to save his sister, and the beauty of it all had been that he could do that and live out his dream of playing baseball for money. He had failed on both accounts and destroyed their family in the process. Mattie's death was the final nail in the coffin.

He lifted one hand in a small wave. The halfhearted gesture was a mere afterthought, delayed and yet almost involuntary. To his surprise, just as he started to pull away, his *mamm* lifted one hand in a tiny salute.

The knock on his door at eleven fifteen that night didn't surprise him. And this time it wasn't raining. He didn't even check the peephole to see who had come knocking. He knew.

"Can I come in?" she asked.

He stepped back and allowed Rachel inside. He couldn't resist looking one way and then the other to see if anyone was spying on them. He had a bad feeling. He'd had it ever since he had stopped at his *mudder*'s house that afternoon. The feeling of being followed, being watched.

Not surprisingly, there weren't any Amish about, no buggies to be seen. One car passed by the motel as Rachel stepped inside. As far as Nate could tell, the driver hadn't given them a second glance.

"Did you talk to them?" she asked without preamble.

"I did."

"And?" she prompted. She was wringing her hands and shifting from foot to foot. Dark circles shadowed her pretty green eyes. She looked as if she hadn't slept in days. She probably hadn't had a good night's sleep since she had found Albie hanging in the barn.

"The sheriff is confident in his decision to classify Albie's death as a suicide."

"I saw my brother," she said, starting to shake with the memory. "He had other injuries. Those boys . . ."

"Sometimes law enforcement isn't as cut and dried as we would like it to be."

"So you're saying they're just going to get away with it?" Her voice cracked.

"Rachel . . . *could* he have committed suicide?" Nate hadn't wanted to ask the question, but it needed asking.

"No," she said. "No."

"An autopsy won't show whether or not someone else could have had a hand in his hanging."

"But it'll show other injuries," she countered. "They won't even need an autopsy for that. His head had been bleeding. His face was black and blue."

"That could have been from lack of air." It was hard enough to speak to a stranger about such matters. It was nearly choking him to talk to her about it. He couldn't bring up lividity and what three weeks in a pine box would do to a body. How utterly useless and painful this whole fight might turn out to be.

"What about DNA evidence? Surely they left some trace of themselves behind."

"Where did you learn about that?" His Rachel was full of surprises.

# The Secrets We Keep

No. Not *his* Rachel. Freeman's Rachel. The woman before him hadn't been *his* anything in a long, long time.

Her lips trembled even as she lifted her chin at a stubborn angle. This was something new. He had never seen this side of her before. "The library." Her eyes dared him to contradict her. "I also know that the boys all used one another as alibis. Isn't that suspicious?"

Nate shrugged. "A little."

"Surely the real killer left some sort of testimony behind." She said the words so confidently. "Albie didn't kill himself," she reiterated. "He wasn't the kind to do something like that."

"Sheriff Walker isn't going to make a case because he has no evidence that a crime other than suicide has been committed."

She waited a beat too long to answer. "What if I have evidence?"

He stopped, blinked. "What are you talking about?"

He could see her weighing it out in her head. She trusted him. At least he thought she did, but she was concerned. She didn't want to say whatever it was out loud. Finally she gave in. "Albie kept a journal. He was always drawing and writing things." She gave a wistful smile of remembrance. "He was a dreamer, you know. But he also wrote about being harassed and chased. Beaten up and such."

"And you saw this?"

"I saw it in his journal, and I knew when he came home with a black eye or a busted lip. But if I give the sheriff that journal . . ." It seemed like the last thing she wanted to do, but she would in order to bring justice to her brother. "He deserves to be buried in the cemetery. Next to Mamm."

"Do you know what you're asking for?"

She nodded.

"Say it," he demanded. "I need to hear you say it."

"I want . . . I want a case. I want the police to investigate Albie's death."

"They'll dig him up."

She swallowed hard but nodded.

"And they'll cut him open." He hated being so harsh, but she had to understand everything she was asking for. Most of it went against their *Ordnung* and even the understood rules of polite *Englisch* society. It was a big deal to unearth a body from its restful sleep, no matter what your religion. "He's been buried for almost three weeks. He wasn't embalmed. I doubt they will be able to determine anything about his injuries or death at this point in time."

"That's why it needs to be done now," she said. "Real soon. Before any more evidence is lost."

She had been doing her homework.

"Please, Nate. What they are saying is not the truth."

"Your father—" he started.

"Will do what the police tell him to do," she said firmly. "But the police don't care. That's why I need you to help. If I take the journal in, will you go with me? They'll listen to you." She had said those very same words to him the night before.

"They haven't so far." He thought back to the sheriff and his good ol' boy attitude. He probably played golf with the senator and would do anything to keep his friend's son out of trouble. But did that *anything* include covering up a murder?

"What does Freeman say about all of this?" The question came out of left field, but there it was.

"Freeman doesn't know."

He stared at her as he tried to think of something to say in return. She was a good Amish woman. And good Amish women didn't keep such important matters from their husbands. But Nate

# The Secrets We Keep

couldn't admonish her for that. He didn't have the right. It wasn't any of his business.

"Rachel, if you go back to the sheriff and demand that they exhume Albie's body and perform an autopsy, a lot of people here in Cedar Creek are going to be upset."

"And if I don't, four young men are going to get away with murder."

"You really think they killed him?"

"*Jah*. I do."

"Not just that they drove him to suicide with their bullying." Which was still a crime, though a lesser offense.

"Albie's stronger than that."

Nate couldn't ignore Rachel's confidence in the matter. "You believe they actually put their hands on him and hung him."

Tears filled her eyes. "*Jah*." She nodded. The tears spilled over her lashes and ran down her cheeks. "I do. I really do."

He sucked in a deep breath and tried to sort through what little knowledge he had of the matter.

"They've started in on another boy," Rachel said softly. "You remember Rebecca Troyer?"

Nate nodded.

"Her little brother, Jeremiah."

Jeremiah Troyer had been eight or ten when Nate left. But even then Nate could tell there was something different about him. Jeremiah was quiet and thoughtful, almost feminine in his mannerisms. He was a born daydreamer.

Nate didn't like categorizing people, but if he was held to the fire, he would say that Jeremiah, if he had been born *Englisch*, would eventually "come out." Life would go on.

But the Amish felt homosexuality was an abomination. Evil thoughts placed in the mind of the afflicted by the devil himself.

Those thoughts had to be eradicated. There were homes and places for "therapy" to help the wayward youngster get his mind back right and live a clean and wholesome life just like the Bible told them to do. If only it were that simple.

And if these boys were bothering Jeremiah as well . . .

"Was Albie . . ." He trailed off, unwilling to voice the words to Rachel. He might have been away from the Amish for years, but old habits and all that. Men and women didn't speak about such matters openly.

"No." Rachel shook her head. "No." The last word was whispered but still spoken with as much confidence as the first. "They didn't like Albie because he was Amish. They are mean and bored," she explained. "And no one is willing to stop them." She waited a heartbeat before continuing. "If they are allowed to, they'll just keep doing this. Hurting people. It has to stop." She hardly paused to take a breath. "Albie hung around with this boy. They didn't like him either."

"Amish kid?" Nate asked. If so, Nate might or might not know him already.

Rachel shook her head. "A Black boy. His name is Keylan."

"Last name?" Maybe he would have some information that Nate could use to further the case.

"I don't think Albie ever said." Rachel seemed to think about it a moment more. "If he did, I can't remember."

Nate nodded. Maybe it was in the journal. A heartbeat stretched between them. The years peeled away and they were back in that bright and warm summer of twelve years ago, when nothing much mattered except getting their chores done so they could sneak away and be alone together.

"So will you do it?" she asked.

# The Secrets We Keep

At the desperation in her voice, he came undone. It was always this way with her. Last night. Tonight. Every time. "Are you positive this is what you want?"

She didn't hesitate. "Albie didn't kill himself."

"And your *dat*?"

A mix of emotions flashed in her eyes. Regret. Resolve. Fear. Samuel Gingerich was not going to be happy at having his son exhumed, and they both knew it. And if he ever found out that Rachel was behind it . . .

"Okay." Nate expelled a heavy breath. "Bring me the journal tomorrow. I'll take a look at it, and we'll go from there." He wasn't promising anything—not even to Rachel—until he saw this evidence for himself.

"Tomorrow's Sunday," she reminded him. "Church."

The Amish held their three-hour worship service every other week. Most times the families went visiting on their off Sunday. Sometimes going to church in a different district. But never taking evidence of a supposed murder to the sheriff's office. Which meant he would have to stay if he was going to help. Was he going to help?

"Please, Nathan."

He must have hesitated too long.

"Monday morning, then." Another day in paradise.

Her expression turned to one of relief. "Monday."

A comfortable yet awkward silence stretched between them.

"Albie didn't kill himself," she said again.

Nate only nodded. What else could he do?

"After Monday, then what?" she asked. He knew what she meant. After she showed him the evidence, what would happen? "You'll take it to the sheriff?"

"If I feel he can use it."

53

There went that chin again, lifting to that stubborn angle he didn't remember ever seeing before.

"And then?"

He shook his head. "I'll go home, I guess." Why didn't his voice sound more certain? Because he had less to return to in Oklahoma than he had here in Mississippi. Some home. Just a cat with one ear and an apartment full of garage sale furniture. It had never concerned him before. So why was all that bothering him now?

Because he was thirty years old and adrift. Thirty years old and he had killed a young man. Thirty years old and alone.

"And Albie?" she asked.

He tried not to shrug. He knew what should be done, but whether or not the sheriff would actually do it was another matter altogether. "If the evidence is compelling enough, the sheriff will open a case. From there they'll get a court order to exhume the body. Then it could be weeks . . . months before they get the autopsy results." Nate would surely be back in Tulsa by then, starting over.

"*Danki*," she said quietly. Her eyes shone with unshed tears. She took his hand in her own and squeezed his fingers. The touch was electric. Just as it had always been. No one moved him like Rachel.

He squeezed her fingers in return.

"I should go." She didn't sound as if she wanted to. But the last time they had been alone this long . . .

It had been the day they buried Mattie. That day Rachel hadn't left. That day she had stayed, and he had found comfort in her. But he had left the next day, and a couple months later she had married Freeman Hostetler.

Freeman had always had a thing for Rachel, but she only had eyes for Nate. Until Nate was no longer there and she knew he wasn't coming back.

Life goes on.

She released his hand and turned toward the door, opening it then stepping out into the humid Mississippi night. There wasn't a soul in sight. But that feeling of being watched returned.

Rachel stopped there on the sidewalk and looked back at him. "You asked me if Freeman knew about me coming here to talk to you."

He swallowed hard. He wasn't going to like whatever she was about to say. He felt it in his bones.

"Freeman Hostetler has been missing for the last three years."

# Chapter Four

*Staying for a couple more days. Feed my cat?*

Nate sent the text to Bree sometime around lunchtime the following day. He immediately received a thumbs-up followed by the three little dots signifying that she was typing once more. But knowing Bree . . .

The message popped up onto his screen.

*I got u. Lmk when ur back.*

He sent the thumbs-up in return and tossed his phone onto the bed next to him. He had already sent an email to his captain requesting a little more time off. He knew it would be granted. Everyone in the TCSO knew he was having trouble adjusting. The simple fact that Nate was still having trouble should have told them all that he was done. But no one wanted to see a colleague go down that way, in the flames of someone else's stupid mistakes. Yet that was what had happened and now it was something Nate would have to learn to live with.

That was easier said than done when a guy had too much time on his hands. He looked around the room with its pine paneling, chipped veneer furniture, and small-screen television bolted to the top of the dresser.

## The Secrets We Keep

The bedspread he sat on was a rust-colored paisley polyester that somehow both matched and clashed with the forest-green carpet. It was home for the next day at least.

What was he doing? What good could come of any of this?

If Rachel found out that her brother had been murdered instead of committing suicide, what would change?

He knew the answer to that. She didn't want the black mark on Albie's standing. But he would still be dead. Yet that was why Nate was staying. Because of her. Always because of her. Because he was a fool. A fool for Rachel.

He sighed and pushed himself to his feet. He needed to eat. It was well past lunch, and the bowl of cereal he'd commandeered from the motel lobby had long since served its purpose.

His stomach growled as if in support of the idea. Food, that was what he needed. A quick bite and everything would be clear again. He palmed the card key to the room and left his phone lying on the bed. He'd walk across the street to the sandwich shop. Easy.

Nate drew in a breath as he stepped from his room. The temperature was already pushing ninety. Looked like it was going to be a warm summer. But he wouldn't be there for that. Just a day, maybe two, and he would be headed back to Tulsa.

The door closed behind him as movement to his left caught his attention. He turned, noting the housekeeper was just a few doors down. He didn't want service. Didn't need much. But he would be back before she got to his room. She could clean it tomorrow after he had already headed out.

She smiled at him, friendly and a little familiar, raising her hand in a quick wave.

Nate returned the gesture—after all, he was in the South—but the action was a bit confusing. Maybe he had known her once

57

upon a time, though he didn't recognize her now. Twelve years was a lifetime, he was starting to find out.

She ducked into the room, and he set his feet into motion toward the road ahead. The sandwich shop hadn't been there when he'd lived in the area. Seemed things did change a bit after all.

It was a Sunday in a small town and traffic was light. Well, nonexistent. Still, Nate checked both ways to see if any cars were coming. And maybe to see if that sense of being watched was founded and not just the feel of being conspicuous in a place where he no longer belonged. But there were no lurking souls in parked cars or buggies waiting to trip him up.

The bell on the door of the shop chimed out a warning to his entrance. The teenage boy behind the counter looked up and raised his chin in acknowledgment. He was already helping a woman and her young son, so Nate took that as *I'll be with you in a minute*.

He got in line behind the woman and waited his turn. Standing there while she asked her child which toppings he wanted on his sandwich made Nate itch. He felt exposed, just *standing* there, and he turned to stare out the window to see if someone was watching.

Pontotoc was making him paranoid. Or maybe it was just Cedar Creek. There was no one there but the four of them—Nate, the young man behind the counter, the mom, and the little boy who wanted only mayo and cheese on his ham sandwich despite his mom's efforts for lettuce, tomato, and pickles.

Finally his turn came. Nate ordered his food and headed back across the street. He had almost traversed the strip of asphalt the motel called a parking lot when he noticed that the door to his room was open. His steps stuttered. He'd shut it. Hadn't he? Of course he had. He would never walk out and leave his room unlocked, much less open, though the door was slightly ajar.

## The Secrets We Keep

Someone had broken into his room in the short time that it had taken to get his food.

He looked one way and then the other. The housekeeper and her cart were nowhere to be seen. Maybe she had left it open. Maybe. But that feeling he had of being watched, being followed, monitored, would not leave him. Someone had waited until he left, then somehow managed to get into his space.

He swore under his breath. His gun was in his truck, his keys on the chipped veneer table in the now invaded room. With any luck whoever had been following him and watching him had accomplished their goal in breaking into his room and had already left in the time it took for supermom to cover every sandwich topping at the deli across the street. With any luck.

He approached the door, heart thumping in his chest. It was just like any other home invasion he had worked, except the only weapon he held now was a foot-long pastrami and Swiss.

Yet what had to be done had to be done.

His feet slowed the closer he got. Three steps and he would be inside.

Three . . .

Two . . .

One . . .

Heart pounding, palms sweaty, he nudged the door slowly open.

The woman sitting on the edge of the bed popped up like an Anabaptist jack-in-the-box.

"Christ, Sarah. You scared the life out of me."

"Nathan." His sister smoothed nervous hands down the front of her faded purple apron. Seemed he wasn't the only one startled. "You shouldn't take the Lord's name in vain."

"You break into my room and that's all you have to say to me." He wanted to sit down, collapse really, and stave off the near heart

59

attack she had given him. Instead he tossed his key card on the table, followed by his sandwich. Food could wait.

"What are you doing here?" she demanded.

"I think I can say the same thing to you," he returned.

"Don't play games with me, *brudder*. You've upset Mamm. Driving by the house, slowing down, parking that big truck of yours and watching. It's creepy, and it needs to stop."

"Fair enough." He supposed it was a bit stalkerish, but now that his father was gone, he held a hope for a renewed relationship with his estranged mother. It was only a small hope that now seemed impossible. "How'd you get into my room?"

She shrugged. "Amanda Troyer let me in."

Amanda Troyer. He'd thought the maid looked familiar. He wanted to ask when she had left the Amish, since she hadn't been wearing a plain dress or a prayer *kapp* when he noticed her a few doors down. Maybe if she had been, he'd have recognized her immediately.

"Where's your buggy?"

Sarah flicked her hand toward the opposite side of the motel. "I parked around the corner."

"I take it Gideon doesn't know you're here."

"Why did you come?"

"He died, Sarah."

"I know, Nathan." Her words held a sharp, impatient tone.

"He was my father too."

"I know." This time soft, understanding. There was a wealth of memories in those two words. Some good, some bad. But there all the same. The shared past, the childhood of bare feet and dusty roads, overgrown fields, and old worn-out hound dogs. Swimming and fishing in the pond and trips to the woodshed when their

# The Secrets We Keep

father had decided they had done something wrong, real or imagined.

Karl Fisher had been a tough *vatter*, a hard man who sometimes held his own twisted ideas about right and wrong. Good and bad, acceptable and not. He would not bend when it came to Nate leaving the Amish, no matter his good intentions.

*The road to hell is paved with good intentions.*

Didn't he know it.

"It's over now," she finally said. "Go home."

He lifted his chin, just a fraction of an inch, but meant it as a nod of agreement. Yeah, it was time to go home. But Rachel . . .

"Don't let her suck you into her . . ." Sarah waved one hand around as if hoping to catch the word in midair.

"Drama?" he supplied.

"There's been some crazy stuff going on around here."

He waited for her to explain.

"She isn't who you think she is. She's changed since you've been gone."

They didn't even have to say her name to know who they were talking about. Rachel had never been on the list of Sarah's favorite people.

"Everyone changes," Nate countered.

"Not like this." Sarah shook her head. "The police investigated her to see if she had something to do with Freeman's disappearance."

"I take it no charges were filed." If they had been, she surely wouldn't be walking around, trying to figure out who might have killed her brother.

"Not enough evidence. But the rest of us still wonder. And then Daniel's wife up and disappears the same day?"

61

"Daniel Hostetler?" Freeman's brother.

"*Jah*, but I don't think they left together."

"Why not?" he asked.

"Rachel came to church with a huge bruise on her face just before Freeman disappeared. Said she knocked a horseshoe off a shelf in the tack room and it hit her in the eye." Sarah paused, pressed her lips together before finally continuing. "That must have been one mighty big horseshoe. And it wasn't only the one time. She always had bruises and such and would scoff if anyone asked about them. Said that they were from this or that or whatever, but no one believed her. Then bang. He up and disappears. No more bruises."

Nate wanted to believe it was a coincidence. But as a detective, he knew: There were no such things as coincidences. Still, he didn't like to think about Rachel being hurt by her husband. By anyone, for that matter. He didn't like the implication that she had something to do with her husband disappearing. It might just be small-town talk or might have a ring of truth. That was what bothered him.

"I figure Daniel must be just like his brother. It runs in families sometimes, you know. So Marie left because she got tired of being Daniel's punching bag."

And Rachel buried her husband for the same reason? He wasn't sure how much of that he believed. Or maybe he just didn't want to believe it.

"She ever come to church with bruises? Marie?" Sometimes the cop in him just took over.

Sarah shrugged. "I didn't come here to talk about them."

"Right." He'd take that as a no. He nodded, then waited for her to continue.

"You need to go home."

# The Secrets We Keep

"I'll be out of your hair tomorrow morning."

She stopped as if considering that statement. "*Gut*," she said, then she turned and made her way to the door. "And stop driving by Mamm's house." With that point made she turned and left.

\* \* \*

Rachel ran her fingers over the worn leather cover of the journal she held in her hands. Albie's journal. Tomorrow she would go with Nathan to take it into the sheriff's office. She would have to give it to them. Well, if they listened to anything she said, she knew they would take it. Use it as evidence. Was there evidence in it? Perhaps.

She smiled down at the rose embossed in the leather even as tears started in her eyes. She had given the journal to Albie, told him that since he was always going around doodling on this and that, he should keep everything in one safe place. It was a quirky little habit that made Albie Albie. When he died—she refused to say that he had killed himself—she had taken the journal from his room, stumbling across it as she searched for a note, a letter, anything that would tell his last words or thoughts. Surely he hadn't left this world without saying goodbye.

It was just one of the many reasons she believed he'd been killed. He wouldn't have done anything like suicide without leaving a note, without telling her his reasons. He just wouldn't have.

She had looked around, for something, anything to hold on to, and found the journal in an old shoebox he kept under the bed. Then she had taken it to her room in order to feel close to him. Read his words, see if there was anything that might shed a light on what he was thinking and doing during those last days. She wanted to find something that would expressly point the finger at the group of *Englisch* boys that she knew was responsible. Yet none of that seemed to be in there.

63

She had flipped through the pages then, smiling at the drawings and sayings, little things that he found inspirational or important. Important enough to jot down. And then she had found the other pages.

Rachel turned to them now, running her fingers over the vile words, hating them as they burned like a fire in her belly. The pages she swore she would never read again. Pages she couldn't allow anyone to read. Not now. Not ever.

If they asked her, she would simply say the book was that way when she found it. She was a terrible liar. She would have to practice it to get it right. And with any luck and perhaps with God on her side, no one would question the lie she had to tell.

She grabbed the side of the pages and ripped them from the book.

\* \* \*

"You don't have to do this, you know." Nate stopped at the door of the sheriff's office. He had one hand raised, paused in midair, waiting before actually opening the door and entering.

"*Jah*," Rachel said solemnly. "I do." She pushed her sister's wheelchair forward as if urging him to go ahead and get this over with.

They had met here this morning as they had planned. It was safer for them not to be seen driving around town together. Plus Rachel had Miri to think about. He knew what it had cost her. Bringing Miri along today meant driving the carriage specially designed for her sister's wheelchair to ride strapped in place.

Miri. The one person who kept Rachel on that side of the Amish line.

He pushed the thought away. No sense going down that road. Nothing would change the past. He had begged Rachel to go with him, and she had stayed for her sister. There was nothing more to it.

# The Secrets We Keep

Miri was so much worse now than he remembered. He thought he'd heard a rumor of her falling and hitting her head, the brain injury only adding more disabilities on top of the Angelman syndrome she had suffered from since birth.

It was heartbreaking to see her strapped into her chair, her perpetually smiling face not giving away anything that was going on inside her head. Was she happy? He hoped so. Was she even aware enough to determine? He had no idea. No one did.

Nate opened the door and allowed Rachel to push her sister's chair into the foyer of the offices. He stepped in behind her, removing his cowboy hat and automatically running his fingers through his hair as he paused for his vision to adjust to the light.

Rachel stopped then as well, waiting for him to take the lead. Her purse slipped off her shoulder, the bag heavy with the weight of the journal she wanted to submit as evidence. She pulled the strap back into place and followed him over to the large semicircular desk area.

Miri laughed seemingly at nothing, the sound joyous but unnerving as it bounced off the marble floor and echoed all around.

"Can I help you?" The compact woman with large glasses who had been at the desk during his last visit looked them over dubiously. Her gaze ricocheted off Miri in her wheelchair with the many support straps holding her in place. Then it hovered on Rachel and Nate, careful not to drop back to Miri. He knew she was taking in Rachel's homemade blue dress, her faded gray apron and white prayer covering. She knew why they were there, but she made him say it all the same.

"We'd like to talk to the sheriff, please."

The deputy nodded as if she completely understood, but from the set of her chin, Nate knew this wasn't going to be easy. "Let me see if he's in." She picked up the office phone sitting on the desk in front of her and made as if to call back to the sheriff.

Nate resisted the urge to hold the button down and end the charade. Instead he nodded toward the black SUV marked PONTOTOC COUNTY SHERIFF'S OFFICE that was parked directly out front. "Oh, I think he's in."

The tiny woman shot him a look, then she turned her back and lowered her voice so they couldn't hear what was being said.

Beside him, Rachel sucked in a deep breath, then trembled as she released the fortifying air. For all her tough insistence on finding out the truth about her brother's death, the situation was quickly unraveling her.

Some of it had to be her upbringing. She had been taught to be a good Christian woman, to respect authority, to submit and to obey. She was doing none of those things at the moment, and he knew it took more than bravery for her to return here today and challenge decisions that had already been made, regardless of how wrong they were.

When she had arrived at the sheriff's parking lot this morning, she had been a bit shaky. She handed Nate the journal, her eyes begging him to find enough information on the pages that he would go with her to meet the sheriff again.

It was a mixed lot, this journal. There were a few drawings of flowers and trees, and one sketch of the creek that ran behind Rachel's house. Nate had been surprised to see Jeremiah Troyer's name there, even though Rachel had told him of the boy's troubles.

The years worked against Nate. When he left, Jeremiah had been just a boy. A little boy. Not a teenager who barely fit in with his own people.

Albie talked about the harassment, but nothing so terrible that it warranted such a drastic measure as suicide. He mentioned

The Secrets We Keep

his friend Keylan, last name Reid, which was helpful, and the names of the boys who had bullied him for years. One name stood out above the others. Chance Longacre. Son of Sean Longacre, state senator and soon-to-be gubernatorial candidate for the great state of Mississippi. Nate had googled him the night before. In a small town like this, a man that powerful was untouchable and his family the same. Though Albie's words were damning.

He wrote about being teased, chased, even roughed up on occasion and for no other reason that he could fathom other than he was "different." They were all different—him, Jeremiah, and Keylan. Keylan wasn't Amish, but he was Black. All had suffered at the hands of the cool kids. If the words held any truth, they were looking at a hate crime.

There was another name mentioned as well. Jay Anderson. Rachel claimed not to have ever heard of him, and Nate believed her. With a name like that, he wasn't Amish. It could very well be that their paths had never crossed. But the relationship between him and Albie wasn't clear. Nate figured he'd be googling again real soon to see what connection Albie had to Jay. The writing simply wasn't clear.

Then at the end of the journal, several pages had been torn out, as if an angry, determined hand had ripped them away.

"What happened here?" he had asked her, pointing to the missing pages.

She shrugged, looked off to the left, and bit the inside of her cheek. "I don't know. It was that way when I found it."

That was a lie. She knew what had happened to the pages. The question was whether or not she knew what was on them and if she or Albie had made the alteration.

Whatever it was, she didn't want Nate or the sheriff to know what they contained.

He could only hope the omission didn't hurt their pleas to open an investigation. Nothing but time would tell. But if the sheriff was smart . . .

The tiny deputy turned to face them once more and hung up the phone. "The sheriff will see you now." She gave a grudgingly curt nod toward the hallway that led to the office door.

"Thanks." Nate rapped his knuckles on the shiny black counter, then turned and nodded for Rachel to precede him.

The wheels of Miri's chair protested against the over-waxed floor as they moved along. Thankfully, the noise ended as they stepped into the carpeted hallway that would take them to the sheriff's personal office. The closer they got to the door, the slower Rachel's footsteps became until she stopped in front of the polished oak and simply stared at it.

Miri laughed. The impulsive sound was part of her condition, he knew, and he was slowly readjusting to it. She laughed at nothing, anything, when there was no reason at all. She simply laughed.

"He knows we're here." Nate kept his voice low and steady, hoping it would lend Rachel some of the moxie she seemed to have lost along the way.

"Are you saying it's too late to turn back?"

"Do you want to?"

She shook her head.

"Then you know what you have to do."

Her first knock was feeble, barely audible to Nate even as he stood directly behind her. Then she pulled in another calming breath and knocked with more force and confidence.

"Come in," a man called from the other side.

Nate reached around the women and opened the door, swinging it wide so Rachel could easily push her sister's chair into the room.

# The Secrets We Keep

Sheriff Walker stood as they entered, his gaze steady and true. Obviously, he had been warned as to who had come calling. The tiny officer might not have remembered their names, but *the Amish woman* and *the deputy from another state* would have been enough to distinguish them. But Ed Walker must not have been told about Miri.

To his credit, he hesitated only slightly when he saw her, then he quickly recovered. Nate supposed that was to be expected; she was a little hard to view. Her disabilities were uncomfortable to most because they were so extensive. If Nate hadn't known her half his life, he would feel the same. He supposed it was human nature to want to stare. To look and see. To count your blessings and be grateful that no one you knew had that many issues. Politeness kept a lot of stares at bay, and some were unable to look at her at all, staring at anything and everything save the poor girl. Perhaps because if they did, they would become one of those who excessively stared.

"What can I do for you folks today?" He looked carefully at Nate, practically ignoring Rachel in his attempts not to stare at Miri.

She laughed.

"I have it," Rachel said. She set the brake on Miri's chair and tugged her purse from her shoulder. Her fingers trembled as she pulled the journal from the bag. She held it out to him. "I don't know if you remember me. My name is Rachel Hostetler." Her eyes closed, and Nate wondered if she was gathering more strength. "This is my brother's journal."

The sheriff stared at the book but made no move to accept it from her.

"My brother is—was—Albie Gingerich," she continued, her lids fluttering open once more. Her chin rose, though her breathing grew more erratic. "I came in to see you once already. This journal contains information you need. I want him . . . exhumed." She stuttered slightly as she said the word. She didn't *want* his body dug up, defiled, but she needed the besmirchment of suicide removed from his life. Nate only hoped that this would do it. That it wasn't all just a waste of time. That it would be worth it in the end.

Walker reached out, took the journal from her, but didn't open it. "Have a seat," he said, nodding toward the chairs in front of his desk.

Rachel sank uneasily onto the faux leather. She remained perched on the edge as if she might jump up and flee at any moment.

Miri awkwardly clapped her hands as if cheering her sister on to victory.

Nate sat down beside Rachel and placed his hat on his lap as he waited for the sheriff to open the journal and look through it.

"I marked a couple of pages," Rachel added helpfully. She flicked a hand toward the book, but Walker didn't look up.

From where he sat, Nate could see where Walker was reading in the journal. The spot that named Albie's tormentors.

"What exactly do you hope to gain from this, Mrs. Hostetler?" He looked up at her then, pinned her with a hard stare.

"My brother did not kill himself. I know he didn't. It's all in there. Chance Longacre and those other boys—" She broke off as he held up one hand to stop her.

"That's a mighty big accusation there." He didn't finish the statement, though Nate could hear it. A mighty big accusation against a member of a very prominent family.

"This isn't just about my brother,"' she said quietly. "There are others. This gang, they prey on the weaker, the different, the gentler. That's not right."

# The Secrets We Keep

Walker sniffed, nodded slowly. "Let's say I do open a case. What do you truly expect me to find?"

"I want justice for my brother," she intoned, her voice firm but low. "And the others too."

"Justice." He looked down into the journal's pages, but Nate doubted he registered anything written there. Walker had that distant, pained look of a man conflicted.

"Albie didn't kill himself," Rachel said. "And I want to know who did."

"You might not like the answer." The words came out almost like a threat.

She shook her head. "He did not kill himself. That much I know. It was one of them. I'm sure of it . . ."

She didn't finish as a knock sounded behind them. Nate turned, only then realizing that he hadn't closed the office door before they'd sat down.

A man came in, holding a file and looking apologetic. He wore khaki tactical pants and a black polo with the sheriff's badge sewn over the left breast pocket. The words stitched below it declared him chief deputy. "Sorry. Didn't mean to interrupt."

The sheriff stood and adjusted his gun belt. It was a move to let everyone in the room know who was in charge. Nate knew first-hand how it was executed. Had done it many times himself. "That's all right, Shane. We're done here."

Nate looked closer at this newcomer. Shane Johnson. They had known each other back in the day. Played ball on the same empty field on the east side of town. Seemed Shane had made good for himself. Odd that somehow they had found themselves in the same profession.

*Not for long.*

71

# Amy Lillard

"Nate?" Shane smiled when he recognized him, extended a hand to shake. "I heard you were back, but I didn't know if it was true or just talk."

"I'm leaving this afternoon," Nate replied simply, even as Rachel swung her gaze in his direction. It was almost tangible, the look she gave him.

"Ah, too bad. I'd have loved to buy you a cup of coffee."

Nate gave a small nod. "Maybe next time."

"Yeah," Shane said with a nod of his own. "Next time."

But there wouldn't be a next time. Nate was leaving Mississippi, and he wasn't coming back. There was too much pain and heartache here.

*You can't go home again.*

"Good to see you, Shane."

"So we're just finished?" Rachel asked, ignoring the two of them and turning her attention to the sheriff. "You're going to open a case?"

"I'm going to think about it."

"He had bruises on his face," she told him, her tone vehement. "Albie did. You don't get bruises from hanging yourself. I looked it up. That means someone else was there. Someone beat him before—well, someone else was there, and the longer you wait—" Her voice broke on a sob, but she quickly pulled herself together.

"I said I would think about it." Ed Walker wasn't backing down an inch. Not from a grieving Amish woman armed with information from the internet.

Her lips pressed together into a thin line. "Can I have my brother's journal back?" The words barely escaped her clenched teeth. She didn't want him to have the book. She didn't believe he planned on doing even one thing about her brother's unfortunate

## The Secrets We Keep

death. Whether he had been murdered or committed suicide, there was no arguing that his death was a tragedy.

Miri laughed, the sound raucous and inappropriate.

"I want to hang on to it for a bit," Walker continued. "Just in case we do feel there's enough evidence to start an investigation." He rested his hand on the butt of his gun. It was a subtle gesture that Nate took to mean *I've heard you, now get out of my office*.

"Come on, Rachel." Nate wrapped one hand around her slender arm. He immediately wished he hadn't. Touching her, even innocently, brought back too many memories.

He nodded to Shane and the sheriff, then gestured for Rachel to turn Miri's chair around.

"Nate?"

He stopped at the door, turned to listen to what Shane had to say.

"I was sorry to hear about your dad."

Nate merely nodded, then ushered Rachel and Miri from the room.

She was shaking as they left the sheriff's office and stepped out into the harsh Mississippi sunlight. But this time her trembling wasn't from nervousness; it was anger. He knew her so well he could tell the difference without her even saying a word.

"He's not going to do anything," she fumed as she unlatched the back of the buggy and rolled her sister inside. "He's all big talk when he wants to be. But the Amish don't vote often enough around here. He doesn't care what we think." Her agitation showed in the stiffness of her movements as she strapped her sister's wheelchair into its space and stomped out of the buggy. He had never seen anyone execute a stomp and a duck walk at the same time, but somehow she managed it. She shut the back of the special carriage, latched it, then turned to Nate.

"I'm sorry," he told her as he settled his hat back on his head.

# Amy Lillard

"It's not your fault." The air left her in a rush, and as quickly as it had come on, her anger dissipated. He could tell that she was disappointed, and he hated the feeling of having let her down. Yet there was nothing more that could be done.

"There's still a little hope," he said, resisting the urge to smooth the wrinkles that marred her brow. "Walker kept the journal. Maybe he'll pass it on to the detectives and they'll start something up." But he knew that wouldn't happen without urging from Walker himself.

"Maybe," she murmured. "What I need is someone on my side doing the investigating. Someone smart who knows the Amish and the troubles we have with some *Englisch*. Someone like you."

# Chapter Five

"That's not going to happen." He said the words so quickly that she didn't believe him. With a little pressure she knew she could make him stay. She had guilt on her side, but she didn't want to be that person. She didn't want to make him do anything he didn't want to do. That was a bad row to hoe. She had learned that lesson long ago, and the hard way to boot.

Just seeing Nathan again was like rubbing lemon juice in a fresh wound. The pain was so sharp, so real, it made her teeth ache. It brought back every bad decision she had made since that fateful day when he told her he was leaving the church to play baseball. The day he had asked her to go with him. The day she had told him no. Every bad decision since then hung around her like a mantle of heavy oak.

She had been taught her entire life to believe that *Gott's* will was final. That she had to accept the tragedies along with the blessings and to be thankful for them both. That was simply life.

But there were times . . . oh, there were times . . . at night, when she was lying in bed alone that she questioned those tragedies. Questioned *Gott* Himself. In the morning she always felt remorseful for her hateful, doubting thoughts. She would pray, ask *Gott's* forgiveness, and she would move through the rest of her day. Things always looked different in the daylight. Then once darkness fell again . . .

"Are you really leaving today?" She hadn't meant to ask, but the words were there all the same.

"I said I was." His voice sounded like water through an old rusty pipe.

"I guess you should be getting back to your life there."

Something unidentifiable flashed through his expression. It was there and gone again so quick that she almost believed she had imagined it. *Secrets,* she thought. Parts of him that she knew nothing about. He had been gone for twelve long years. He had a life without her. A career, friends. Everything without her. There had been a time when she knew everything about him. Could tell him his own thoughts before he even thought them. But that was a long time ago.

It was a time when he knew everything about her. No longer. There was so much now that she was ashamed to admit. So many things she would never tell another soul. Not even Nathan. Especially not Nathan.

"Be careful driving home," she told him.

From habit she stepped closer to him as if to kiss him goodbye.

He cleared his throat. Took a step back.

"Sorry," she murmured, not because she had almost pressed her cheek to his but because she no longer should. She was sorry for that, for the distance, the gulf between them, sorrier than he would ever know.

\* \* \*

"What was that about?"

Sheriff Ed Walker stared at the leather-bound journal a moment more before tossing it onto his desk. There was something fishy about the whole thing. Rachel Hostetler was a little too willing to hand over evidence all of a sudden. And those missing pages . . .

"Nothing." Ed finally answered Shane's question. Then he shook his head. "That Amish boy who killed himself."

"An Amish suicide?" Shane raised one brow, then sat down in the chair closest to him. "When did this happen?"

"While you were on vacation. Franklin's working it." But that wasn't the truth. It had landed on his desk, but Franklin was too close to retirement to give much attention to anything. Add in the fact that no one wanted to mess in Amish affairs . . .

Ed couldn't blame the men. The Amish were too much like a cult for his liking, and he wished daily that he could scoop up the whole lot of them and move them up to Ohio or Pennsylvania where they belonged. Because they sure as hell didn't belong in Mississippi.

Damn it. One Amish kid offs himself and now all hell was coming down on him. Since the father had buried the boy without notifying the police, Ed could get him for moving a corpse, but did he really want to? It sure wasn't what Rachel Hostetler wanted him to do. The whole thing was more trouble than it was worth.

"What does this have to do with it?" Shane asked as he leaned over and plucked the journal from the desktop.

Ed flicked a hand toward the book. "I guess he kept a diary, and now the sister thinks that he was murdered."

"Murdered?" Shane's head snapped up. "That's the last time I take time off."

"There's no real evidence to support her claim." Without evidence, they had nothing to go on. The body had been cut down and buried. The clothes the boy had been wearing and the rope he had used to hang himself destroyed, burned. Or at least that was what the sister had told him the first time she had come into his office calling foul play. But then she hadn't had the journal.

77

The journal that stated four boys from four very well-connected families might have been bullying those different than them. Just as the sister had alleged. One Black boy; two Amish.

If that was the case, then the evidence he had just claimed they lacked could be rotting away in a grave at that very moment. "Now that she's got that idea in her head, she wants me to order an autopsy, have the body exhumed, the whole nine yards."

"Want me to look into it?" Of all his deputies, Shane was the one most involved with the Amish community. In truth, there were some affairs where he trusted his chief more than his under-sheriff. Anything to do with the Amish by far. So out of sheer habit, most of the calls that came in about the Amish went to Shane Johnson. Not that there were that many. The Plain folk mostly kept to themselves. Just how Ed liked it.

Come to think of it, it was something of a fluke that Ed hadn't given the complaint to Shane to begin with. Fluke. That was better than saying he had handed it off to Franklin because Shane was off and Ed hadn't cared one way or the other.

But that was before he knew Chance Longacre might be involved.

He shook his head. "That's not necessary." Let sleeping dogs lie, he always said. Soon the sister would give up and accept her father's decision and quit trying to blame prominent young men in the county for something that couldn't be proven.

"Chance Longacre?" Shane glanced up from the pages of the journal and shot Ed a concerned look.

The one thing about the case that couldn't be forgotten.

"Yeah, Chance Longacre."

The senator's unruly son was the exact reason Ed wouldn't let himself get any more involved in this mess than to allow a courtesy visit with the sister and her law enforcement friend from out of

# The Secrets We Keep

town. Let her get it out of her system and let the cowboy go back home. Then everything would die down and return to normal. He was counting on it.

"These boys are . . ." Shane trailed off. He didn't need to finish the sentence for Ed to know what he was about to say. All four boys came from the best families in the area. Taylor Bennett's father owned Bennett Ford over in Tupelo. Ely Thatcher was the son of the preacher at the First Baptist Church, and Leo Davidson's father owned and operated the largest sawmill in the area. Then there was Chance.

"I can't do a thing. Not to Chance Longacre. Politics." He didn't like the look on Shane's face.

"Ed, we've known each other for years. You taught me everything I know about the law. Do I really need to remind you that politics go in both directions?"

Ed didn't need for him to, and yet he had forced Shane to say the words all the same.

Nope, Ed couldn't let this dog lie. He had to kick it awake and hope it ran off on its own. Damn, he hated kicking dogs. He liked things nice and quiet. Simple country life. Kicked dogs tended to yelp, bark, and bite those who had kicked them.

The clock ticked behind him. The clock Margie had bought him when he'd first been elected. The face bore his name and a depiction of the badge he wore clipped to his belt. Every second that went by was one more second that the only real evidence they might have was decomposing in an unmarked grave outside the Amish cemetery.

"Was he beaten?" Shane asked. "Like she said?"

Ed shrugged. "No idea. The father buried him the very next day."

It wasn't illegal in Mississippi to bury someone without embalming them as long as the burial was within forty-eight hours of the death. The illegal part was not notifying the police at the time and in the moving of the body itself. That was the coroner's job.

Shane seemed to mull over that tiny detail. That tiny, gigantic detail. "If she kicks up a fuss about this . . ."

She wouldn't. She was Amish. Coming into the office to complain was as much of a fuss as she would make. But if word got around that a body had been moved . . . Amish or not, everyone would start to think they could do whatever they wanted in their peaceful little community. So long, simple country life.

"Ed? If what I'm thinking she's saying is really what she's saying, you might just have a hate crime on your hands."

Hate crime. Hate felony. One thing that could not be overlooked. "Damn it all to effing hell," Ed muttered, then picked up the phone.

\* \* \*

Nate threw his bag into the back of his truck and slid into the driver's seat. Time to go home. But just like the first time he left, a rock of longing settled in his stomach.

He cranked the motor, the ache increasing. He wanted to drive out to his mother's house one last time. He wanted to see if she would visit with him, even for just a little while. He knew she wouldn't let him in the house, but maybe they could sit on the porch. Or hell, maybe even stand out in the road so he wouldn't be on her property. But she wasn't ready for that, and he had promised Sarah he wouldn't. His father had only been gone for a week or so, and Emma King Fisher was still very much under the influence of her husband, Karl. Maybe one day she could see her way to letting Nate back in. But today was definitely not that day.

And the truth of it was, Nate wasn't coming back. Not until they buried her.

*You can't go home.*

When he left today, he would never see her again. That was the hard truth of it. And that was what allowed the burning ache to spread inside him until he could hardly breathe.

A knock sounded on the window of his truck. Nate jumped at the intrusion into his thoughts. He turned to see who was tapping.

Shane Johnson stood outside, motioning for Nate to roll down his window.

Heart thumping, he did just that.

"I know you said you were leaving today, but I'd like to talk to you about the Albie Gingerich case."

Nate looked at him carefully. "So there's a case now?"

"Something like that. The sheriff made the call to exhume the body. But I want to know what you know before you leave. Buy you a cup of coffee?"

Nate wanted to say no. As much as a person couldn't go home again, leaving was getting harder and harder as the what-ifs and what-might-have-beens pressed in on him. "In this heat?" Nate asked. "How about an iced tea?"

"The Grill?" Shane suggested.

"Meet you there."

Shane nodded and moved away toward his own vehicle, an unmarked, dark-blue Ford.

Nate had been so lost in his own thoughts he hadn't even seen the SUV pull into the strip of a parking lot. It was past time to get himself together. Way past time to get himself back to Tulsa. Back where he belonged.

But even as the thought crossed his mind, even as he put the truck into reverse and backed out of the space, even as he pointed his front bumper toward downtown Pontotoc, he wondered if he would feel like he belonged anywhere ever again. But one thing was certain: He surely didn't belong here.

"So, tell me what you know about this." Shane tossed the journal onto the table between them.

Nate resisted the urge to pick it up and flip through the pages once more.

The two were seated in the Grill with tall glasses of iced tea complete with fresh lemon wedges sitting in front of them.

"Not much at all," Nate admitted. He didn't know a lot about what was going on, and everything he had came exclusively from Rachel's point of view. Law enforcement had taught him one hard, fast lesson: There were always at least four sides to every story. Sometimes more. Hers was merely one. "Rachel told me that Albie died, that everyone thought he had committed suicide, but she didn't believe it."

"How did you end up at the sheriff's office with her?"

Should he remind Shane that he had always been a fool where Rachel was concerned? That the only time he had ever told her no was when he had left to play baseball?

It was a decision he regularly questioned. Sure, it had made him who he was today, but there were times when he didn't necessarily like who he had become. Too many of them to even keep track of, especially lately.

He shoved that thought aside. *Take care of business, then hit the road.* He could drink this tea with Shane and still get home by ten.

"She asked me to help her. Said she went in by herself and didn't feel like anyone took her seriously."

Shane wagged his head back and forth. "We're taking it seriously now."

# The Secrets We Keep

"Not because of me," Nate added.

"That journal." Shane punched down his ice with his straw and shot Nate a look. "What about those pages? You know what was on them? Where they are now?"

"No to both," he replied. "Rachel said the book was like that when she found it." Not that he believed her.

"She found it," Shane repeated. "What exactly does that mean?"

Nate suddenly felt a bit bristly. Something in Shane's tone had shifted. At first his voice had been open and friendly, but now it had taken on a different edge. The shift between friend and investigator. "You'll have to ask her."

"Did she say where she found it?"

"Nope."

"Did you look at it? Is it really in Albie's writing?"

The hair on the back of Nate's neck stood at attention. This conversation was beginning to get more than a bit trying.

"Why don't you talk to her about that? I don't know what Albie's writing looks like." He reached out and thumbed through the pages. "He was twelve years old the last time I saw him. And most of us tend to write very similarly."

"Us?"

"Amish. Ex-Amish." He shrugged.

"It does seem to have been written by the same person throughout. But if what you're saying is true . . ."

"What?" This conversation was really hard to follow. Or maybe he was just having trouble keeping his mind in one spot.

"It could be Rachel's journal that she's trying to pass off as her brother's."

"Why would she do that?" Nate did his best not to scoff at the idea. Sometimes his training really paid off. He'd been told he had a helluva poker face.

Still, it took everything he had to remain calm, seated, and continue this farce of a sociable glass of tea between old friends. He wanted to know where this was going. What Shane was truly trying to get at. If the information was worthy, he would pass it on to Rachel and then get the hell out of Dodge. Otherwise he would just get up and walk away that very moment.

All for Rachel.

"To convince us to open a case," Shane said. He watched Nate closely.

"If there's no case, then she wouldn't have been in to talk to you. Twice."

Shane made a dubious face. "All those drawings?"

"Those are Albie's. Rachel can't draw two convincing stick figures." That much he knew for certain. Though he wasn't sure why he felt it necessary to share this information with Shane.

Normally Nate was as closemouthed as they came, but all this therapy lately seemed to have loosened his tongue. But not his suspicions. "Rachel truly believes that Albie didn't kill himself."

"And because she believes it, you do as well?"

He wasn't even going to validate that with an answer.

"I know you and Rachel had a thing back in the day."

A thing. That was what he was going to call it? It had been more than *a thing*. If it hadn't been for Nate's arrogance and prideful nature, he and Rachel would be married. He would never have left. His family would not have shunned him. He would still be Amish. He wouldn't have killed a young man. A thing. Yeah, it was much more than *a thing*.

"I'm not trying to point any fingers," Shane continued.

*Not yet, anyway.*

"But tell me it's not weird that those pages are missing. The last entries that Albie wrote in the book are gone. Whatever was on

# The Secrets We Keep

them is important. Most likely a secret, but someone doesn't want anyone else to know that secret. So who tore them out? Albie? Rachel? Someone else? You tell me."

"How should I know?" He didn't like being questioned in this manner, not as a witness but as a potential suspect. Or perhaps an accessory. That was what this felt like. Shane might not be writing anything down, but he was recording it in his thoughts. Trying to trip Nate up, make him say things that maybe he wouldn't otherwise.

And it hit him then. Shane didn't know what Nate did for a living. How could he know unless someone else had told him? So Shane didn't know they were on the same team, on the side of justice and the truth.

But Nate had to wonder if Sheriff Ed Walker wanted the truth or if he just wanted all of this to go away. Moreover, Nate didn't know how firmly entrenched Shane might be in the sheriff's camp.

"And where are those pages now?" Shane continued. "Hidden away? Burned? In the bottom of someone's birdcage?"

"I don't know that either."

They sat in silence for a moment as the eatery geared up for the lunch crowd. "Why are you on the case?" Nate finally asked. "I thought another guy had it."

"There are some very prominent people being accused of some pretty bad dealings."

"Prominent people's children."

"Same thing," Shane said. "The truth needs to be discovered."

"What happens if it turns out that Rachel is telling the truth, that these kids are involved? What then?"

Shane shook his head. "I guess we cross that bridge when we come to it."

85

*Burn it, more likely.*

"I thought you were a fair and square fella." Nate shook his head and stood. Then he took out his wallet and tossed down a couple of ones for the waitress. "Thanks for the tea," he said. Then he reached down and snatched the journal from the table. Without another word, he turned for the door.

He had thought they could talk about this as friends, but that clearly wasn't the case. Shane just wanted dirt on Rachel. Nate wasn't leaving any ammunition behind. Whatever it was that had made the sheriff want to open a case, it wasn't in the journal.

"Wait." Shane stuck out a hand to stop him.

Nate could have easily stepped to the side and continued on his way, but he allowed Shane this one last say.

"You're not going to take that." Shane nodded toward the journal.

"I am." His words dared Shane to defy him. They weren't the only ones that could be intimidating. "If you want to look at it again, you'll have to arrange that with Rachel."

"What about your contact information? In case we need to talk to you again."

Nate gave him a cold look. "Ask your sheriff. He knows where to find me."

# Chapter Six

Nate's phone buzzed from the passenger's seat, where he'd tossed it when he'd gotten back into his truck. He picked it up. Bree.

*Satchel is missing you. Be home soon?*

He doubted very much that the cat even realized Nate hadn't been around. Not with Bree filling his bowl and scratching him behind his one good ear. It was Bree who was wondering when he was coming home. Bree who was worried about him.

Come to think of it, he was a little worried about himself.

He pitched the phone back into the passenger's seat and gripped the steering wheel. He had said he wouldn't come back out here, but he couldn't leave town without seeing her just one last time. However, in the ten or so minutes since he had parked his truck and left the engine idling, he hadn't seen his mother even once. Gas prices were too high to sit here burning fuel and stalking the woman who had given birth to him. She obviously knew what his truck looked like. And it seemed plain to him now that she was avoiding him.

Nate grabbed his phone again and typed a message to his neighbor. One word. *Soon.*

Then he put his truck into gear and pointed the nose toward the cemetery.

His father's grave was still no more than an unmarked mound of freshly turned earth, but Mattie . . . He hadn't visited her when he had come before. He'd lost his focus when he'd seen Rachel and those two sets of eyes staring at him from the back of the buggy. After that, all he could think about was that she had gone on without him.

Of course she had. In a sense he supposed he had as well, but he hadn't fallen in love. He hadn't married another. There were times when he wished he could love Bree. Those times when he saw a spark of something more in her eyes. But he had given his heart to Rachel, then he had broken it to pieces when he left her behind. There wasn't enough left to give anyone else.

Mattie. He had to see her before he left. He made a quick stop at the gas station, where he filled up his tank, picked up a couple bottles of water and a bag of M&M's, before heading off the main road. Back at the cemetery once more, this time he looked to see if anyone else was around. But no buggies lurked behind the tall grasses. He was alone.

A narrow path bisected the small cemetery. His father was on one side and his sister the other. He turned toward Mattie's grave, barely remembering where it was yet instinctively finding it at the edge of the field. He remembered now, hovering watching as they laid her to rest. Not able to speak to anyone, unable to attend the wake since he was under the *Bann*. But he remembered where they had put her, thought it kind of fitting that she was barely in the cemetery at all. It was as if her spirit were so bright it could barely be contained. Or maybe that she could dance away like she never had been able to in life, escape in death from the pain that living had caused her.

He squatted down next to the small cross that bore her name and the year of her death. He took off his hat, set it to one side, then sat fully in the grass next to her.

# The Secrets We Keep

"Well, here we are," he told her. He wanted to apologize for not being successful in saving her, not making enough money to pay for her to have a new heart. For not staying and spending those last four years of life with her. For being arrogant enough to think he had the talent to play with the *Englisch* kids who had been fed competitive baseball since they were in diapers.

But what good were the words now?

Instead he pulled out the packet of M&M's and smiled a little to himself as he opened one end. He poured the candies into the palm of his hand. Three yellow came out first with a blue and a red. He picked the last two out and ate them, then placed the yellow ones near her marker.

The yellow ones had always been Mattie's favorite. She swore they tasted different than the rest. Said the yellow were little bits of sunshine that you could carry in your pocket, eat, then you could keep them with you always. So you were never without the sun.

There were five yellow total, and he placed them all next to the cross. They wouldn't last long in the heat, not even with their candy coating. Then he sat there and ate the rest of the bag, not really wanting them. Because they didn't taste like the sun, and as much as he wanted to regain the feelings he'd had before he left, that time was over.

He crumpled up the bag and shoved it into his pocket, then he redonned his hat and pushed himself to his feet.

*You don't have to go home, but you can't stay here.*

It was time. Whether he wanted to or not. It was time to go home.

He brushed the grass from his jeans, then turned to leave, stopping as another mound of dirt captured his attention. It was outside the fence, though he had been too lost in the past to see it earlier. Now that he had, he knew immediately what it was. Albie Gingerich's grave.

# Amy Lillard

According to Shane, the coroner would be digging it up soon. Maybe even as early as tomorrow. If they truly thought there were clues to be found, time was of the essence. Mississippi heat and an unembalmed dead body where not conducive to preserving evidence. They might even start today. But by the end of business, he would be halfway back to Tulsa.

He removed his hat and nodded once in Albie's direction, then replaced it and turned toward the cemetery's exit.

The rattle of a buggy slowed his steps. Just what he needed, some mourner coming out and finding him there. Well, he supposed that was too bad. Who were they going to complain to that would listen? No one. And he'd be long gone.

His steps stalled as a familiar figure swung down from the buggy. Rachel. A small girl, no more than four or five, climbed down and stood next to her. She was the miniature of her *mamm*. Both wore purple dresses cut from the same cloth, but whereas Rachel's apron was dark green and her prayer covering white, the little girl's apron was black and her *kapp* gray. And though she had Rachel's grass-green eyes, her hair was a dark chocolate brown. Just like that of Freeman Hostetler.

Rachel stilled when she spotted him. He realized then that she had come out to see Albie. Perhaps after Nate had left Shane at the grill, the detective had gone on to question Rachel once more and to tell her that the coroner would be performing the autopsy she had demanded. Nate just hoped she understood what she was asking for. What she was up against. Not only were the odds stacked against finding any evidence of a cause of death other than suicide, but she risked facing discipline from the church as she prepared to fight a family more powerful than any other in Northeast Mississippi.

There was still the off chance that the unknown Jay Anderson might have something to do with Albie's death. But it seemed unlikely. Albie's journal appeared to point straight to the senator's son.

# The Secrets We Keep

Rachel waited for Nate to come near, holding the little girl's hand and talking to her though he couldn't hear what was being said.

"I didn't expect to see you out here," she said when he was finally close enough that she could speak without raising her voice. "I thought you were on your way home."

He stopped just in front of her. "I was. I am." *Home.* That word didn't have the same meaning for him any longer. He didn't think it ever would again. "I just came to see Mattie."

"And now you are leaving?"

"Yeah." It would do no good for him to be hanging around. It wouldn't change any of the facts, but the thought of leaving her at the mercy of the uncaring sheriff and the suspicious detective made him a little sick. Like he was abandoning her all over again.

"I talked to the chief deputy. The sheriff is opening a case for Albie."

She nodded. "He came by the house."

Perhaps that was why she had felt compelled to come here. To tell Albie she had finally gotten her wish.

The girl pulled on Rachel's hand. Rachel looked down into her inquisitive face. "*Jah?*"

"Is he a cowboy?" the cherub asked.

Rachel smiled but only just.

He supposed she didn't want her little one to think she was laughing at her. And he knew this petite *maedel* was a handful. Something in the sparkle of her eyes brought back memories of Rachel's adventuresome streak. A trait she seemed to have lost with age. Hell, life had the power to do that to anybody.

"I don't know, Kate," she replied. "But you may ask him yourself."

Kate turned those meadow-green eyes to him, and he felt as if he had stepped back in time. A better time. "Are you a cowboy?" she questioned.

91

"Not exactly." It was the best answer he could give her that she could understand.

"But you wear a hat like one," she continued.

"Yes." Nothing like the demands of a preschooler to put a person on the spot.

"That's enough now," Rachel said.

For a moment, he thought the girl might protest, argue back, but it seemed she was smart enough to know when to pick her battles, and he was not one that she was willing to take a stand for.

"Thank you," Rachel said. She didn't have to finish the rest, didn't have to tell him what she was thankful for. He knew.

Nate nodded. Though the sheriff's backtracking wasn't his doing. In fact, none of it seemed to be. Nor had it been Rachel's willingness to hand over the journal, or Shane would never have let him leave with it. Something else must have happened after they left the sheriff's office that had made him change his mind, and Nate couldn't help but wonder what it was.

They stood that way for a moment, just looking at one another. Needing to say something, unable to say anything. Unwilling to move forward. Unable to go back.

He couldn't do this forever. Well, he *could*. But he just couldn't. He moved to go past her, the scent of her teasing his senses as the years fell away. "Goodbye, Rachel."

"I have no right to ask you."

He stopped two paces behind her. He turned slowly but still didn't face her. "Ask me what?"

Out of the corner of his eye he could see her shake her head, the tremble of her shoulders as she pulled in a deep breath. Then she visibly stilled. She was stronger now. Stronger than he had ever seen her. How much of that resilience could he lay at his own feet

# The Secrets We Keep

for the pain he had put her through? How much was from the twelve years that had passed?

"They are . . . exhuming his body tomorrow."

He turned and faced her fully. "You don't need to be here for that."

"Nathan." The one word, just his name, held a weight of emotions.

"Rachel. Please. Tell me you won't be here."

"Who else will be here for him?" Tears thickened her voice.

Nate closed his eyes, gathered his own strength. When he opened them again, she had composed herself. The tears were gone, absorbed back into her pain. "It's past that now," he said.

He couldn't tell her what it would be like. That digging up a grave in any situation was a terrible, unthinkable endeavor. But this . . . they would exhume that box and take him out of it. They would place his decomposing remains in a harsh black body bag, then take him away in the back of the coroner's van. The police would save the coffin for evidence. Though they would do all this outside, the smell would be unbearable, even for those most seasoned in dealing with death. The people who got paid to witness such an event would be haunted by it for months, maybe years, but for a sister . . . "Just promise me," he said.

"I can't do that." She shook her head.

He dipped his chin in Kate's direction. "You have bigger responsibilities."

Her mouth twisted into an ugly frown, part grimace part pain. "I know what my responsibilities are." *And you don't have the right to remind me of them.*

He could hear her thoughts though she didn't give voice to them. Didn't tell him that he had given up that privilege the day he left.

"Rachel."

"What am I supposed to do, Nathan?" She propped her hands on her hips and faced him down, a mother hen defending her chicks. "Kate, go get in the buggy."

Kate looked from one of them to the other, assessing the entire situation and coming up with only heaven knew what as the cause of this friction. "I thought cowboys were the good guys."

"Buggy, Kate. Now." Rachel didn't take her gaze off him as she fairly spit the words from her mouth.

One more heartbeat passed before Kate decided to obey her mother. She seemed reluctant, most likely wanting to question him more on the whole cowboy angle. Instead she turned on one bare foot and made her way back to the carriage.

"They are my children," Rachel told him as soon as Kate was out of earshot. "And I take care of them. I am both mother and father to them. And have been for the last three years."

"I was only suggesting that you concentrate your time on the living. Allow the others to take care of the dead. They'll let you know what they find."

"I'm sure they will."

He could hear it then, the distrust she had for the police, perhaps even her father and the bishop. She believed Albie had been wronged, and the list of culprits was growing.

"Just go," she said, the venom leeching from her tone.

He didn't know if she meant away from her at the moment, or home to Tulsa.

"Goodbye, Rachel." How many times would he be forced to say those words to her?

She didn't respond, just closed her eyes.

He hesitated only a moment before turning and making his way back to his truck. He didn't want to leave like this. He didn't want to leave at all. And yet he couldn't get out of there soon enough.

It took almost everything he had to not look back as he walked away. It was harder that way. Maybe easier in the long run. He didn't need any more memories of her to haunt him. He climbed into the driver's seat of his pickup and slid his hat onto the dash.

Kate's innocent words swam around him, in and out of the heat his truck cab had picked up during his short stop at the cemetery.

*I thought cowboys were the good guys.*

They were, mostly. But they couldn't save everyone. That lesson he had learned the hard way. Was still dealing with it daily.

He started the engine and pulled out onto the gravel road. He wanted to speed away. Put as much distance between him and his past as quickly as possible, but the road was rutted and dry. No matter how fast he ran, it would always catch up with him.

He eased his foot off the gas and did his best to enjoy the ride. Just a couple of miles and he would be back on the highway. Then he could breathe easier. And it would be easier, once he got started. Once he was headed home.

His foot hit the brake when he realized he still had Albie's journal. He'd mail it back to Rachel once he got to Tulsa. He had to get going. He punched the gas once more.

He noted the houses he passed with familiar eyes. It was strange watching them go by from air-conditioned comfort. He almost expected the view to be set to the soundtrack of buggy wheels and the clop of horse hooves. Not the hum of a V-8 engine.

It was his life now. It was different. Changed. He was changed. Everything had changed. Even if it didn't look as if it had. People were no longer the same. Faces transformed. Children were born, old folks died. Life went on.

And it would go on for Rachel.

He needed no other proof than the green eyes that had surveyed him so precisely. Not hers, but Kate's.

*I thought cowboys were the good guys.*

He slowed his truck as he neared the intersection with Highway 9.

They were the good guys, he thought as he waited for the logging truck to go by. They were as good as they could be. But cowboys were human as well.

Just a few more miles to 278 West.

*Go west, young man.*

He slowed as he neared the water tower for the community of Cedar Creek.

All he had to do was keep going. But he felt like he'd hit some kind of force field. Like he was magically unable to continue. He wanted to. The conscious part of him knew that was what he needed to do. Yet another part of him seemed to have a different idea. He whipped into the gravel lot surrounding the water tower.

The car behind him sped past, honking their horn as they made their way. He must have been slowing down for yards before finally making the decision to pull off the road.

He shoved the gearshift into park and laid his head against the steering wheel. He closed his eyes, sucked in a deep breath. Then another. He needed to go home. He wanted to go home. He couldn't go home.

A quick rap sounded on the glass beside him. He looked up into a stranger's face.

Nate rolled down the window for the old man.

"You all right, son?" he asked. He wore well-broken-in bib overalls over a crisp, long-sleeved blue shirt. Great tuffs of white hair sprouted from his ears, and a grease-stained baseball hat advertising the local co-op sat atop his head. His eyes were blue, wide with concern. "You need me to call anybody?"

# The Secrets We Keep

Nate pulled a smile up from somewhere. "No. I'm good. I'm just . . ." *I'm just what? Swamped with memories? Trying to figure out where I belong in the world? Once again leaving behind the only woman I've ever loved?* "I spilled my drink in my lap."

The man's gaze flicked from Nate's face to the cupholder with nothing in it. He hadn't even taken the bottles of water he'd bought at the convenience store out of the bag the cashier had put them in. The man gave him another concerned look.

"I'm fine," Nate said. "Really."

The man didn't want to leave him, Nate could tell, but there was no reason for him to stay. "You take care of yourself, hear?"

Nate nodded. "Yessir."

The old man dipped his chin only once, then limped his way back to the shiny vintage Ford pickup he'd parked behind Nate's Chevy.

Nate waited for him to get his truck steered back toward the road. He waved to let the Good Samaritan know he was thankful for the concern, then put his own truck into gear.

Now all he had to do was pull back onto the highway. Point his truck west and let the asphalt and the big engine do the rest.

Except he couldn't. He had walked away twice already. A third time just wasn't in him. He had failed her on so many levels, in so many ways. When he left the first time. When her mother had died and he didn't come back for her. When Mattie had died and he came back, then left again. This time he couldn't do it.

He didn't know what difference his presence would make in the investigation of Albie Gingerich's death. None, most likely. He had no sway with the Pontotoc County Sheriff's Office, and he was fairly certain any assistance he might give would be viewed instead as interference. But he sure as hell didn't have much waiting for him at home. A career he no longer wanted, a one-eared cat, and a woman he couldn't give his heart to.

97

# Chapter Seven

"A deputy sheriff?" Shane collapsed into the seat in front of the sheriff's desk and shook his head. "You didn't think that might be something you should have told me before I ran him down and questioned him like a common criminal?"

Ed tossed the paper clip he had been messing with back onto his desk blotter and gave a small shrug. "I figured you knew already. Weren't you guys friends back in the day?"

"Yeah, but that was over fifteen years ago."

"No one told you to mistreat him."

"I didn't mistreat him." Shane just wanted to do his job the best he could. And his job was to protect the sheriff and the citizens of Pontotoc County. Not necessarily in that order. But it would have been helpful to know that he and Nate were on the same side.

Or maybe they weren't. He might not remember everything about those days. But one thing that stuck out to him the most was how much Nate had loved Rachel. When he wasn't lamenting over baseball, all Nathan Fisher could talk about was Rachel Gingerich. But once Nate had made up his mind that he could save his sister by leaving and turning pro, it was as if he had set all other feelings aside. Perhaps he thought he would be able to come back and pick up where he had left off. Perhaps he had thought that

Rachel would cave and go with him to wherever his career might take him.

Shane had been one of the few who had tried to talk Nate out of such dreams. Professional baseball was a hard game to crack, and to walk away from everything and everyone he knew or loved for money hadn't seemed logical. Not even when millions of dollars were at stake. But Nate hadn't been after the money for himself. He had merely wanted to cure his sister. Once the notion that he could had settled in on him, there was no changing his mind.

Shane wondered how Nate felt about that now. If he looked back and wished he'd kept the blessings he had and not reached for the stars.

Then there was a part of Shane that envied the bravery it had taken for Nate to just go for it. Shane had done everything by the book. Wrangled a scholarship to Ole Miss, prayed a scout would find him. Played his best games, ate the right foods, didn't party, didn't do anything, and he had wound up right back where he started.

Not that he minded being in Cedar Creek. He loved his hometown. But there were still days when he wondered if there was more out there for him.

"You don't have anything to worry about," the sheriff said. "He's leaving town today."

"I suppose."

"And you're going to be out there tomorrow." It wasn't quite a question.

"If that's where you need me to be." It was perhaps the last place Shane wanted to be, watching them dig up a dead body that had been buried for almost three weeks. There was nothing he would be able to discern from the corpse itself. It would be more than a mess. That chore would fall to the coroner. Who knew when they would get that information back? The office they used for autopsies was backlogged clear into the following year.

"I want you there. I want you to see who shows up. How they're acting. I want to know if there's anything else in that box."

"Like the pages from the journal?"

Ed nodded. "Like the pages from the journal."

"Will do." At least he wouldn't have to stand too close to the grave site to gather that kind of information. "About the journal . . ."

"Yeah?"

"Nate took it."

"You let him have it," the sheriff countered.

"He wanted it, and I didn't figure there was much in it that we needed. Those missing pages, that's where the good stuff is."

"So find 'em," Ed demanded.

"Right." Shane stood and checked his watch. "If that's all . . ." He might still be able to get in nine holes before he needed to be home for supper. Tomorrow's weather was promising to be even hotter than today. Much too hot to stay on the fairway, and golf wasn't nearly as much fun in the trees.

The sheriff shook his head. "One more thing."

"Yeah."

"I need you to find this Keylan Reid."

"The boy mentioned in the journal?"

"That's the one. He just might be our star witness for this case."

\* \* \*

Nate sat down on the bed in his motel room and flipped open the steno notebook he'd picked up at Walmart. He'd also bought a few T-shirts, a couple of pairs of sweatpants, underwear, new socks, and a stack of notebooks and a packet of pens, as well as detergent and fabric softener to clean the clothes he'd brought with him.

He was no longer kidding himself that he was going back to Oklahoma anytime soon. He couldn't stay until they got the results

# The Secrets We Keep

of the autopsy back. He knew how slowly those wheels turned even in a big place like Tulsa. He could imagine that they moved at a crippled snail's pace here. Add in that the vic was Amish, and foul play questionable; multiply by the political power of the family being accused . . . it might be years before they could find out the truth. But he wanted to write down all the information in the journal that might be useful. Including the fact that the last couple of pages were missing. He wanted to record it all and take it to Rachel. Then she would have the ammunition she needed to keep the sheriff in line. If there was an Amish woman alive who could cow the sheriff, that woman was an angry Rachel Gingerich.

*Hostetler,* he corrected. That was something he needed to remember. Her husband might be missing, but in the eyes of the church she was still very much married until he showed back up, alive or dead.

It was the perfect excuse, though, to write everything down. The excuse to stay. The excuse to see her again. The excuse to not go back. The excuse to quit his job and figure out what he wanted to do before continuing on. Okay, so maybe he wouldn't quit his job outright, but he could take all his PTO and stretch any remaining vacation days to give him a week or so to work on things. Here was as good a place as any for self-reflection.

Though he could use more modern surroundings, beggars could not be choosers. He had driven from the water tower straight back into town, right back to the motel.

*Quizzical* was most likely the best word to describe the look on the woman's face when he asked for a room after checking out only three hours before. But he didn't acknowledge the questions in her eyes. He just gave her his credit card, told her again that he was the only one planning to occupy the room and he didn't know when he'd be checking out.

**Amy Lillard**

"Is that a problem?" he asked her.

She shook her head. "If it's more than a week, we'll need to close out this invoice and run your credit card again. Motel policy."

"Fine," he told her. He didn't plan on staying more than a week. That was what he'd texted Bree and Travis, at any rate. They texted back almost immediately saying they would see him when he returned and to be safe coming home.

Home. He might not have much of a life waiting for him, but surely in a week he'd get tired of his own company. Surely in a week he could get whatever this was out of his system enough that he could move forward. Right now, he was in some sort of holding pattern, a limbo of bad choices and new decisions.

He'd gotten a different room this time. Same side of the motel still facing the sandwich shop across the street. Same green carpet and rust and green paisley bedspreads on squeaky full-sized beds. The pictures on the wall above them were black-and-white photographs, enlarged and framed. At first glance he'd thought them to be vintage pics, but after a little careful consideration he could tell they were recent snaps of small-town life, action shots from what looked to be the Bodock Festival held annually there in downtown Pontotoc.

After Nate had procured himself a room, he went shopping, bought himself a sandwich from across the street, and settled in with his notebook.

*Jeremiah Troyer.*

The name popped out to him like it was highlighted in shocking yellow. He, like Albie and his friend Keylan Reid, had supposedly been bullied by Chance Longacre and his gang.

Maybe Nate could get Jeremiah alone somewhere. Maybe Rachel could help him arrange a meeting so the two of them could talk.

**102**

*Jay Anderson.* The name wasn't as much of a jolt as that of Jeremiah and Keylan Reid, but he might hold the key to the investigation. Though right now Nate knew nothing about the man except his name.

He needed whatever information he could find if he was going to help Rachel.

And this time he was going to help her.

That was what he needed to move forward: a clean conscience. Maybe wiping that slate would help him in other matters. Like Bree. She deserved more than he could give her. Satchel too, come to think of it. Leaving the Amish had stunted Nate's emotional growth, and he was bound and determined to somehow change that. Un-stunt it or whatever. Get himself back on track.

A knock sounded on his door. "Housekeeping," the young voice called.

Nate checked his watch. Housekeeping? It was almost suppertime, and he had just moved in. "I don't need anything," he yelled in return.

But it was too strange an occurrence to allow it to pass. All those times when he first arrived, the feeling of being followed.

He silently rose from the bed and eased his way toward the door. The face on the other side of the peephole wasn't familiar at all. It wasn't Amanda Troyer, whom he had seen the day before. This was a young Black girl. She had on a T-shirt with the Americana Inn logo on the front and a bandanna tied around short braids, each with three white beads gleaming in the afternoon sun.

"I don't need anything," Nate said, not quite as loudly this time. "Thank you."

He watched through the peephole as she nodded. "Okay. If you don't want any service, just put the Do Not Disturb sign on the door. 'Kay? And let the front desk know if anything changes."

"Will do," he said, still carefully monitoring her every move.

She turned away from the door and stepped closer to her cleaning cart. She released the brake on the device and pushed it toward the next room.

*Paranoid,* he thought as the space in front of his door cleared. He was beginning to get paranoid.

Nate heard her knock on the door of the room next to his. No muffled voices in response, but he could tell she had entered the room. He opened his own door, stuck the Do Not Disturb sign on the knob, and shut it again with a comical swiftness. That should take care of that.

He checked the bolt on the door and chuckled at himself as he returned to the bed and his waiting notebook. He might be a little more high strung these days. Killing a man could do that to a person, whether that killing was ruled justified or not. The deed was still there. But these were powerful people being accused of what was essentially a hate crime. At least that was how he figured the DA would view it. If a fair DA got involved.

Albie and Jeremiah were Amish. Keylan was Black. Bullying a minority in the sport of intolerance equaled hate crime.

There was no telling if it would ever make it that far. But in Nate's experience, when powerful people were involved, less powerful people tended to get hurt.

\* \* \*

Rachel bit back a groan when she saw the familiar buggy and horse in the driveway as she pulled in that afternoon.

Even though she didn't make a sound, she somehow alerted Kate. "What's wrong, Mamm?"

"Nothing, *liebschdi,*" she murmured as she drew the horse to a stop. "Dawdi has a visitor, so when you go into the house, go straight up to your room, *jah*?"

## The Secrets We Keep

Kate nodded in that exaggerated way she had that caused Rachel to have to employ five extra bobby pins to keep the *maedel*'s prayer covering in place.

Rachel waited for her daughter to scramble down from the buggy and skip into the house before unhitching the horse. She led him into his stall and stored the carriage in the open port at one end of the barn before backtracking to the beast once more.

She might have taken a little extra care with the gelding today. Maybe brushed him a little more than necessary. Maybe even stood at the door of the stall and just stared at his beautiful chestnut coat. But sometimes it was good to pour affection onto the animals in your life, even if they weren't treasured pets but simply the means to get from one place to another.

At least that was what she was telling herself. It was what she would tell her *dat* when she got to the house.

And she needed to be getting into the house. Because she wasn't only thinking about the horse and caring for the beast. She wasn't only putting off the inevitability of seeing Daniel Hostetler face-to-face. She was daydreaming about Nathan Fisher and how handsome he still was. How he still made her heart beat out of her chest and her breathing unpredictable. Even in those *Englisch* blue jeans and that cowboy hat he seemed to have on everywhere he went, she saw him, and he was the same Nathan she had known before. The same Nate she had fallen in love with. The same Nate who had broken her heart. The same Nate who would turn around and leave once more.

*But you asked him to stay.*

She didn't need to be reminded of that. But she did need him. He might not think it important, but without him, there would be no case for her brother. They wouldn't be performing an autopsy. There wouldn't be any investigation. That was what she was really

**105**

after. *Jah*, she'd told the sheriff that she wanted justice for Albie. That she wanted those responsible for his death and for the torture of others to be brought to justice. But more importantly she wanted the mark of suicide removed from Albie's name. He deserved that much. Regardless of what anyone else said, she knew—she *knew*—he hadn't committed such a vile act. It wasn't in him. It just wasn't. That meant someone else had been in the barn that night. She just didn't know who.

She shook her head at herself. She might have asked Nate to stay, but he had headed out like the devil himself was on his heels. He was gone, and everything else that needed to be done for Albie's case now fell on her shoulders. But she could do it. She had to do it, she thought as she turned to finally make her way into the house. It seemed that Daniel wasn't up for leaving just yet, and she was certain by now that Lydie had had her fill of caring for Miri.

Her sister was a lot better these days, but she was still something of a challenge, and her care fell exclusively on Rachel. She welcomed the responsibility, but it proved to be a hardship when she needed time away. Like today. And tomorrow.

Lydie lived next door to them and was a sweet soul, always willing to help. Her wrinkled face and wizened eyes told Rachel that she was at least seventy. Yet she was as spry as someone half her age. Her bones popped when she stood, and her hands were knotted with arthritis, but she wasn't one to pay that sort of thing any mind.

Regardless, Rachel worried when she left Miri alone with their neighbor. She worried about the seizures Miri still sometimes had, some violent enough that those around her got hurt. But so far the new medicines that Rachel had gotten from the doctor were helping, and Miri hadn't had a seizure in days.

It was always that way, though; a new medicine would work well for a time, then all of a sudden it wouldn't work as well, then

## The Secrets We Keep

not at all and they would be back at the doctor looking for a new treatment. She could only pray that the miracle continued.

Rachel closed the door quietly and made her way to her sister's room. She knew that was where she would find Lydie and Miri, since her father was home.

"There you are." Lydie closed the book she had been reading to Miri and pushed herself up from the rocker as Rachel eased into the room.

Miri clapped her hands and waved them in the air as was her habit. She made a noise that said nothing itself but told Rachel that Miri was glad to see her. Her sister might not be able to walk or talk or even care for herself, but she knew those around her and she knew who cared for her and who . . . didn't.

"Hey there," Rachel said, using the greeting to encompass them both. "Sorry I'm a little later than I thought I would be."

"I heard Kate go up the stairs a bit ago."

Rachel nodded. "Where's Amelie?"

"Been up there since school let out." Lydie made a face. "He got here just before."

That was over an hour ago. Surely he was about ready to leave. Rachel could hope he was leaving soon, anyway. Daniel might be her husband's brother, but there was something about him that set her teeth on edge. Something that made her want to stay as far from him as possible. Which, these days, was more than difficult. Especially since her father had recently sold him the house and the two acres of land it sat on at the back side of their property. Since then Daniel seemed to find one reason or another to come by the house and talk about the improvements he had already begun.

Truthfully, Daniel had never done anything to Rachel, but she still avoided him every chance she got. She had even instructed her girls to stay as far away from him as possible. That was easy

**107**

enough for the most part, and if Daniel noticed anything odd, he never mentioned it. Somehow it worked out, maybe because he wasn't one of those doting uncles who carried around hard candy or gum to give to the little ones. Thank the good Lord for that, at least.

However, Daniel's relationship with Albie had been a different matter altogether. Daniel had started picking on him right after she and Freeman got married. He had teased the boy about not being tough enough to hack it on a farm. It was true that Albie was not very athletic, but it surely didn't warrant such abuse. *Abuse* was perhaps too strong a word, but she couldn't think of one better. Daniel had teased him and bullied him, all in the name of making him a man.

Rachel pushed that thought away and concentrated her attention on her neighbor.

"She's been real excitable today," Lydie was saying. "I hope you're not in for a bad night."

So did Rachel. Tonight was bath night, which was always a chore, but even worse if Miri was already keyed up from the day's events.

Rachel bit back a sigh. Some days were just like that. "Can you come again tomorrow?" she asked as Lydie prepared to leave.

Nate had said Rachel shouldn't be there when they dug up Albie's body, but she didn't care. She was going. He was her brother, and she would witness the event. Maybe if only to make sure it happened. She had signed the papers giving permission, but that didn't mean the sheriff would actually go through with the exhumation. She didn't trust him as far as she could throw him.

"Tomorrow?" Lydie seemed to think it over, probably looking for an excuse not to tend to Miri. Caring for her sister was a little easier these days, but she still needed someone mobile to look after her.

# The Secrets We Keep

"I wouldn't ask, but it's important."

"*Jah*?" Lydie cocked her head to one side.

Rachel took a deep breath. "They are opening a case for Albie's death," she finally said. "Tomorrow they are going to exhume his body and take it for an autopsy."

Lydie blinked in surprise. Not that she didn't know Rachel felt Albie's death was somewhat suspect. Most everyone in their district knew that. But the surprise came, Rachel supposed, at the thought of her having won over the people who mattered enough to get them to take a second look at an Amish youngster's death. Yet that feat she could only attribute to Nathan. She just wished he'd be there tomorrow. She had the feeling she was going to need all the moral and emotional support she could get. "I hope you know what you're doing."

"I have to do something or whoever killed Albie will just get away with murder and he'll always be branded—" She shook her head. She couldn't stand the thought of the black cloud that would always hover over any memories the people of the community had of Albie. He had been a good kid, faithful, honest, obedient. He didn't deserve this. And whoever had done it, they needed to pay.

They they they. She didn't even know who *they* were, but *they* had all the power.

"If you say so." Lydie picked up her copy of *Martyr's Mirror*, pulled the strap of her handbag over her shoulder, and started for the door. Rachel didn't understand why Lydie brought her own copy of the book that outlined the struggles the Anabaptists had faced for centuries, the strife and the persecution. It was rumored that every Amish household contained the tome. Rachel wasn't sure if anyone had ever tested that statement for truth. One thing she did know: Every Amish house that she had ever been in had a copy, including her own.

109

"So can you?" Rachel asked, running through her mental list of people who might be able to care for Miri on such short notice if Lydie denied her this. It was a very short list.

Lydie pressed her lips together in a disapproving frown. "I suppose," she finally said. "But don't you go thinking that I believe what you're doing is right. You should leave that boy to rest."

"*Danki.*" Rachel released her breath, not realizing until that moment that she had been holding it.

"Does your *dat* know?"

Rachel slowly shook her head. "I don't think so." But he would soon enough. He hadn't been at the house when the deputies came. But knowing her luck, Daniel had already figured out what was going on and was relaying all to her father.

Lydie's nod matched Rachel's, a slow, reluctant movement. "Okay, then. I'll see you tomorrow."

Rachel walked Lydie to the front door, the anxiousness of the upcoming confrontation with her father weighing heavy on her, making her palms sweat. "Come early," Rachel said as she let the old woman out of the house.

Now for her father.

She had been hoping that in the time she had been checking on Lydie and Miri that Daniel would have found the call to leave, but she could still hear his voice coming from the kitchen. She imagined that he and her father were inside, talking, laughing, drinking something or another from an unmarked bottle. Daniel seemed to have a great many unmarked bottles. She had asked once what was in them, but he had just laughed and smiled at her the way one does at a silly child.

Perhaps she didn't want to know after all.

Rachel pulled in a deep breath and marched confidently into the kitchen. She would have to start preparing their supper soon.

# The Secrets We Keep

Maybe by then the unmarked bottle would be empty and Daniel would be on his way.

But there was no bottle on the table between them, just half-full glasses of water, one for each.

"I'm thinking about making a new driveway, but I haven't decided yet." Daniel stopped talking when she entered the room. He turned to face her. "There she is."

Rachel forced a smile. "Here I am."

Daniel was nothing like Freeman. Truly they shared a great many physical traits, the same brown hair and dark eyes, the same gentle overbite. Yet where Freeman was large and sturdy, Daniel was on the thin side, too short to be considered lanky. Freeman's smallish eyes made him seem like less of a threat. On Daniel the same looked ferrety. Or perhaps that was just how she saw him. He had never done anything to her to make her feel this way, and she silently begged forgiveness for her unkind reflections. After all, she had to believe that he had Albie's best interests at heart as well. She had been raised to respect the men in her life, their opinions and wishes. And yet . . .

Rachel pulled her thoughts away from Daniel as her father scowled.

*He knows.*

Her father knew that she had meddled in the affairs of Albie's death. As far as he was concerned, the event was over and done. There didn't need to be an investigation. There shouldn't be any disturbing of the grave. As far as he was concerned, Rachel was having trouble letting go of her brother. Of accepting *Gott*'s will and moving on. As soon as Daniel left, she was bound to hear about it.

"What about the well?" her father asked, thankfully turning his attention back to his guest. "There's not any water out there."

Their *Ordnung* might not allow for running water in their houses, but a person needed a water source on their property in order to survive. Not that she gave much thought to Daniel's ability to thrive on his new acreage. He would be too close for her liking. But her father said he needed the money the sale of the land would bring. The cost of Miri's medications had gone up recently, as it seemed everything had these days.

The house Daniel now owned was originally the one Rachel and the girls had shared with Freeman. She had wanted to keep it, in case of his return. But as the months went by, it became harder and harder to believe he would come back one day. She had heard the rumors that he had left town with Daniel's wife, but she knew in her heart that Freeman was dead.

"I got a few of those big containers of water from Walmart. I found a man to dig the well, but it's expensive, even though we're going to use the same spot that Freeman had picked out before . . ." He shrugged without finishing.

Just before Freeman vanished, the well on their property had gone dry. Freeman had gone to all the trouble of having a dowser come out and search for water. The waterfinder had located the spot and Freeman had even begun digging the well, then he disappeared. Just another reason to believe he was dead and gone. Why would he go to all that trouble just to up and run away, with or without his brother's wife?

Her father nodded. "Let me know if you need any help."

Daniel shook his head. "It's just a matter of time."

Rachel turned away from them, their conversation secondary as she began to pull the ingredients for tonight's supper from the larder and the propane-powered refrigerator.

Both the stove and the refrigerator ran off propane. Rachel's community was even allowed to have a couple of propane-powered

# The Secrets We Keep

lamps, but each household was permitted only two, the thought being one for the upstairs and one for the downstairs. But since the Gingerich-Hostetlers had to sometimes check on Miri in the middle of the night, their second lamp was in her room. Far from her reach, of course. And it was only turned on in case of an emergency.

Rachel lit the pilot light and began to fill her pan with water from the five-gallon bucket next to the cabinet. Once she got the pasta going, the meal was a breeze from there. She tossed the rest of the ingredients into the large baking dish for tonight's casserole. A can of soup, a package of cream cheese. She needed simple and easy, but it seemed these days her life was turning out to be anything but. She opened the jar of home-canned chicken and started layering the meat into the pan.

Behind her, chairs scraped as the men stood. The joy of Daniel leaving was eclipsed by the thought that her father would soon be free to question her concerning the day's events.

Her heart began to thump in her chest. She had learned long ago not to cross her *vatter*. Yet some lessons were harder for her to remember than others. She was headstrong. She had been told that enough times that she believed it for gospel. However, she had learned to be careful, and she picked her battles with careful determination. She might have her own mind, but she was cautious as well. She didn't bring trouble onto herself if she could avoid it.

This time she couldn't avoid it.

It had been a long while since she had disobeyed her father. She would just have to make certain it was another long while before she defied him again.

# Chapter Eight

Six more days, Nate told himself as he pulled on his boots. Six more days *max*, and he was out of here. He grabbed his hat and his keys, then let himself out of the motel room. He kept telling himself that. The time he had left in Pontotoc. In Cedar Creek.

If he wanted to help Rachel, then he needed to get some results for her. The first would come with checking out the scene at the grave site when the coroner exhumed the body. He had no idea what time they would be out there. That was something Rachel hadn't told him. He hoped for her sake she had taken his advice and stayed home. Surely she hadn't dragged Miri or Kate out to such a gruesome event. He wasn't sure exactly how old Kate was, but she was too young to be in school just yet, though she talked like a little Rachel.

His plan had been to get up early and head over, hang around until he could find out something. He figured if he called the sheriff's office, he'd just get the runaround. What else did he have to do but wait?

The exhumation appeared to be in full swing when he pulled his truck to a stop on the dusty gravel road. There were two sheriff cars parked down one side, one city police, and a car he supposed belonged to the coroner. A large, dark-colored van with PONTOTOC COUNTY

# The Secrets We Keep

CORONER on the back in white block letters was parked in the field next to the cemetery. The field where Samuel had laid Albie to rest.

Everyone stood around the small Bobcat that was gently scraping the earth away from the grave. They would stand back even farther when the box actually came out of the ground. There was nothing worse than the smell of death.

He spotted her then, not around the grave but in the driveway of the cemetery where she had pulled her carriage to a stop. The entire area had been cordoned off with yellow caution tape that declared it a crime scene.

She was talking with Shane Johnson, and she looked anything but happy. Nate supposed it wasn't a day for happy, but the best he could figure was she wanted to be closer and Shane wasn't allowing it. Good man.

"That is my brother," she was saying as he came up behind her.

"I know." Shane's tone was patient and firm, one that Nate himself had used many times with many distraught family members.

She must have heard him walking up behind her. She whirled around, shock lighting her eyes as her hand flew to the large bruise under one eye. It wasn't a black eye per se, like she had been punched, but her cheekbone was swollen and puffy, the skin an angry shade of blue.

She lowered her hand and stared at him defiantly. "I thought you were going home."

"I never said that," Nate replied. Though he kind of had, now that he thought about it. Then she had asked him to stay. What was a man to do?

"What happened to your face?" he asked, thinking back to his sister's veiled accusations that Freeman Hostetler was free with his fists. If Freeman had been gone for the last three years, then he couldn't have left the bruises Nate was seeing now.

115

"Nothing. I fell." But that was a lie and they both knew it. Still, he wouldn't call her out in front of Shane.

"Tell him to let me pass," she demanded, glaring at Nate with an anger he hoped was directed more toward Shane than him.

"I can't do that," Shane said as Nate shook his head and replied, "That's not a good idea."

"That's my brother they are digging out of the ground." Her eyes blazed green fire as she spoke, the words pushed between clenched teeth. She looked from one of them to the other, he supposed trying to find a weakness to exploit.

"Why are you here, Rachel?" Nate asked as softly as he could.

"That's my brother," she said again.

"Why?" he demanded, sterner this time. She was deflecting.

"Because I don't trust them." She nodded toward the field where the deputies and the one city cop were hovering around. Nate had no idea why a city cop was there, unless he just wanted to be in on the action. He had no jurisdiction way out here. This was county land.

"And the coroner?" He cocked his head toward the tall woman patiently waiting off to one side. She was dressed for the apocalypse. The white Tyvek suit covered her from shoulder to foot. The hood was down now, but he knew it would be in place just as soon as they removed the body. She held a face shield in one hand and had a mask around her neck. Her protective goggles were pushed onto the top of her head, ready to be pulled down as the body came up.

That time was not far off. The men who were digging had fastened ropes around the coffin and were preparing to pull it out of the hole.

"I don't know her," Rachel said.

"I do," Shane put in. "She's a good apple."

# The Secrets We Keep

Rachel shot him a look that clearly stated that she had no value for his opinion, but she didn't say the words. "I want to see him."

"No, you don't." Shane and Nate spoke at the same time.

Nate ignored his onetime friend and turned his full attention to Rachel. "You don't know what you're asking. You know that's his grave. You know that they're digging him up and they are going to perform an autopsy and let you know of the results. That should be enough. It needs to be enough," he reiterated.

"They, they, they," she muttered.

"Trust me on this one, Rachel."

She looked about to protest once more, then the starch went out of her shoulders. "I just—" she started to say, but increased activity from the grave site had everyone's attention swinging in that direction.

The coffin was out of the ground and sitting opposite the mound of dirt the Bobcat had dug up.

It wasn't a coffin like the *Englishers* used, sleek and shiny, with ornate trim and side rails for the pallbearers. Most Amish communities had one coffin maker who made all the coffins for their district. Each one was essentially a box within a box, but with no padding, silk, or decoration. It was merely a humble pine casket, modest and unassuming, lined with only a white cloth.

"You shouldn't watch this," Nate said as one of the workers pulled out a crowbar and a hammer. The coffin would have to be dismantled in order to remove the body. Nate had seen bodies left to the elements after weeks had passed. They no longer looked like people. This one had at least been in a casket, but that was little protection from the Mississippi heat. It was May, after all.

Lifting the remains out of the depths of the casket would be tricky to say the least. He had already worked it out in his head, the best way to remove the corpse, and it seemed that he and the coroner were on the same page. Take the sides off the casket, then move the rest as carefully as possible into the thick, black body bag.

Rachel gasped as the sides finally fell away. But Nate couldn't see many details and figured she couldn't either. But he didn't need a good look to know. The body was discolored, bloated, the skin starting to slough from the bones.

The realization that it was really happening was setting in. Rachel rose onto her tiptoes as if to get a better look.

"Rachel. Seriously." He didn't need to tell her again.

"I really want to see him. Just one more time." Her voice bordered on a whine, a near-hysterical cry. "I didn't get to say goodbye."

He turned her to face him and held her chin so she was forced to look at him and him only. He waited until she mentally got herself together again before speaking. "No one gets to say goodbye." It was a lesson he had learned with Mattie.

Out of the corner of his eye he saw the cops that surrounded the casket take a step back, their hands pressed over their noses. He was glad the wind was with them today.

"Nathan, I—"

"Let them do their jobs," he said simply. "They will figure out what happened." Dead men always told tales. At least they did in these days of heightened technology. DNA, blood types, lividity. All that played a part in what tale they had to tell.

He was very aware of Shane watching the two of them. It seemed he and Rachel always had an audience. Except for that one time . . .

Shane cleared his throat.

Rachel pulled away from Nate, but not before he saw the flash of something in her eyes. Regret, longing, perhaps even a small sliver of the love they had once shared. But they both knew that was over.

# The Secrets We Keep

He turned his attention back to the grave. They were moving the body into the bag they would use to transport him to the funeral home, where he would wait to be shipped out for an autopsy. This was a delicate process considering how much time had passed since his death.

"Rachel," Nate said, trying to get her attention back on him and away from the sensitive procedure being performed just a few yards away.

Albie's body dropped a few inches even though the man still had ahold of his hand. The shift was enough that Nate knew what had just occurred. The boy's arm had been pulled out of its socket. Too much decay.

Rachel gasped and turned away, obviously recognizing what had happened as well.

A small sob escaped her as she turned and raced back to her waiting buggy.

Shane pinned Nate with a quick hard stare, then Nate took off after her.

"Rachel," he called.

She stopped before pulling herself up into the carriage, but she didn't face him.

"I'm sorry. Is there anyone who can sit with you?" Now was not the time to be alone. Nor was it the time for *I told you so*.

"The neighbor is at my house," she said quietly. "Sitting with Miri."

"I don't think you should be alone."

She turned then and flashed him a watery smile. "I'm never alone."

Nate watched as she backed her horse out onto the road and climbed into the buggy. She didn't wave as she drove away.

119

He tried to tell himself that she would be all right. She would have someone with her when she got home. Miri, the neighbor, maybe even Kate.

As the dust cleared, Nate turned and went back to where Shane was waiting.

"Why didn't you tell me you're in law enforcement?" he asked as Nate returned.

"You didn't ask."

"We're on the same team, you know."

"Are we?" Nate asked.

"Yeah. We both want the truth."

But Nate was not convinced that put them on the same team. He was on Rachel's side. He wanted her to have the peace she needed over her brother's death. Shane was on the sheriff's side. He needed to solve the case and keep it as quiet as possible considering all the political ramifications. And if they were both on the side of the truth, well, that was where things got a little problematic. Whose truth?

"So what made him change his mind?" Nate prodded.

"I talked to him about it, and we determined it might be something we should look into a bit."

Politics, Nate decided. But he had a feeling that if too many fingers started pointing in Chance Longacre's direction, the investigation would sputter to a stop.

"What about the old man?" Nate asked. "Are you going to charge him with moving a corpse?" That sentence alone could carry up to seven years.

"Haven't decided yet."

Which meant they were waiting to see what the autopsy said. If Albie had indeed killed himself, then chances were that concealing

## The Secrets We Keep

foul play wasn't the motive for moving his body after death. But if it was more than that . . .

"I did talk to Chance Longacre," Shane finally admitted.

"Oh, yeah? How'd that go?"

Shane shrugged one shoulder. "He's an entitled ass, but I don't think he's malicious enough to start murdering people."

"It's a hate crime," Nate reminded him. And the accused was an entitled ass with a powerful daddy who would do anything to keep his son out of trouble. Factors like that tended to push those teetering bad seeds to fall completely off the edge. Someone not so malicious suddenly became one of the dangerous ones. He had seen it happen before.

"I don't think he did it," Shane said quietly.

Nate didn't answer.

The workers slammed the door on the back of the van, and the driver slowly pulled out onto the dirt road. Thankfully, they were going in the opposite direction Rachel had just gone. He could only imagine her driving down the road and the van pulling around her. She had been distraught enough when she left. That would send her over the edge for sure.

"What's the word?" Shane asked as the coroner came near. He had been waiting there for her to finish. No doubt to take the news directly to Ed Walker. Seemed the other detective was off the case for now.

The coroner had removed her gloves at the scene but now pulled the shield from in front of her face. She looked to Nate as if determining how she should answer.

"He's with me," Shane told her. Nate figured Shane was trying to make up for treating him like a suspect, but truly, wasn't everyone a suspect until they weren't?

"At first glance it's hard to say. I did see a skull fracture, which is odd. Didn't you say he hung himself?"

Shane nodded.

"Never had a skull fracture commit suicide, if you know what I mean."

Nate did. The head injury alone would be enough to knock a man out. How did a person get a wound that severe, then turn around and kill themselves?

"From there it's hard to tell with the amount of decomposition that we're dealing with," she continued.

That much was a given.

"We'll know more once we get the autopsy back."

"Don't forget: The sheriff wants a rush on that," Shane reminded her.

She started to release the zipper on her Tyvek suit, but she only pulled it down enough for Nate to see she was wearing a simple white top underneath. "I've already contacted the lab. But Ed knows that rush may mean he gets it back in two months instead of twelve, right?"

"As soon as possible," Shane said. "We need to put this matter to rest."

No one more than Rachel.

The coroner nodded at both of them, then moved back toward the group of cops and workers. She pulled off the white suit and stuffed it into the trash bag before scrubbing her hands with sanitizer. Then she pulled her keys from her pocket and started for the car Nate had already suspected was hers.

"I thought you were leaving town," Shane finally said.

Nate shook his head, still watching the men laugh and joke as if they hadn't just exhumed the dead and decomposing body of a boy who was most likely murdered. Or maybe they were laughing and joking because they had just completed such a distasteful,

## The Secrets We Keep

odious . . . *god-awful* task. Cops and other emergency workers all had to keep their sanity one way or another. Making light was sometimes the only way to get through it.

"Don't you need to be getting back?"

Nate shook his head once more. He wasn't spilling all to this man whom he had once called friend. Too many years had passed, too much time, too many forks in the road. Too many miles traveled. Neither was the same person they had been twelve years ago. Though Nate had put walls up to protect himself from this town and the people he once knew, they were easily destroyed. Or scaled. Somehow Rachel always managed to get to him. He couldn't let Shane in as well.

"I've taken leave." It was the best answer Shane was going to get.

"Because of your dad." Shane nodded knowingly.

"Yeah." He didn't need to know the truth. Nate wasn't up for telling him that he'd been on leave after a fatal shooting. Talking about it didn't help the situation.

"Are you staying for a while?" Shane asked. "I want to know, as a friend."

*Yeah, right.* Nate didn't believe that for a minute. "A couple of days, maybe. I want to make sure Rachel's all right." *And I want to talk to Chance Longacre myself.*

Shane whistled under his breath. "That bruise . . . But what do you do if no charges are filed?"

*Something,* Nate thought. *Anything. Nothing.* But he wasn't going to leave until he knew she was okay. Who in Rachel's life would hurt her? The first and foremost suspect would be her husband. But he was missing. Then came her father. Her brother was dead. Then there was the chance that it truly was an accident, and he was letting his cop brain get away from him.

123

But it was the look on her face when she had seen him that made him think otherwise. She hadn't wanted him to see. Because . . . because she knew he would worry. That he would want to find out the truth, and she didn't want anyone to know that truth.

"Maybe it really was an accident," Nate said, borrowing the words of every abused spouse since the dawn of time. Then he gave a small salute to Shane and headed back to his truck.

If he had wanted to leave that afternoon, there was no way he could now. No way he would go back home without making sure Rachel was safe.

First he would make a few more notes about the group of kids who had bullied Albie and the other victims of their shenanigans. Which started with Jeremiah Troyer.

The farm belonging to Marvin Troyer looked the same as it had when Nate left twelve years ago. The tree in the front yard was bigger and the dogs lying under it unfamiliar, but the house, the outbuildings, the garden to one side all seemed to have come straight from his past. Some things were slow to change.

As he pulled his truck to a stop, a young girl came out of the house and beelined for the small shack that sat near the road.

Almost every house had a "store" where they sold the goods approved by the bishop. Woven potholders, all sorts of home-canned goods, extra produce, and even soaps and lotions, depending on the farmer. Apparently, the girl had been sent out to mind the store while the *Englischer* shopped.

Nate followed behind her into the small building. He had never met her before, and judging by her size, she might not have even been born before he left the area.

# The Secrets We Keep

She started lining up the jellies all in a row on the shelf closest to the table where the money box sat.

He took off his hat and cleared his throat to get her attention. "I'm looking for Jeremiah Troyer," he said.

He knew the Troyers still lived in the house. Their name was painted on the dented and dusty mailbox that perched next to the road.

"Jeremiah?" she asked.

He felt like she had heard him but didn't know how to answer so she just repeated his name. "That's right. I want to talk to him for a bit. Is that possible?"

"You don't want to look at stuff?" She gestured around her. It was obvious that she had expected a certain response from him, a particular way of interacting. He wasn't playing his part correctly, and she was struggling with her lines because of it.

"No. I just came to talk to Jeremiah. My name is Nate Fisher. I used to live here."

"But now you don't."

"No," he said. "Now I don't, but I used to be friends with Rachel Gingerich." He stopped, closed his eyes for just a moment. He was forever messing up her name. "Hostetler," he corrected. "I was told that maybe Jeremiah might know something about Albie Gingerich's death."

Her eyes grew wide. "Let me see," she said. She all but ran from the shack back to the house. The screen door slammed behind her with a thwack, and he heard her call for someone.

A few moments later, Marvin Troyer came out of the house. He was fatter and grayer than he had been the last time Nate saw him. His beard a good deal longer. He still wore the frown that was as much a part of him as his intelligent blue eyes.

125

# Amy Lillard

Nate stepped from the store building and waited for the man to come near. He kept his hat in his hand as he stood there.

"You need to head on out," Marvin said the moment he figured Nate could hear him without shouting.

"I just want to talk to him."

"You left the church. The only reason I'm talking to you now is to tell you to move on. No one in this house has anything they need to say to you."

Nate started to protest once more, but he knew the man was right. At least by Amish standards. Nate had joined the church before he left, and he was under the *Bann*. He wasn't supposed to talk to anyone, nor they to him. He couldn't take money, eat at the same table—pretty much no interaction at all until he asked for forgiveness and came back into the fold.

It was the one thing that most *Englischers* didn't understand about shunning. It wasn't about punishment; it was about coming back.

"I'm sorry to have bothered you."

Marvin crossed his arms and stood that way until Nate redonned his hat, walked over to his truck, and backed out of the drive.

\* \* \*

Rachel wiped the tears from her eyes and did her best to paste on a smile as she entered her house. She should have gone by the school to pick up Kate, but she didn't want her daughter to see her this way.

When Rachel needed time for personal errands, she left Kate with Martha Yutzy, her cousin and the teacher at the Amish school. Kate was allowed to play with the other children at recess and color at a table in the back of the room. Rachel tried not to do it often, but today was an exception to be sure. This whole month seemed to be an exception.

# The Secrets We Keep

Her father was nowhere to be seen when she arrived back at the house, which was another blessing she could count. She made her way to the living room.

Lydie looked up as she entered, the unspoken questions lighting her eyes.

Rachel tried to smile and shook her head. She blinked back the tears and swallowed the lump in her throat. The last thing she needed right now was someone's compassion. One kind word and she would fall to pieces.

"I'll just be . . ." Lydie stood but didn't finish the sentence.

Miri flapped her hands and laughed that bold, inappropriate laugh that came with Angelman syndrome. Rachel wanted to fall down onto her knees, bury her face in her sister's lap, and hold on to her the best she could. She was precious. They were all precious. Life was precious.

Today made her wish for simpler times. Like the days when she would sneak away and meet Nathan at the creek behind her house. She would follow it to the edge of the property as far away as she could go. There was a big oak tree planted on the bank. Most likely grown from an acorn dropped there by a mockingbird or the like. It served as both cover and shade for them when they met during the day. Mostly they snuck out at night, holding hands and stealing a *verboten* kiss from time to time. But those simpler times were gone. And they were never coming back.

All her life she had been taught to accept, not look back, move forward, love God. But today . . .

"I'll see myself out." Lydie adjusted her purse strap and started for the door.

Her movement shocked Rachel from her stupor. "Hang on," she said, wiping away the fresh tears. She had to get a grip. The last thing she needed to do was start feeling sorry for herself and lose sight of everything that was important. Everything right under her nose.

She rushed into the kitchen and grabbed the plastic container off the counter, then hurried back to where Lydie waited. "These are for you."

Lydie accepted the gift with a smile. "*Danki.* What is it?"

"Oatmeal cookies. I made them last night."

"I don't know if I'll be able to eat them." She grinned a bit wider, showing that most of her back teeth were missing.

Rachel couldn't help but laugh. Something about the way she looked with her lips all spread apart. "Miri has the same issue," she told Lydie. "Just soak them in milk for a minute and eat them with a spoon."

Lydie's smile returned to normal, and there was a twinkle in her eyes. "Girl, I like the way you think."

\* \* \*

When all else fails, head to the Grill and order fried green tomatoes and caramel pie.

Not exactly the words of Gandhi, but it was a philosophy Nate could get behind . . . occasionally. If he got behind it too often, he would end up as big as a house. Especially with everything that was going on here. Plus, the Grill was exclusive to Pontotoc. No one in Oklahoma could fry green tomatoes like they could, and he would be on his way home soon enough.

Home. He would call it that whether it felt that way or not. *Home is where your cat is,* he decided. And his cat was in Tulsa.

He leaned back as the waitress approached, carrying a plate in each hand. She slid them onto the faux-wood laminate tabletop and checked his glass of tea. "Unsweet?" she asked.

# The Secrets We Keep

He nodded. "Please." He'd drained half of it already, needing the coolness after the heat of the morning.

She fetched the correct pitcher and returned in seconds, since the restaurant consisted of only seven or eight tables total. Those were crammed into the small space with no room to spare.

"Can I get you anything else?"

"Maybe some information?" She was about the right age: late teens, early twenties.

She turned away, her attention pulled from him to the rowdy laughter coming from the corner table. He might not have lived in the area for a while, but he knew who they were from the entitled way they dined and the in-your-face Gen Z attitude. Chance Longacre and his cronies. It was apparent to Nate that they thought they owned whatever place they currently occupied.

He didn't want to make rash assumptions, but he couldn't rein in the thoughts fast enough.

"They come here often?" he asked.

She sighed and nodded. "I should probably go check on them. Unless you need something?"

"Nah, I'm good." She would be by at least once more to bring his check. He would ask her then. It was still a little early for the lunch rush. He had plenty of time to talk to her.

His eyes kept straying to the corner table and the loud group. While he ate, he checked them on Instagram, putting a current mental picture with the names in the journal.

Taylor Bennett. Ely Thatcher. Leo Davidson. Chance Longacre.

Their feeds showed parties, drinking beer, girls, stunts, and typical wild southern-boy activities.

They were boisterous and unruly, but were they murderers?

There was one other name he needed to check—besides the Amish kids involved. No, cell phones and internet were not allowed in the community, but that didn't mean none of the Amish youth broke that rule. But with the conservative climate in their community, he suspected he wouldn't find anything on Jeremiah Troyer or even Albie Gingerich.

There was also nothing on Jay Anderson. He tried Jason Anderson, but there wasn't anything showing up for that name either. It was worse than a needle in a haystack if Jay was an initial/nickname and not a name proper. Instagram was a dead end. He'd try Facebook next, though not many of that generation posted on there the way they did on Instagram. Just a fact of life.

The boys finished eating well before Nate did, and he surreptitiously watched as they haggled over who had what, who needed to pay for the appetizers the table shared, and what drink went with what tab. Again he wondered if they were truly responsible for Albie's death. Here, midmorning with other people around, they were unpleasant, but they did not appear dangerous.

Yet he knew from personal experience that none of it amounted to a hill of beans when people were alone in the dark. In the night, with no one else watching, people found themselves much more capable of acts they would never have thought of committing in the light of day.

They walked past him without paying him any mind. He thought for a moment about following them to see where they were going, but he decided to stay. He wasn't out to solve the case. Hell, he wasn't even on the case. He was merely helping an old friend find peace after her brother's death.

"No hurry," the waitress said as she slipped the ticket facedown onto the table in front of him.

"Hold on," he said, reaching into his back pocket.

The Secrets We Keep

She stopped.

He fished his credit card from his wallet and handed it to her. "Question."

She picked up the ticket once more. "Yeah?"

"You know a Jay Anderson?"

She seemed to mull it over for a moment. "Is he a singer or something?"

Nate bit back his smile and shook his head. "I don't think so. What about Keylan Reid?"

If she thought the question strange, she didn't show it. "Yeah. I mean, we're not really friends or anything, but I know who he is. We went to school together."

Nate nodded. "And if I wanted to talk to him about something, how would I go about it?"

Her eyes narrowed. "Are you a cop or something?"

"Or something," he said. "I just want to ask him a couple of questions about an Amish kid who died. He was a friend of mine."

"You don't think he did it. 'Cuz Keylan isn't like that. He's real sweet, you know."

Nate shook his head. What was she trying to say? Like everyone else, "sweet people" could be pushed beyond their normal boundaries.

She cocked her head to one side. "Sweet."

Nate waited for her to continue. He was starting to get the idea of what she was saying, but he had learned long ago to let people keep talking. They would eventually get there.

"You know, like gay. He isn't the kind."

"You don't believe that gay people can commit murder?"

She shook her head, obviously realizing she had given an objectionable answer. "That's not what I'm trying to say. He's a kind person. He's nice. And he's Black."

131

Nate waited a heartbeat before responding. "I don't follow."

She closed her eyes for a minute as if to gather her thoughts on the matter. "They were in here that night. The two of them, whispering. Looked like they were planning something. Then Chance and the others came in." She rolled her eyes. "They basically chased them away."

"Casey!"

She visibly jumped at the sound.

A man stuck his face through the little window that connected the kitchen from the dining room. "Order up!"

Obviously, he had said those words more than once. Or maybe he didn't want Casey talking about Chance, Keylan, and Albie.

"Sorry. I'm making a mess of this, but I gotta go."

"I understand."

She started away from the table, then spun back to face him. "I haven't seen Keylan around in a while. But his sister works at the Laundromat. Maybe she could tell you how to find him."

# Chapter Nine

After Lydie left, Rachel swept the floor and waited until it was time to walk her girls home from school. On the way, she heard a buggy approaching her from behind. Not an unusual happening, but she could tell that the driver was slowing the carriage down to pull alongside her.

Rachel turned to find her brother-in-law driving—close.

"Pretty day for a walk," he commented, barely glancing at the sky before turning his gaze back to her.

"*Jah.*" She really didn't have anything else to say. It was a pretty day, but there was no need to excessively discuss it.

"Going to the school to pick up the girls?"

"*Jah,*" she grudgingly admitted. She wasn't sure why, but Daniel gave her the creeps. He just did. He was as different from her Freeman as one man could be to another and still be kin. She often wondered if he'd had anything to do with his brother's disappearance. But every time those thoughts rose, she pushed them away. And now Albie . . .

Again she shoved the thought aside, yet it crept back in. Made itself known. Daniel might have tried to push Albie into being more like what he considered to be a man, but surely he wouldn't go as far as to—

"I could give you a ride," Daniel offered.

133

Rachel shook her head and kept walking.

Daniel kept pace with his buggy. "It's quite a fer piece."

"Not really."

Once the words were out of her mouth, Daniel sped up his horse and turned sharply, blocking Rachel's track. She stuttered to a stop, the horse chuffing, so very close.

"Daniel!" she gasped, pressing one hand to her heart. This sort of behavior was the reason she didn't like him. He had no cause to scare her half to death. Not merely because she had refused a ride.

"You don't like me much, do you?"

She sucked in a deep breath, trying to calm her nerves and devise a plan for escape all in the same moment. "I wasn't aware that us liking each other was a requirement."

"Oh, I like you just fine." His words sent chills skittering down her spine. "But you seem to have something against me."

She shook her head. "You're imagining things." She did have something against him. A bad feeling, but that was all it was. Just a bad feeling.

"It's a shame about Albie."

She really didn't want to have this conversation. She started to ease around the front of Daniel's buggy mare, but he pulled forward. To go around, she'd have to step down into the ditch. Something about that seemed a little too desperate, and she was afraid he would somehow use that against her as well.

"I just wish I could have done something more for the boy," Daniel mused.

"Like what?" Rachel quietly asked. Had Daniel been there that night?

"Like taught him how to be a man. Maybe he wouldn't have killed himself if he was a man."

## The Secrets We Keep

Rachel sucked in another breath to soothe her sudden anger. It didn't help much. "He did not kill himself."

"Your *dat* told me you would say that."

She remained standing there, unwilling to take that first dire step into the ditch to get around Daniel and his buggy. "It's true." She believed it with all her heart.

"Well, if someone had strung him up, I suppose being more of a man would have helped him then too."

"Can you—" She fluttered one hand out in front of herself, motioning him from her path without saying the words.

"Am I in your way?" he asked innocently.

Lord save her from the mean idiots in her life.

"I need to get to the school and get the girls."

Daniel nodded as if the conversation they had just had was of no more importance than what was for dinner. "I can still give you a ride. Since we've been wasting time jawing, you know."

She hadn't been *jawing* at all. She had been trying to get away, but pointing that out to him wouldn't benefit her in any way.

"No, *danki*. I prefer to walk. It is a beautiful day, after all."

He studied her for a moment more, then pulled his horse around and headed out in front of her.

Rachel kept walking, wondering why. Why was her life filled with trial after trial? If it wasn't someone calling Adult Protective Services on her sister, it was her family dying, her husband disappearing, his brother making untoward advances. Nate Fisher coming back to town. Problem after problem. Though she would like to see Nate again. Maybe in a time where she wasn't asking him to help her solve her brother's murder or the coroner exhuming his decomposing body.

Just the thought sent shivers howling through her.

*Jah*, she wished she could see Nate and tell him the truth. Stop hiding. But what good would it do? None. None at all. It would only hurt them all the more.

\* \* \*

Dead end. Dead end. Dead end.

He just couldn't seem to catch a break in this case.

He shook his head at himself as he neared the city limits. It wasn't a case. Or rather it wasn't *his* case and he had nothing to do with it other than wanting to help an old friend. And if he had any sense at all he wouldn't be driving around his hometown trying to figure out what to do next.

He almost passed them, but slammed on his brakes and pulled his truck into the parking lot. Thankfully, no one was behind him and he didn't cause an accident as he swerved off the road in front of the drive-in.

Buddy's was as much a staple of Cedar Creek as the Grill was to Pontotoc. The old-fashioned drive-in looked like something out of the old television show *Happy Days*, though the servers weren't on roller skates. There were three wooden picnic tables out front, but otherwise patrons—mostly teenagers—ordered at the window and took their food back to their cars. Or buggies, as the case might be. Two black carriages sat off to one side, and Nate could just see the smiling faces of the Plain teens as they grinned at each other and ate their hamburgers. Two girls sat in one buggy and two young men in the other. No one he recognized, but he had been gone a lifetime.

However, they were not what had drawn him into the drive-in.

Leaning up against the tailgate of a shiny red Ford were Chance Longacre and his three faithful buddies. What luck that Chance just happened to be next on Nate's list of people he needed to talk to. He supposed he should have connected with him sooner, but truthfully Nate hadn't made up his mind about Albie one hundred percent. One thing he had learned being out in the *Englisch* world was that you never truly knew what someone was thinking. What was in their heart. If asked, he would say no, that there was no way Albie Gingerich would commit suicide, but he also knew that anything was possible, all the time.

He stopped next to the truck, gingerly donned his hat from its place on the dash, and got out.

"Hi, boys." He greeted them each with a nod and a smile. "Nice day for an ice cream." He glanced to the soft-serve cones the boys held.

Chance frowned at him but took a swift lick before answering. "Yeah. It is." His tone was wholly dismissive. He turned back to his friends, chalking Nate up as a weirdo.

"Thought I might come introduce myself."

The younger man turned around slowly as if distrustful of the reasons why Nate was still there. "And why's that?"

"I believe we have mutual friends."

Chance waited, jaw tense, for Nate to continue.

"Albie Gingerich."

Chance waited an extra heartbeat, as if he didn't immediately recognize the name. "Oh, yeah. Too bad about old Albie."

The other three laughed. Nate wanted to smash their smug, self-righteous faces in but managed to keep both his calm and his temper.

"Yeah, and I promised I would help them find out who killed him."

One of the boys frowned. From his Instagram page, Nate knew him to be Taylor Bennett. "Didn't he off himself?"

"That's what I heard," Leo Davidson chimed in.

Only Ely Thatcher the preacher's kid remained silent. He stared down at the tops of his sneakers as his ice cream melted in his hand.

"The police think otherwise," Nate said. Sure, he was stretching the truth a bit, but honestly, what better way to test the waters?

"What?" Leo looked surprised. He immediately swung his gaze to Chance.

But Chance remained eerily still. "They think someone killed him?" Nate could see the light dawning in his eyes. Chance was nothing if not smart. At least when he wanted to be. He saw the truth now. He was a murder suspect. He and the three guys surrounding him.

It wasn't bad enough that their actions might have driven a young man to kill himself, but being charged with murder was a whole 'nother thing. Fear took the place of understanding.

"Could it be possible that the four of you might have some information about that night?" Nate pressed.

Chance shook his head. "I don't know what you heard, but we have nothing to do with them. We went to my house and watched movies all night. Right?"

"Right," the three chorused behind him. But Chance's jaw had lost the cocky angle and his eyes seemed dulled by the weight of Nate's revelation.

However, Nate hadn't said anything about anyone other than Albie, yet Chance had said *them*. There was more he wasn't saying. But was it enough to prove murder? Hardly.

Talking to the boys made him realize just how young and immature they truly were. Bored and entitled summed it up perfectly. That could be a lethal combination given the right circumstances. Yet Nate wasn't convinced.

"I didn't say anything one way or the other," Nate said. "But I thought you should know."

"Know what?" Chance asked, his voice quiet and dangerous.

"That you're being looked at in the case."

# The Secrets We Keep

Something in his tone struck a nerve with the others. They immediately bristled, but Chance held up one hand to quiet their grumblings.

"Is that all?" Chance asked.

Nate nodded. "That's all," he said, then headed back to his truck. He stopped halfway there. "Nope," he said as he turned to face the teens once more. "Any of you know a Jay Anderson?"

Chase scoffed. "Why would I tell you even if I did?"

Nate studied the young man's expression, doing his best to read between the lines of teenage stubbornness and puffed-up ego. But he saw no hint of recognition there. "Right," he said, then made his way to his big black Chevy.

* * *

*Meet me at the creek tonight. Nine o'clock. Please.*

Nate sat on the edge of the bed and stared at the small piece of paper. It had been on the door when he arrived back at the motel.

On Casey the waitress's recommendation, he had gone by the Laundromat first. Keylan's sister, Aisha, wasn't working. But at least he had a name and a start. He would swing back around tomorrow and pay her a visit. While he was there, he might wash a load of clothes. A twofer.

But when he saw the note shoved between the doorframe and the doorknob of his new room, all assured thoughts of two birds and one stone had fled.

Who could have left the note? Anyone. Anyone Amish, that is. The handwriting was familiar, but every Amish person he knew wrote the same way. They all learned to make their letters the same. Variations were frowned upon, and consequently their writing was very similar.

*Meet me at the creek tonight. Nine o'clock. Please.*

139

It had to be Rachel. She was the only person who would leave him such a message. She was the only person he had snuck away from home to meet at the creek after dark. But he had a feeling she wasn't just being nostalgic. There was an urgent current running through her words. An urgency made all too real by the events of the day.

Her words from the cemetery haunted him. *I'm never alone.* He couldn't figure out if she meant that to be a good thing or a bad one. Maybe it was neither. Maybe it was just a statement of fact. *I'm never alone.*

And the bruise on her cheek. He had wanted to ask again how she got it, but he had known she would lie, just as she had when he asked her the first time. But who was she covering for? Was she protecting the person who hurt her or merely ignoring the fact that she was hurt?

It took everything he had to wait until almost nine o'clock before heading out to the creek. Going early wouldn't help anything, but neither was watching stupid game shows on the motel television. There were channels now that played nothing but, and out of all the stations available in this modern world, there weren't many choices at the Americana Inn that didn't involve bad plots and naked people.

That feeling of being watched returned as Nate stepped from his motel room and made sure the door locked behind him. He shook it off. He was being paranoid, he decided. He needed to relax and go see what was happening at the creek.

He had already decided that Rachel had left the note, and the urgency he felt in the words she had written was a side effect of too many years in law enforcement. The same went for the feeling of being watched and followed as he drove through the town. He had been trained to be on constant alert. It was all he had known for many years. No wonder he was having trouble letting go of that conditioning and just enjoying himself for the time he was to remain in Pontotoc.

## The Secrets We Keep

He had forgotten just how dark it got out among the Amish houses as nighttime fell. The *Englisch* and the Amish lived side by side as much as farmhouses separated by fields planted with soybeans, peanuts, or corn could be. There was enough room in between that the security lights and the lamps in the windows of the *Englisch* houses didn't carry far enough to illuminate any of the Amish homes he passed.

The yellow flames from kerosene lanterns and the few propane-powered lamps lit the Amish houses with a warm glow that didn't quite match the blue-white light from the *Englisch* dwellings.

Nate drove past Rachel's house with intent, not slowing down so as not to alert anyone inside of their plans. He parked down from the house, far enough away that his truck lights could no longer be seen.

They would meet at the old oak tree. She didn't have to tell him where to go for him to remember it. He liked that she took that for granted. It had been "their" spot. How many kisses had they shared there? How many plans had they made, back when the idea that he might be able to save his sister hadn't occurred to him? They were going to get married, he and Rachel, have a passel of kids, as many as God willed them. He would farm; she would bake pies and wipe dirt from the faces of their little ones. Their life would be sweet.

Until it wasn't.

The opening was still in the same place as it had been back then, and Nate let himself into the fence by the light of the moon and the glow from his cell phone. He used the flashlight app to make his way across the pasture and down to the banks of the creek. Everything looked basically the same, though even in the darkness he could see a few small changes. The creek was low; they needed some rain. The oak was larger and the banks not as trampled down as they had been when he used to come down to see Rachel back in the day. Back when they were in love.

But she had married another.

Amy Lillard

He stopped just under the branches of the tree. The light from his phone bounced off nothing as he surveyed the area. He had expected her to already be there. She always came first.

But she wasn't there.

He didn't even bother to call her name as the truth hit him.

Had he really been that stupid?

Had every bit of training he'd had just flown the coop when his hormones got involved? Like anything was going to happen between him and Rachel right now. Even if she wasn't married . . . even if she didn't have two children by another man . . . He was leaving in a couple of days.

Then he knew. She hadn't left that note. If she had wanted to see him, she would have merely stopped by his motel room, just as she had done before.

Stupid. Stupid. Stupid.

Nate turned and headed back toward his truck. His feet couldn't take him fast enough, but it was slow going. He had to turn off his flashlight. He couldn't draw any more attention to himself.

Someone had lured him down to the creek. That meant they either wanted to get him alone where they could have him at their mercy, or they wanted him out of his motel room.

It took way too long for him to finally make it back to his truck. Each footstep carried with it the expectation of being ambushed. But the closer he got to the road, the more he began to realize that whoever had left that note wanted him away from his motel room. Or maybe they simply wanted him out of town, perhaps in a controlled place, and they knew that he and Rachel used to meet at the creek under the large oak.

That narrowed it down to a handful of people—his brother Leroy, his sister Lavinia, Rachel's sister Nancy, and possibly his

*The Secrets We Keep*

*mamm.* But he couldn't see any of those people trying to lure him away. Lavinia and Nancy both lived in Tennessee.

Nate sighed as he slid into the cab of his truck and jabbed the keys into the ignition. The idea that someone wanted him here instead of in town still burned within him. But why? There was nothing of value in his room. His sidearm was in the glove box of his truck.

He was finding it harder and harder to carry it these days. When a man held a gun, he put away all other options and the weapon became the solution. *When all you have is a hammer, everything looks like a nail.* If he hadn't had a gun that day, what would have happened? It could be argued that he would be dead. But . . . if he hadn't had the gun, perhaps the kid wouldn't have pulled his first. And the boy would still be alive. *Might* be alive.

Nate shook the thought away. They couldn't go back. He knew it. He shouldn't dwell on what-ifs. Yet they crept up on him at the strangest times.

Still, he felt the need to have this sidearm close. Training would do that to a man. So he followed his gut and kept it near, but not in hand.

He started the truck and pointed the headlights back toward town. This had been a fool's errand. Perhaps that was what the author of the note intended. Some kind of practical joke. Maybe they just wanted him to burn time and gas. To get agitated. To think the worst when nothing at all was afoot.

That kind of prank would fall to Sarah. His sister wanted him gone from Mississippi. She had told him not to come out to the house again, and he had. So she had left the note to run him around and show him that he didn't belong there. Like he needed her telling him that.

He just couldn't remember if Sarah knew much about his and Rachel's relationship from back in the day. He supposed someone could have told her.

It didn't matter. He was leaving soon, and he had already promised himself he wouldn't drive out and stare at his mother's house again before he left.

The motel was quiet when he pulled back into the parking lot. He cut the engine and sat in the truck for a moment, watching. He could just see the strip of soft light coming through the space between the curtains. Nothing moved inside the room. But that feeling of being watched returned.

He needed to get out of Pontotoc. He wasn't being followed. He wasn't being watched. His sister had played a prank on him. He half expected her to come out of the bushes, laughing at his foolishness. Even so, he knew she was at home with her family, secretly cackling to herself. He was not in danger. He was just being paranoid, a feeling that the therapist said would go away in time.

Nate slid from the cab and used the fob to lock the doors. The horn honked and the lights flashed to let him know the vehicle was secure.

He pulled the key card from his back pocket and slid it into the reader. The light turned green and the door clicked. He twisted the knob and eased the door open.

He had only a moment to register a couple of strange and hard facts. He had turned the bathroom light on when he left, but it was off now. He had left it on, hadn't he? He hadn't realized at the time that the detail would be important. The light he saw through the drapes was from a flashlight that had been dropped. A real flashlight, not a cell phone app. Who had a real flashlight these days?

He had only a split second to realize that someone was in the room with him, behind him, before the pain exploded in his head and fractures of light sparked before his eyes. Then everything went dark.

# Chapter Ten

❧

"Nathan? Nathan . . ."

The sweet voice penetrated the fog of his mind.

He stirred.

"Nathan?"

Then he woke fully, remembering. He had just been coming back to his motel room. The door had been locked. Everything had been in place. He'd waited to make sure. Then he had come inside. There was a shadow, and then—

He pushed her hands away and scrambled to his feet, bracing his palms on the doorjamb as he leaned outward. He looked both ways, but there was no one there. No one running away. No cars speeding off. Nothing out of the ordinary. Whoever had attacked him was gone.

"Nathan, you're bleeding."

Rachel.

He turned around, swaying a bit as he raised one hand to the knot just at his hairline on the left side of his head. His fingers came away sticky. Blood. He looked at it as if mesmerized. He was bleeding. And he was going to have one helluva headache come tomorrow morning when the adrenaline wore off.

"Come sit down." Rachel was on her feet in an instant, clasping his arm and leading him over to one of the squat wood-and-vinyl

145

chairs that crouched around the laminate-topped kitchenette table. He stumbled over something on his way there. The baseball bat he had placed behind the door for emergencies. He had been attacked with his own weapon.

"What are you doing here?" he asked. That was when he felt it, the warm trickle down the side of his face.

She didn't answer, just grabbed a couple of tissues from the box on the table and dabbed gently at the wound.

He sucked in a hard breath.

"What happened?" she quietly asked.

"I was coming back, and someone was waiting for me in my room. They hit me on the head, then I guess they ran away."

"It's deep," she said. "You need to go to the doctor."

He shook his head, then immediately regretted it. Forget tomorrow; his brains were beginning to throb now. "No doctor." He didn't want to have to explain how he had gotten bashed in the skull. Not until he knew who did the bashing.

The hospital would call the police, who would certainly call the sheriff. Who would want to know all the details. That wasn't a can of worms he wanted to open.

On the flip side, if the perpetrator had indeed used Nate's bat, then his fingerprints could possibly be on it. But what good would it do if he happened to be Amish? Most Amish didn't have their prints on file. Of course, most Amish didn't go around breaking into motel rooms and conking people on the side of the head. But the hat . . . He thought he had seen a hat, a bit battered and made of straw just like all the Amish wore there. Or maybe he had imagined it. The details were a little fuzzy and the room had been dark. It was hard to file away particulars after being bashed in the head.

## The Secrets We Keep

If the offender wasn't Plain, then he was surely smart enough to wear gloves when prowling around Nate's room uninvited. No, he could see no benefit to including others in this mess.

"But it's bleeding," Rachel protested. Like he didn't know.

"I can't involve anyone else."

Rachel fell quiet. "I didn't mean to bring this on you."

He wanted to tell her that she hadn't, but they both knew it wouldn't be the truth. Instead he said, "Go to the front desk and ask if they have any superglue."

She nodded and went without protest, rushing out the door and heading in the direction of the front motel office.

Gingerly, Nate cradled his head in his right hand.

Someone had broken into his motel room, and he had messed up. He had let his guard down and allowed this assailant the upper hand. If they had wanted to kill him, he would be dead right now. Which meant they didn't want him dead.

They wanted something he had.

The journal!

The whole thing, the note from Rachel, the trip out to the farm, it had been a decoy, meant to get him away from his room so whoever could come in and—

He was on his feet in an instant, his head throbbing with the movement. He had left the journal on the bedside table; it was no longer there. It wasn't on the floor near the bed. He dropped to his knees, a small wave of dizziness washing over him as he did so. He closed his eyes against the sick feeling in his gut, not knowing if it was from the obvious concussion he had or the underlying knowledge that the journal was no longer in his room. Whoever had attacked him had undoubtably taken it.

"Nathan?" Rachel's panic-filled voice rose at the end. "Nathan?"

147

"Here." He braced his arms on the side of the bed and somehow managed to hoist himself into a standing position. He wasn't even swaying. At least he thought he wasn't. It was hard to tell with the blurry edges at the sides of his vision. Blood was still dripping down his forehead and trying to get into his eye.

"Please let me take you to the doctor."

"No." He managed not to move his head as he said the word. He was learning.

Rachel pressed her lips together in disapproval. Or maybe it was to keep from saying more. Instead she patted the backrest of the chair closest to her, motioning for him to sit.

Nate rounded the end of the bed and did as she bade. The dark flanks of his vision were clearing. By tomorrow he would be right as rain. Though he wouldn't have the journal. Not that it contained much. At least he hadn't found anything more than the boys' names.

"We need to clean this first. Do you have any rubbing alcohol or antiseptic?"

"Really?" he asked. "I was supposed to stay one night before heading back to Tulsa."

She pulled away as a strange look flickered over her face. But his head was hurting too bad for him to completely dissect it. However, he did see regret, remorse, and a touch of fear. He had no idea what any of it meant. Then she turned from him before he could ask.

She moved toward the bathroom, wetting one of the white washcloths the motel provided and bringing it back to where he waited.

He winced as she pressed the cool cloth to the cut on his head. The lady at the front desk was going to love his bloody laundry come tomorrow.

"They took the journal," he said quietly.

Rachel said nothing right away, though her sharp intake of breath let him know she had been listening. "How did you get it?"

## The Secrets We Keep

Right. She didn't know about his meeting with Shane.

"Long story. But it's gone now."

"Are you sure?"

"Pretty sure. It's not where I left it. Whoever broke in didn't come here to hurt me or I would be hurt."

"You are hurt," she countered.

"I mean bad." He wouldn't get into the details. Rachel didn't need to know all that. "They came for one thing only."

He felt her part his hair and wipe the cut once more.

"The bedside drawer," he told her. "There's some . . . alcohol in there." He nearly choked on the word. He should have had her ask the front desk for a first aid kit. But he hadn't been thinking as clearly as he should. Now he was revealing secrets. He hadn't wanted to admit to actually having booze. Hadn't wanted to say out loud that being back in Mississippi had him drinking to get through the days. Or was it the nights?

*You can't go home, but you can't stay here.*

She studied him for a moment, then moved away once more toward the nightstand. She pulled open the drawer, and there it was, lying right next to the Gideons Bible. A pint of Jack Daniel's. Half of it already gone.

A frown settled itself between her brows as she came back to where he sat, but she said nothing as he reached for the bottle. He uncapped it and took a swig, then handed it back to her. "This is the best we're going to get."

She nodded, then leaned closer to him, her scent surrounding him, sweet, familiar, forbidden. Even more so than the amber-colored liquid courage she was about to pour over the cut on his head.

"Are you sure you don't want me to take you to the hospital?"

"In your buggy?" he asked, hating the sharp note his voice carried.

"Right."

149

Then he sucked in a breath as, without warning, the alcohol splashed over the open wound. That would teach him to sass her. Rachel Gingerich might be a docile Amish woman, but she was no doormat. Never had been. Yet he had seen less of that spirit since he had been back. His head stung like hell, but he was glad to know it hadn't left her entirely.

Rachel *Hostetler*. And once again he had to remind himself.

"This is going to make a mess," she warned. "You'll probably end up with half your hair glued together."

"It don't matter." He wore a hat most times anyway.

"I could stitch it up," she offered.

"I'd rather have half my hair glued together."

"Here goes."

He sat as still as possible as she worked. "Make sure it's all covered," he instructed. It wouldn't be as good as what the medics and EMTs would have in an ambulance, but it would do for now.

"Okay." She stepped out from behind him. "I hope I did it right."

He resisted the urge to reach up and test it. "Is it still bleeding?"

She shook her head.

"Then it should be fine."

"It's surely going to scar if you don't let someone who knows what they're doing see to it."

He shrugged. Then they both fell quiet.

"What are you going to do, Nathan?" She eased into the chair opposite him.

"About what?" His head? Staying in Mississippi? Going back to Tulsa?

"About the journal," she explained. "I was hoping the police would find something in there to help."

He had too, but there was nothing there. "I looked through it three times, and I couldn't find anything. Whoever took it must have wanted to do the same." But who could that be? The only person he knew who had a vested interest in the journal was Shane. But Nate couldn't imagine his onetime friend setting him up that way. Had Shane even known that Nate and Rachel used to meet at the creek behind her house? The two men had been friends, but had they been that close? Nate couldn't remember. Only a handful of people knew that secret, and he was pretty sure Shane hadn't been one of them.

Unfortunately, Nate hadn't seen the person who hit him. Not really. They had come from the rear as if they had positioned themselves behind the door and lain in wait for him. He must have heard them when he walked in. Something had alerted him, and he had started to turn when the pain burst inside his head like a sharp white light. Attacked with the only other weapon he had brought with him, the Louisville Slugger he kept behind the seat of his truck. He might not have seen his attacker, but Nate had the distinct impression that the man was Amish.

There were so many things wrong with that theory. Pacifist dogma aside, what Amish man knew he had the journal and/or would want it so badly as to trick him into leaving his motel room to steal it? Then there was the whole Ten Commandments thing. Thou Shalt Not Steal. So there was that. No. It wouldn't have been an Amish man, but the thought wouldn't leave him.

"Do you have any idea where those missing pages are?" he asked, but he knew what she was going to say.

"No." Just like before, he knew she was lying.

She was Amish. She wasn't built for deception. Every time an Amish person went against their upbringing to the point that the *Englisch* got involved, the news was everywhere. But those times weren't as prevalent as some might think. The way of their fathers was strong. Strong training, strong upbringing, strong values. And yet she wasn't telling him the truth.

He didn't want to press her on the matter. There would be time for that later. Or there wouldn't. When it was time to go, he was going. He had to. He might owe Rachel this much, helping her discover the truth about her brother's death, but after that . . .

She was married, and nothing short of the death of her husband could change that for her. Even then she would have to leave the church to be with Nate. It wasn't as easy as they made it look in movies and on TV. It was a traumatic and terrible process. He wouldn't wish it on her and her girls. Not even to be with her. Their love that once had been could never be again. Too much stood in their way now. Too much stood between them.

"Those pages probably hold the key to all this," Nate fished.

"What are you going to do tonight?" Rachel asked, deftly trying to change the topic of their conversation. She didn't want to talk about the pages. Another reason to believe she knew exactly where they were and exactly how they got there. His only concern was that they were ash at the bottom of the burn barrel.

"What am I going to do about what?"

"You shouldn't go to sleep with your head." She shook hers. "It's dangerous to sleep too much when you have a concussion."

He wasn't even going to argue with her amateur diagnosis. He'd been hit in the head with a baseball once and felt about the same as he did now. His mother had stayed up all night making sure he didn't slip into a coma as the hours passed.

"I'll set an alarm on my phone," he said.

"Which will do no good," she started, "if you . . . fall asleep and don't hear it."

"The whole point is to have someone there to take you to get medical care if you don't wake up. What are you going to do? Drag me to the truck and drive to the hospital?"

She sniffed. "I have my buggy and horse."

152

# The Secrets We Keep

"I weigh over two hundred pounds. There's no way you could get me into the buggy or the truck. So it doesn't matter."

"It does. I'll stay until the morning," she said. "If I get up really early, I can be back at home before Dat wakes and the girls are up. That way we know you'll be safe."

He wanted to tell her to leave, that he didn't need her. That he didn't want her to stay. But none of that was the truth.

"You would do that for me?" Risk her father's temper. The admonishment of the church if anyone found out she had spent the better part of the night with him—regardless of the innocence of it all.

"*Jah.*" The word was whispered and sweet. "Do you have Tylenol for the pain?"

"No." Of all the things he had scored from Walmart for this trip, Tylenol was not one of them.

She moved toward the desk, and for the first time Nate noticed that her purse was sitting on its side next to the wall as if it had been tossed there by urgent hands. She unzipped it and pulled out a rattling plastic bottle. She shook a couple of the pills into the palm of her hand and offered them to him.

"Thanks," he murmured. He gingerly tossed them back, then headed for the sink to get some water. The mound of bloody towels still sat on the counter. He grabbed one of the wrapped plastic cups the hotel provided and got himself a drink. That was when he got a good view of himself. He looked like a character from the set of a horror film. Dried blood streaked down his face and the side of his head, circling his ear before dropping down onto the shoulder of his shirt. He had a knot the size of Georgia and an angry-looking cut that gaped from his temple clear up into his hairline. Yeah, extra in a slasher movie. The first victim of the psychotic killer.

He grabbed one of the towels and started to wipe at the blood that smeared over his face, but it wasn't enough. He needed a shower. As much as he welcomed having Rachel around, he knew she couldn't stay, not really. But he couldn't ask her to leave. He didn't have it in him. Not right now. Not tonight.

Nate turned back to her. "I'm going to take a shower," he started, hoping she would get the hint. He couldn't allow her to stay. She needed to go home now. Then again, he didn't know why she had come in the first place. "Why are you here?"

She gave a small shrug and looked off to one side. "I just wanted to see you again. To thank you for helping me." Once again she wasn't being truthful, but he didn't have the energy to question her. His head pounded. The Tylenol had not taken effect yet.

She made no move to leave.

"Rach," he started, his voice a little rusty. "As much as I appreciate you trying to help me, we both know that you can't stay here." There was too much at stake, and she was the only one with anything to lose. He couldn't let her risk everything—her standing with her family, with her church, with everyone and everything she had ever known and would ever be a part of.

For a moment he thought she might protest further, but instead she looked down, away from him. She started to pick at a hangnail. "I'll go," she finally said. "But after you shower. I wouldn't be able to forgive myself if you fell and there was no one here to help you."

He wanted to protest, to tell her that he wasn't going to fall, that she wouldn't be able to lift him if he did. But it was a compromise he could accept. He raised his chin ever so slightly in agreement. Then he got a pair of the sweatpants he'd bought at Walmart, a fresh T-shirt, and a clean pair of boxer briefs before heading into the bathroom. He closed the door behind himself and resisted the urge to slump against it. He felt shaky, weak, and he tried to tell himself that was the reason he was glad she was there.

# The Secrets We Keep

He started the shower, adjusted the water, and stepped beneath the spray. He was careful not to let the stream hit directly on the injured spot, but he wanted as much of the blood gone as possible. It bothered him. Maybe because it just kept reminding him of the failure of it all. But it had been a matter of *hurry up and wait*. They had to rush to get the body exhumed, then rush to get the autopsy, and now . . . wait. Hopefully it would only be a couple of weeks before the results were back. He wasn't sure how much urgency they would give the alleged suicide of an Amish kid, but he could hope. For Rachel's sake. Though he wasn't sure how she would react if it came back that Albie had died from asphyxiation. But Nate supposed he could only cross that bridge when he got to it.

He washed himself, washed the blood and some of the worry down the drain. By the time he toweled off and dressed, the Tylenol had started to work. It had only taken the throbbing edge off his pounding head, but it was better than nothing.

When he made his way back into the room, Rachel was sitting cross-legged on the bed, her back against the headboard, her knees tucked up under the skirt of her dress. He knew she shouldn't be there. He knew he shouldn't compromise for her own sake, but tonight . . . for his . . .

She smiled a bit when she saw him.

He made his way toward her and laid down, stretched across the bed, and let the years fall away. With his head in her lap, he closed his eyes against reality, the room and all the reminders that it wasn't twelve years previous, before things had gone sideways for them both.

Then her fingers were in his hair, brushing the strands gingerly away from the throbbing cut on his head.

Just for tonight.

"It'll be okay," she murmured.

He almost didn't respond, unwilling to make the effort, unwilling to have his own words cut through the utopia of the past swirling in his mind. "Will it?" he rumbled in return. But he drifted off before he heard her reply.

\* \* \*

His hands shook as he opened the book. The small leather-bound journal that had once belonged to Albie Gingerich. He flipped through it, a little awed by the muted colors of the beautiful drawings. He hadn't realized the boy had that much talent. It wasn't something that was praised among the Amish. But it wasn't the artwork he was looking for. Truthfully, he didn't know what he was looking for, only that it wasn't artwork. Maybe he'd thought he'd find some sort of clue as to what had been going through Albie's mind that night. The night he died.

Had Albie seen something he shouldn't have? He wanted to know. He *needed* to know.

He started to read some of the entries. Albie had been bullied by a group of boys, and apparently he wasn't the only one. His friend Keylan and another Amish boy had also been the subject of their ridicule. Albie talked a little about leaving the Amish, what such a move would cost him. He wrote that he believed his sister would stand by him, even if in secret. But he suspected that his father would not go against the rules of the church. He was probably right about that one. But what was a man to do? Leaving the Amish was a hard and terrible situation for all involved. Everyone knew that. He had seen it before.

Most outsiders thought the Amish *Ordnung* too strict and confining, but it was what it was, as far as he could tell. Who was he to say any different? Who out there truly knew what God wanted from them? Man struggled along, hoping and praying that his worship was the right one. That his beliefs would get him into heaven. What choice did a man really have when faced with the impossible task of going against everything he had ever known? Everything he had been taught his entire life?

And then the trials. What trials they all endured! How was a person supposed to keep their faith when the land was dry, the crops rotting from too much rain? Again and once more, over and over. It was an endless cycle that could drive a man mad. Drive a man to do the unthinkable.

At the end of the journal, there were several pages missing between the last entry and a series of blank pages.

He flipped through once more, trying to see if the loose pages had been tucked into a different spot. No. He flipped through again. And again. He turned the journal open side down and shook it, but nothing fluttered free.

As far as he could tell, the missing pages were from the week Albie died. They would have been his last entries. If he'd had an explanation for why he wanted to leave the Amish or even what drove him to do what he did, it would have been in those missing pages.

But they weren't there.

He dropped the book, then picked it up, closing it properly once more. After everything he had gone through to get the book, there was nothing in it to help him. Nothing at all.

\* \* \*

"Mamm?"

"Hmm . . . ?" Rachel stirred as the sweet, familiar voice called to her from the doorway of her room.

As she had promised, she had stayed with Nathan long into the night, waking him periodically to make sure he hadn't taken a turn for the worse. He was groggy every time and she seriously doubted he would remember any of it, but he had answered with his full name and who was president. What state he lived in and other such questions. As far as she could tell, he was fine. He would wake this morning with a serious headache, but there was not much more that could be done about that. She had left the bottle of Tylenol on the nightstand for him to find when he awoke.

"Why are you still sleeping? It's almost time for school." Kate barreled into the room, jumping onto the bed just as Rachel sat up in a panic.

They nearly butted heads, only missing because Rachel reached for the windup alarm clock that she kept by the bed. It was already seven thirty.

"I overslept," she told her daughter.

"I know. That's why I woke you up. Dawdi said I needed to."

Great. Her father was back at the house wondering where his breakfast was and why she was still in bed instead of downstairs cooking it for him.

"It's a good thing you did," she said, planting a kiss on her daughter's forehead. "I might have slept all day." She pushed herself from the bed and stood, fighting back the wave of exhaustion that washed over her. She felt as if she could go right back to sleep, but she didn't have that luxury. She had too many things to take care of. Starting with breakfast, getting her daughter off to school, and helping her sister get washed and dressed. None of that could be done without first getting herself up and ready for the day.

She lifted Kate from the bed and set her bare feet on the floor. At least her feisty daughter had dressed herself today. That was an improvement. "Where are your shoes?"

Kate made a face. "I don't like shoes."

# The Secrets We Keep

"I'm aware of this," Rachel said dryly. "But you have to wear shoes to go visit at the school. Where is your sister?" No doubt downstairs still in her nightdress, her nose in a book.

"I would like some shoes like your friend has. Those boots."

Rachel gently shook her head. "Cowboy boots are not part of the *Ordnung*."

"Hiram Esh wears cowboy boots."

"Hiram Esh is a boy." She pointed her daughter toward the door. At the rate they were going, Rachel wouldn't be dressed and downstairs until lunchtime.

"That's not fair," Kate stated as Rachel nudged her from behind.

"There's a lot that's not fair," Rachel countered. "Now find your sister and get downstairs."

"Amelie's not lost. She's in the barn with the puppies."

"Of course she is." Rachel prodded her daughter once more, and this time Kate got the hint.

"I'm going," she groused. "But I still want a pair of cowboy boots."

"I'm sure you do. Now get." She closed the door behind her daughter and stripped out of her nightclothes. She donned the same dress she had worn the day before. It was hanging on one of the peg hooks to the left of her bedroom door.

Rachel had stayed with Nathan until four, then sneaked away and back home, knowing that her father would be up at five to start the day's chores.

Two and a half hours of sleep was just not enough. But for today it would have to do.

Rachel took her hair out of its ponytail holder and quickly brushed through it, then twisted it into a bob at the back of her head.

Ten more minutes and she was downstairs, facing her father.

"Where you been?" he asked, eyeing her with a skepticism she had never seen before. Not even in those long-ago days when she and Nathan were sneaking out whenever they could.

"I overslept," she explained simply. She wouldn't overexplain; when she did that, she usually got herself into trouble.

It took her father too long to answer. "*Jah.*" He said the word slowly and without conviction.

She wanted to ask if everything was all right, but she wouldn't. The less she said, the better. But—

But what if something had happened in the night and she wasn't there? If something had happened with Miri and Rachel was gone, their father would have had to see about her and Rachel was sure to hear about it . . . eventually.

She turned toward her father, pasting on the brightest smile she dared muster. "Are you all right today, Dat?"

She had to stop this madness. She had to stop seeing Nathan at his motel room. She had to stop thinking about him and start concentrating her every thought on finding her brother's murderer. But that led her right back to Nathan.

"I'm *allrecht*," he said, but his eyes still held a watchful light.

He knew. She didn't know how he knew. But somehow she had been found out. Rachel could only hope that her father didn't know the whole truth about where she had been last night. It wasn't the best, but he could know that she had been away from the house. She could explain that away easily enough. But if he somehow knew she had been with Nathan . . .

Aside from reprimanding her for being married and running around all over the place at all hours, he would tell her about the temptations of the flesh. Temptations she knew all too well.

## The Secrets We Keep

She turned her attention to her oldest as Amelie walked through the door, Kate trailing behind her.

"I found her." Kate proudly beamed. Honestly, they really needed to work on the girl's humility, but Rachel found it hard to break her spirit. *Jah*, the Amish faith was firmly rooted in conformity, but she enjoyed Kate and her radical ideas and thoughts. Like wearing cowboy boots. But it wouldn't be allowed. Not in their community.

She sighed and turned back to the stove. "Did you wash up?"

Their settlement was what some called Swartzentruber Amish, one of the most conservative sects of the Old Order Amish faith. There was no indoor plumbing, and it was much easier to wash up outside at the spigot than it was to wash up inside using the always-at-hand bucket of water.

"Yes, Mamm." Amelie came to stand beside her. "Can I help you with breakfast?"

As much as Rachel loved her youngest daughter's spirit, she appreciated her oldest daughter's care and concern. She just wished she didn't come across so melancholy all the time. Rachel knew people like her in their community. Just as there were bubbly children and adults, there were more serious ones as well. But something about Amelie's seriousness struck her as more than a quirk of personality. Her daughter hadn't been quite this serious until Freeman disappeared.

"*Jah. Danki.*" Rachel handed the spatula to Amelie. "Serve everyone their eggs, and I'll go get Miri ready for the day."

Rachel hated the rushed feeling that was coming over her. It choked her and took her breath away. There were Amish families with ten and twelve children, but she could barely get herself and her two daughters ready for the day.

And of course Miri. Miri took a lot of extra care.

She was already sitting up in bed, a testament to Rachel's late start. But as she always did, Miri laughed and clapped her hands when she saw Rachel.

"Good morning, *shveshtah*," Rachel greeted her sister. She loved Miri, she really did, but sometimes she wondered if her life was something worth living. What had God had in mind when He made her this way? What purpose could she serve Him in the state she was in?

Rachel pushed those thoughts away. It did no good to question God's plan. It only led to more questions. Questions that had no answers.

"Let's get you up and ready for the day." She grabbed Miri's dress, which was hanging by the door, and laid it at the foot of the bed. Then she fetched her sister's wheelchair from the far corner of the room. They kept it as far away from Miri as possible at night. She had a tendency to try to get up without assistance. Those nights had resulted in more than a few bumps and bruises. And when she broke her arm, they knew something more had to be done.

Rachel placed her arms under her sister's and scooped her up and into the chair. Thankfully, Miri had a little muscle movement left in her limbs. But it was spastic at best. Still, it was enough to allow Rachel to get her sister into her chair without anyone else's help. When that ability was gone, she didn't know what they would do.

Adult Protective Services had been out more than once to make sure Miri was being well cared for. Rachel didn't know who had called about them, most likely some *Englischer* in town who thought they were doing the family a service. All they had done was bring down her father's wrath. Onto Rachel. Like the whole of the situation was her fault. He had resented being watched and checked in that manner, and the APS visits always made him surly. But Rachel had used their suggestions to her advantage and did for Miri

# The Secrets We Keep

everything they had recommended. Still, she worried that one day they would come and scoop her sister up and take her away forever.

The thought was freeing and crushing all in the same instant.

She was just tired, Rachel thought as she pulled the nightdress over Miri's head. Her sister's arms flapped, slowing the process even more. Rachel hadn't gotten much sleep. She was worried about Nathan. She was worried about who had the journal now. What had they expected to find? Surely not the pages Rachel had stuffed into her mattress. She couldn't throw them away or burn them in the trash barrel; they were her brother's last words. She couldn't allow anyone to see them, but she couldn't destroy them either.

"Miri woke up last night."

Rachel jumped as her father spoke from the doorway. She had just pulled Miri's dress down and was reaching for her apron when he spoke.

She glanced at him over one shoulder, then turned back to the task at hand. "Oh?" The word slipped from her lips, as innocent sounding as a new *boppli*. She held her breath as she waited for what was next.

"I had to come in here and see about her."

Their father hated caring for Miri. Rachel couldn't understand why but had decided that Miri made Dat feel helpless. Samuel Gingerich could pray for rain. He could ask God for guidance, wisdom, and strength, but asking for his daughter to be healed . . . well, that was a miracle the almighty power refused to perform. Not only that, but incident after incident had made her condition worse. Or at least her life.

This was the hardest part of dressing her sister. So many times, Miri started rocking. Not a gentle sway but a violent crash from side to side and back and forth in an uncontrolled manner. Too many times Rachel had come away with a black eye or a bruised cheek, even a busted lip.

"Be still now, sister," Rachel cooed. She tried to pretend her father wasn't watching her every move, judging and calculating.

"Did you hear what I said?"

"I'm sorry." Rachel finished tying her sister's apron without incident and went behind her to start her hair. She wasn't going to stop her chore because her father was upset. She was behind enough as it was. Truthfully, she was too exhausted to have the conversation at all. Maybe somewhere deep down inside she thought that if she didn't stop, he would go away and not criticize today.

But she knew that was never going to happen.

"Where were you?" he demanded.

"Sleeping." It wasn't really a lie; she had been sleeping, just not in her bedroom upstairs as her words implied.

"You weren't. I checked."

"Dat, I—" But she had no idea what she was going to say. She certainly couldn't tell him the truth and have him understand. And she couldn't lie anymore. It was too hard on her conscience.

He raised one hand and marched into the room.

Rachel flinched, terrified for one split second that he was going to strike her. She closed her eyes and braced for the moment, but it never came.

She opened them again to find him staring at her oddly, as if she were some new insect that he had never seen before.

And that maybe he wanted to squash under the heel of his shoe.

"Things have been off around here," he started.

Rachel continued to brush Miri's hair and didn't bother to point out that her brother, his son, had been murdered. *Jah*, things were definitely "off."

"Ever since he came back to town."

## The Secrets We Keep

She glanced up from her sister's long hair to her father. She didn't need to ask him who he was talking about. Doing so would be an insult to them both.

"I think things went off course before then," she gently said.

"Stay away from him, Rachel. He's no good."

"*Jah*." She twisted Miri's hair into a bob and started to pin it. No easy task, as Miri could never sit entirely still. It was easier to fix Kate's hair than her sister's. She had just slid the pin in place when he reached out a hand to stop her.

"I mean it, *dochder*. Stay away from him if you know what's good for you."

Stay away from him.

How was she supposed to stay away from him? Aside from the fact that she was depending on him to find out the truth about her brother, Nathan Fisher was like a magnet, pulling her toward him.

Rachel wanted to pretend she was showing up at his motel room once again because she needed to talk to him about Albie. And maybe even that she was doing the Christian thing and looking out for Nathan by checking on him. After all, he had received quite a blow to the head the night before.

But she had had enough of lying. Even to herself. She wanted to see him again. Last night hadn't been enough. But it would never be enough. She was still married in the eyes of the church. It didn't matter that no one had seen her husband in over three years. She was married to him until she died if no one could prove his death. That was the way it was.

But even if she weren't married, Nathan was shunned. He had left the Amish and she hadn't. She couldn't. She had Miri to think about. Her sister needed her care, and she certainly couldn't care for

165

her if she was no longer part of the community. For all their father's bitterness toward Miri, Rachel knew he would never let her go.

She hadn't asked Nathan if he would ever consider coming back into the fold. She knew the answer in her heart even if she couldn't say it out loud. He could never come back. Too much time had passed. Too many conveniences in the *Englisch* world. Too much bad water under the bridge.

They were stuck in the roles they had made for themselves.

She raised her hand to knock on his door, but it opened before her knuckles met the painted wood.

"Nathan." She pressed the hand she had raised to her rapidly beating heart.

"Rachel." Her name on his lips came out like a prayer. Perhaps a little rusty, but filled with emotions as old as time.

"I . . ." She what? She had to come by and see him? She couldn't manage to keep herself away. "I was worried about you."

He shook his head, grabbed her elbow, and pulled her into the room. She turned just in time to see him look both ways before closing the door behind him and locking it.

"Did anyone see you come here?"

"I don't think so. What's wrong? What happened?"

"Last night. The journal." He looked at her as if she had taken leave of her senses.

Her eyes grew wide. "You don't think they would come back? They have the journal." What more could they need?

"Yeah, but they don't have those last pages. I have a feeling what's in them is more important than either of us know."

She didn't want to believe that. She didn't want to believe the words her brother had written on the last pages of his journal were any more important than the first ones.

*Then why did you tear them out and hide them?*

# The Secrets We Keep

She shook her head. When was this going to stop? She was hanging on by a thread and couldn't take much more. She shouldn't have come here. She should not come here anymore. Not again. Not until they knew for certain what had killed her brother. After that, Nathan would leave and the temptation of him would go dormant once more, like Bermuda grass in the wintertime. Brown and dead looking but waiting to be revived again.

"I'm sorry," she said, not even understanding what she was really apologizing for. For coming here again, when she should be as far away as possible? For tearing out the pages he seemed determined to find? For not going with him all those years ago?

She moved toward the door, intent on leaving and never coming back. He could have the sheriff come and tell him what had killed her brother. After all, they would be the ones who would go after the terrible boys who had done this to him.

Before she reached for the doorknob, a knock sounded.

Rachel jumped, but Nathan was as cool as ever, as if he had been expecting someone to stop by. The culprit from the night before?

But a burglar wouldn't knock.

Nathan used one hand and pushed her behind him. He eased toward the window and looked out. Then he swore under his breath. His mother would have had a heart attack upon hearing him say those words had she been there.

He let the curtain fall back into place, then urged her farther into the room. "Go. Hide in the bathroom. In the shower. Pull the curtain closed."

Nathan rushed her across and into the bathroom.

"Don't come out," he told her. "Even if he comes in here, don't let him see you."

"Who?" Rachel asked, her voice whispered urgency.

"Leroy," he told her. "My brother is here."

**167**

# Chapter Eleven

Nate pulled the curtain closed behind her and shut the door to the small bathroom area just to be on the safe side. He was fairly certain his brother hadn't stopped by to use the facilities. With any luck, he would state his business and be on his way.

Nate hurried across the matted carpet to the door of the dingy motel room. He stopped there and took a deep breath. There was only one reason his brother had come to see him. Only one reason he would stop by and talk to his shunned sibling. Only one reason at all.

With more confidence than he felt, Nate opened the door. "Leroy," Nate greeted him.

His brother frowned. Then without a word, he pushed past him and inside.

"Okay." Nate shut the door behind him and turned for the verbal lashing he knew was to come.

Leroy was definitely the new patriarch of the family, a role he had been preparing for his entire life. Of all the brothers, Leroy and Nate were the most alike. Dark hair and clear blue eyes they had inherited from their mother. Though Leroy was two years older, Nate had a couple of inches and a few pounds on him. Always had. Which was why when they were growing up people thought they

**168**

were twins. The idea had always bothered Leroy. After all, he was older, the firstborn. He would be in charge if anything happened to their father. He would run the family. He was all in with the community. On the school board and the first one called when something needed correcting.

Nate had been as close to his brother as was possible with the pot of envy bubbling between them. It wasn't like they hadn't had good times growing up, but the older they got, the worse the contention became. And when Nate left, it had roiled over, spilling out to soak everything in its toxins.

"You have to stay away," Leroy said. "You made the choice to leave. Now you can't just come back and try to upset everything."

*You can't go home again.*

"I'm not trying to upset everything. Or anything."

But Leroy wasn't there to listen. "It's upsetting to Mamm, you coming by and sitting out in the road. You must stop it."

He hadn't been by in a couple of days, but he wasn't about to argue for argument's sake. So he nodded instead. Truthfully, Leroy was right, but she was his mother too. Despite what anyone else might think, he loved her. He hadn't left because he hated the lifestyle and wanted to escape. He hadn't changed his mind about the doctrine they taught—not at the time, anyway. He hadn't wanted to get away from everything Amish, including his family. He had stupidly and naïvely wanted to help. And the truth was, he missed her. There wasn't a day that went by that he didn't miss her, didn't wish it all had turned out differently. These days even more than ever. If he hadn't left when he did, a young boy might still be alive.

"You knew what would happen when you left. You knew and you went anyway. There's no coming back now."

Didn't he know it.

169

"I'm leaving soon," he said.

"*Jah*?" His brother seemed skeptical of the news, like why would Nate want to be anywhere but Cedar Creek now that he was back.

Nate gave a small nod. His head was still throbbing, and he didn't want to move it unnecessarily.

"What happened to your head?" his brother demanded.

"I bumped into a baseball bat." Let his brother make of that what he would. He was tired of defending his actions. Tired of being told by his family that they didn't want him. It was Rachel. She was the reason he was staying around. It had always been Rachel.

His brother's eyes narrowed. "Go home, Nathan."

If only it were that simple.

Then his brother turned on one heel and marched to the door in a way only Leroy Fisher could manage, head held high, back straight, not giving an inch.

"Lee," Nate started, before his brother could step one foot outside and shut the door behind him. "You know anyone named Jay Anderson?" It was a long shot. Anderson wasn't an Amish name, and his brother was already riled up. But the detective in him had to ask.

Leroy didn't bother to face him. "No." Then he was gone.

Nate waited five full seconds before moving behind him and locking the door. "You can come out now."

He could hear the sound of the shower curtain being pulled to one side, and then she was there beside him.

"Is it safe to go?" she asked.

"I'd give him a little more head start," Nate told her.

She stood next to him, staring at the closed door of the motel room, and all at once he was more aware of her than he had ever been. Them sneaking around and trying to not get caught. It was their past together all over again.

Rachel started laughing, the sound high and thin. She doubled over, wiping her face as the tears started, then she hiccupped as those tears of mirth became sobs. "I have to go." She shook her head and wrenched at the door, but it refused to budge. She pulled again, finally realizing that the door was locked. Somehow she managed to unlock it before trying a third time.

It all happened so fast. Nate just stood there watching, trying to figure out where everything had gone wrong. She had been beside him, laughing, then crying, then leaving.

She stopped just on the other side of the doorframe, so close but out of reach all the same.

"Leroy's right, Nathan. I was wrong to try and keep you here. Go home. There's nothing left for you here."

*You don't have to go home, but you can't stay here.*

It was past time for him to leave. His head was killing him, not from the wound but from thinking and worrying and wondering about things best left in the past. He had spent a restless night nursing what was left of the bottle of Jack, perhaps even giving Rachel a little more time to come back. She hadn't. Now it was morning and the undeniable truth was that he had hidden out long enough. There was nothing for him in Cedar Creek but bad memories and people who wanted to forget he had ever existed.

And Rachel? If Albie had a skull fracture like the coroner was saying, then something had happened to him before he was strung up. There was a small chance it could have happened after he had been cut down, but the coroner would be able to tell that as well. If it had been post or premortem. If Nate had to bet on

## Amy Lillard

it, he would say pre. The dirt floor of the barn was hard but not that hard. Which meant someone else had had a hand in Albie's death. Whether or not it was Chance Longacre and his gang was another matter altogether. Nate would leave Shane to sort it all through. Nate had done what he promised to do: He had helped Rachel prove that her brother had not committed suicide. Well, at least he had started the ball rolling. He just hadn't finished it. He would call Shane from the road and tell the detective he was going home.

That wasn't the worst part, leaving it dangling. The worst part was all the loose ends that awaited him in Tulsa. The only things he knew for certain were that Satchel would expect his food bowl to be filled and Bree would welcome him back, no questions asked.

A man could do worse.

Nate was grabbing up the last of his things when a knock sounded on his motel room door. He stopped, listening for some clue as to who it was. His family had made their wishes clear. Surely it wouldn't be any of them coming again so soon to chase him out of town. He had no other ties in Mississippi. Not any longer. He owed no one an explanation of his plans. After yesterday, he was fairly certain it wasn't Rachel coming back to smooth things over between them. That kite had flown.

Hearing nothing, he moved to the window and peeked out the side of the curtain. A thin young man stood there. Amish. Nate had never seen him before. At least he didn't remember seeing him. The man raised his hand and knocked again, looking from side to side as if an answer were going to sidle up next to him. But as he turned, something in the angle of his chin sent recognition searing through Nate.

He released the chain and opened the door. "Jeremiah Troyer?"

172

# The Secrets We Keep

The youngster swallowed hard, his Adam's apple bobbing as he nodded. "I heard you were looking for me."

\* \* \*

Rachel pasted on a happy smile. She hoped it looked happy, anyway. Today was supposed to be a fun day. The last-day-of-school picnic. Lunch on the ground and games, prizes, and an all-around good time to celebrate the end of another school year. As Amelie was a first grader, this was her first picnic, and she was excited. Rachel couldn't allow her own sour mood to spoil her daughter's good time.

"Are you ready?" Rachel asked as she pushed Miri through the house and out onto the porch. Kate danced excitedly beside her. Amelie waited patiently by the door, eyes twinkling but feet still.

"*Jah*," Kate gushed.

Amelie being Amelie, she was excited, but her enthusiasm couldn't touch that of Kate. But that was Kate being Kate. Her daughters might look alike with their sweet dimples and matching green eyes, but their personalities were like their hair color—exactly opposite. Their bright differences brought a smile to Rachel's face. She didn't know what she would have done without them these past couple of years. And she knew their love and joy would get her through the rest.

She had told Nathan to leave. She was the reason he was still here, and she wondered if he had headed home already. And if she would ever see him again. But those thoughts dimmed her smile, the corners of her mouth pulling down. She consciously smiled a little wider, hoping she didn't look demented. She wasn't going to think about Nathan today, and he had entered her thoughts so many times already without any invitation from her. But it had always been that way. Even when she wasn't thinking about him,

173

it was as if he had never left her. But nothing would ever come of it. Anything they'd ever had between them was suspended in a time neither one could return to. He had made his choices, and she had made her own. Life moved forward.

Amelie ran ahead and jumped in the back of the custom buggy they took when Miri went along with them. She waited patiently there to help strap her aunt into the safety harnesses that had been installed to keep her wheelchair in place. A man in Ohio had designed the carriage, and it had been a lifesaver for the whole of their family.

"Off to somewhere?"

She was just about to push the clapping and laughing Miri into the carriage but stopped, stiffened, when she heard Daniel behind her. She turned slowly to face her brother-in-law. "Hi, Daniel. *Jah.* It's the last day of school."

He nodded sagely. "Picnic, huh?" He should have said more, perhaps even offered to help her, but he just stood there, watching, his thumbs tucked underneath the sides of his suspenders.

She waited until after she had her sister secured in the carriage and the back latched into place before asking, "Did you need something?"

"Samuel around?" he finally asked.

She shook her head. "He's in town. At the co-op."

Daniel nodded. "Okay. *Danki.* I was hoping to ask him a question about the well."

"He should be home later this afternoon." She turned to Kate, who was listening with rapt attention. "Get in the buggy, Kate."

Her daughter nodded and scrambled inside.

Rachel turned back to Daniel. She didn't like the way he was looking at her daughter. She took a side step to block his view of

# The Secrets We Keep

the girls. He had never made any sort of overtures toward them, but the light in his eyes was somehow off. She didn't like it. Not one bit. "Is that all?"

He nodded. "*Jah*. I wanted to tell him that I got the pump working on the old well. Seems it wasn't quite dry. So at least I have a little bit of water now."

"I'm sure he'll be home in a bit," she reiterated. Her *vatter* should be home long before she would be, and Daniel would be over as soon as he caught whiff that her *dat* was back. She didn't need to relay any messages.

Yet he continued to stand there, watching her as if he could see straight through to her bones. She shook the thought away.

How she wanted to ask him what he had meant the other day about teaching Albie to be a man. Did he know more than he was saying? She might never know. She wasn't sure if Daniel was capable of giving her a straight answer. It seemed every time the subject came up, he avoided responding.

She waited, crossing her arms and silently urging him to go. He hesitated for a moment longer, then turned and strode away, past the barn and in the direction of the house. Rachel closed her eyes, took a deep breath, then made her way around the buggy.

Kate was bouncing in place and swinging her legs, so excited to be going to play with the school kids again. She had one more year at home before she would enter the first grade, and Rachel planned to make sure they made the most of that time. Sometimes it was hard, when a person had so many responsibilities, to make sure they spent enough time with their loved ones. It was a struggle, but Rachel was mindful of it every day. Especially now that Freeman was gone.

She drove the short distance from her house to the school, then pulled her buggy into the schoolyard. She parked in the line of

**175**

carriages that had already formed. The picnic goers were getting settled, spreading quilts to sit on and placing their sack lunches on the long table the teacher had set up for that purpose.

The school building itself was a small, white clapboard structure that sat in a field contained within a wire fence. The only phone shanty in their district sat off to one side, made from the leftover materials that remained after the school was built.

"Do you need help with Miri?" Amelie asked as she and her sister climbed down from the carriage.

Rachel shook her head. The girls were fairly humming with excitement, and for Amelie, that was saying something. But she was a good girl offering to help even when she wanted to run and play with her friends. "No, but I do need one favor." Rachel handed Amelie the paper bags containing their sandwiches. "Take these to Martha. And you"—she turned to Kate—"find us a place to sit. Next to the building, please. So Miri can have shade."

"*Jah*, Mamm." Kate took the quilt and started off after her sister.

The girls quickly made their way across the field toward the side of the school where the picnic had been set up.

It took only a few more minutes for Rachel to unhook Miri and roll her out of the back of the buggy, but it was another thing trying to navigate the lumpy field that served as the school's playground. She carefully picked her way along, then she crossed the packed dirt drive and over to where Kate had dumped the quilt they would sit on.

Out of habit, Rachel set the brake on Miri's wheelchair and started spreading out the quilt. The school faced north, and thus the area where they were would be shaded most of the morning and even some of the early afternoon. After that, Rachel supposed she would gather her girls and take them home whether the picnic was over or not. It was hard enough to sit with Miri all morning

**The Secrets We Keep**

long without her having a nap. It was too much to expect her to sit all morning and all afternoon in the blazing southern sunshine.

"I'm glad you could make it." Martha Yutzy was a few years younger than Rachel, as dark haired as Rachel was fair. Truthfully, they were only cousins by marriage, but they had connected early on and used that tenuous relation to their advantage.

"I don't think either of the girls would have been happy if we hadn't come." Rachel shot Martha a smile. Her cousin returned it, but her lips seemed stretched a bit by the movement. "Is everything okay?" Rachel asked.

Martha nodded. "Of course." But Rachel had a feeling she was hiding something, though she had no idea what it might be. "I heard Nathan was back in town."

Leave it to Martha to change the subject in such a dramatic way. "*Jah.*" Rachel sniffed and tried to play it off like it didn't keep her up nights knowing Nathan Fisher was just down the road. For so long she had held her feelings for him in check. It had been easier when he was gone, out of sight. But having him back in Cedar Creek . . .

"I suppose that's why you've been dropping Kate off at school?"

That was something she really didn't want to talk about. "He's leaving soon," Rachel said, hoping like everything that he had taken her advice and was driving west even as she was speaking. She could only hope.

"I see." Martha nodded, then turned as someone called her name. She looked back at Rachel. "I need to go see what that's about. It's almost time for the games."

"Go to it," Rachel said, and settled herself down on the quilt next to her sister's wheelchair. Martha was a busy person and the picnic was busy for the teacher. But Rachel had the feeling that Martha had been looking for a way to escape their conversation. She shouldn't care anything about Nathan being in town, so it seemed to Rachel that she was avoiding what it was that had her frowning even through a smile.

But in truth, Rachel had enough of her own problems to keep her busy many times over. She had to trust that if Martha needed her she would come and ask for help. It was the way it had always been between them.

"Mamm, Mamm." Amelie rushed over, cheeks pink from exertion. "Come, come! It's almost time for the three-legged race."

Rachel glanced back at Miri. She seemed content and stable, strapped in her special wheelchair, but Rachel knew better than to leave her alone for long. It seemed that every time she did, something disastrous happened. She really couldn't deal with disastrous today.

"I'm sorry. I can't, *liebschdi*. I have to stay with Miri. You know that."

Amelie bounced up and down on the balls of her feet. The strings of her prayer *kapp* had come untied, and they danced around her small shoulders. "Please. Just this once. Please."

Rachel shook her head and pushed to her feet. She reached down and tied the covering strings in a neat bow. "Go see if your sister will race with you."

"No." Amelie grimaced. "She can't run that fast, and all the other girls are running with their mothers."

"All of them."

Amelie nodded sternly.

"I'm sure not all."

Amelie continued to frown. "Please, Mamm."

"Go get your sister or sit down and watch. Those are the choices you have."

"That stinks," Amelie groused as she flounced down on the quilt.

"What was that?" Rachel eyed her daughter sternly.

**178**

# The Secrets We Keep

"I'm sorry, Mamm. I didn't mean that."

Rachel nodded, then eased down next to Amelie. She ran light fingers over her daughter's prayer covering, smoothing it down out of sheer habit. "I know it's hard when you have a loved one that needs special care, but you have to remember that God chose us for this burden. And we gratefully accept it because it means we have Miri with us, on earth." Once again she had to push away musings on what quality of life Miri had. Yet what was the alternative? Miri was here until the good Lord saw fit to take her home.

"Is Dat ever coming home?"

The words sliced through Rachel like a hot knife through butter. She could handle almost any question except this one.

"I don't know." It was the only answer she could give. In truth, she felt the answer was no. Somehow she knew that her gentle giant of a husband was long dead. She didn't know how she knew it, but in her heart, that was the truth.

"Do you think Jesus will bring him back?"

"I suppose if he comes back, we should definitely thank Jesus."

"Kate prays every night that it's the Lord's will that Jesus brings Dat home." Amelie plucked a stray blade of grass, then tossed it away. She picked at another.

"There's nothing wrong with that," Rachel said. Kate also prayed that it was the Lord's will that the buggy horse have a colt. Which truly would be a miracle, seeing as how he was a gelding, but Rachel certainly wasn't getting into that with Amelie. Or Kate.

"Thomas Byler says that he's not coming back. That he ran off with Marie. Why would they run off? Where would they go?"

Rachel winced at the words. "I think we should talk about this some other time," she said gently. Honestly, she didn't want to talk about it ever, but she definitely didn't want to talk about it with so many little ears around. Not to mention all the big ones. Gossip was rampant in a close Amish community. Rachel knew that the talk stemmed from caring, but still, it was hard to know that your friends were talking about you behind your back. Wondering if your husband had truly run away with another woman or if he had gotten messed up in something that he shouldn't have. Or maybe he was just tired of Amish life and had to get away. There were a thousand reasons to account for a person leaving everything they had behind, and yet none of them seemed big enough to Rachel to amount to action.

For a moment she thought Amelie might protest.

"Why don't you go see what your sister is into?"

Amelie nodded slowly, then pushed to her feet. She brushed her hands down the back of her dress and sauntered off in the direction of the other children.

Rachel breathed a quick sigh of relief, but she knew it would be short lived at best.

\* \* \*

What kind of luck did he have that the one person he wanted to talk to had come to find him only minutes before he got ready to leave Mississippi for good?

"Come in." Nate moved back to allow Jeremiah to enter the room.

The boy stepped inside and perched on the edge of the unmade bed. Then he seemed to think better of it and relocated to the nearby chair. The very chair that Nate had sat in when Rachel glued his head back together two nights before.

Jeremiah Troyer was barely sixteen, thin as a rail, and nervous.

He waited until Nate shut the door before speaking.

"I suppose you want to talk to me about Albie." Jeremiah slouched in his seat, appearing somewhat browbeaten as he did so.

## The Secrets We Keep

But Nate could see why he might be bullied as Rachel had told him. The description of Keylan from the young girl in the Grill suddenly jumped to mind. Sweet. Jeremiah's demeanor was definitely sweet. Not flamboyant, but he had the kind of flair that wouldn't slide under the radar. Maybe it was the tilt of his chin, or a specific mannerism, a flick of the wrist or a wave of the hand, that called him out. He was gay, and there was no denying it. The problem was what it all had to do with Albie. And what the sheriff was willing to do to protect the Amish from further hate crimes.

"What can you tell me about him?" Nate asked. It seemed the best place to start.

Jeremiah smiled, a wispy curve of the lips that usually came after knowing someone for a long time. Or maybe just intimately. And that was what Nate needed to find out. Had they shared secrets? Could Jeremiah tell him what might be on those final journal pages? "He was a good kid. The best. And he didn't deserve what they gave him."

Nate nodded and sat down into the chair opposite the boy. "So you believe that Chance Longacre and his running buddies killed Albie?"

Jeremiah looked one way and then the other as if there was a chance he might be overheard. "Of course. Everyone believes that, whether they say it or not. A lot of . . . people around here are scared of them."

"I got that impression. Just Amish?" he asked, hoping this conversation might lead him to others who knew Albie as well. Others he might have shared his plans with.

"No." The young man shook his head, his black hat rattling a bit with the motion. Then he took it off and laid it on the table. His hair was a medium brown, not dark or light, and the chilibowl haircut did nothing to soften the angular blades of his cheeks.

"Keylan Reid?"

He sat up a little straighter at the mention of the other boy's name. "Keylan and Albie were good friends," he started. "The best. Even though they were different."

"Because one is Black and the other was white?" Nate asked.

"Because one is *Englisch* and the other Amish."

Nate nodded. Growing up, he had had more than his fair share of *Englisch* friends, much to his father's chagrin. But he knew he was the exception and not the rule. He should have known. Change was slow in a small town. "But they had stuff in common. Things that drew them together."

"They were supposed to leave that night. They told me they were going. Then something happened, and the next thing I know everyone is saying that Albie killed himself." He shook his head. "Albie didn't kill himself."

Nate thought about the coroner's unofficial report. *I've never seen a skull fracture commit suicide.* "It appears that the autopsy is going to show that."

"Good," Jeremiah said simply. "He deserves to rest in the cemetery by his mother."

"I agree." For his sister's sake if no one else's. "So what about Keylan?" Nate asked. "Where's he now?"

Jeremiah shrugged. "He left."

"Why? He wasn't running from his religion or his upbringing. Why did he leave without Albie that night?"

"He was trying to get away from Chance and them others." Jeremiah didn't look at Nate when he said the words.

"What about a Jay Anderson? You ever heard of him?"

Jeremiah shook his head.

"Okay," Nate started. "Kid gloves off."

"I don't know what that means." Jeremiah met his gaze. The boy looked scared.

## The Secrets We Keep

"It means now I'm going to ask the really tough questions."

He swallowed hard. "Okay."

"Was Albie gay?"

Jeremiah wagged his head back and forth like a hound dog trying to shake off fleas. "No. No, no, nonono."

Nate stood, leaned forward, and gripped the arms of the other chair. "Did he like girls? Do *you* like girls?" He needed Jeremiah to admit the truth, whether he wanted to or not. Had Albie been gay, and had Chance Longacre targeted him for his sexual orientation as well as his religion?

Jeremiah stopped, the look in his eyes shifting from scared to terrified. "No," he whispered, his gaze glued to Nate's. "I don't want to be sent away."

It was a common practice among the more conservative of the Amish sects to send away the afflicted so they might be cured of the evil thoughts that plagued them. The Amish didn't believe that a person was born gay. They only considered the doctrine that it went against the Bible, against their teachings. The stigma would not allow a person to enter the kingdom of heaven, and therefore such behavior could not be tolerated.

Nate knew the elders meant well. They had the best intentions. They wanted to help the person get back with God, stop what they believed to be evil ways, and walk with Jesus again.

But it wasn't that simple. A person couldn't "therapy" gay away. He'd had enough sensitivity training to know that. And even if it could, not everyone would want to fall in line.

Nor would anyone want to be sent away. Once they returned, Nate knew the Amish would invite them back into the fold as if nothing had ever happened. But still everyone knew. The shame of that mark would follow the offender the rest of their lives.

# Amy Lillard

"I don't want to be sent away," Jeremiah said once more, this time a little quieter.

"No one's going to send you away." Nate eased back into his seat. "What we talk about stays right here. I won't tell anyone. I'm just trying to get to the truth of what happened to my friend's brother." Calling Rachel a friend seemed like more of a lie than anything else he'd said. He wouldn't say a word about Jeremiah, but he had to know about Albie for the sake of the investigation.

"I think so. Keylan and Albie." He shook his head. "They weren't a couple or anything. They just had that in common, I guess."

"And you?" Nate pressed. "Is that why the boys are harassing you?"

"I don't want to be sent away." Jeremiah flattened his lips. "I'm only telling you this to help Albie. It is going to help Albie, right?"

Nate nodded. He would have to dig a little more. "The thing is, I need to be able to pin this on Chance and his buddies so it sticks. If I knew of someone that they have been bullying for the same reason, it would build a stronger case for when it comes time to make arrests. Do you understand that?"

"I don't want to be sent away." Jeremiah stood and grabbed his hat. "Maybe you can find Keylan."

"Do you know where he went?" Nate asked, following him to his feet.

Jeremiah placed his hat on his head and grabbed the doorknob before answering. "No, but his sister works at the Laundromat."

# Chapter Twelve

He should be doing exactly what he had told Rachel to do: be patient and wait for the coroner's report to come back. It would answer some, if not all, of their questions. But the detective in him couldn't let it rest. He had to talk to Keylan.

Hell, he had been leaving. Halfway out the door and he got dragged back into this crazy town with its crazy dichotomy between the *Englisch* and the Amish.

Nate unlocked his truck and swung himself into the driver's seat. The pain in his head had faded to a dull ache, and it only hurt when he touched it. Especially when he touched it. Or wore his hat. He had placed the straw Stetson on the Chevy's dash until it healed a bit more. He felt somewhat naked without his head covered, and whenever he met someone, they looked at the wound curiously. Yet he offered no explanations.

He started the engine and headed across Cedar Creek to the Laundromat that sat between the tiny town and the larger Pontotoc. Not that Pontotoc was big by any stretch, but Cedar Creek consisted of a post office, a water tower, and a handful of houses.

Nate put his truck into park and turned off the engine. This could end up being another dead end. Everyone he had talked to had sworn that Keylan was gone for good. He wasn't sure what the

185

boy's sister might be able to tell him, other than the actual truth of where Keylan was, but leave no stone unturned.

He didn't even pretend to be doing laundry. He simply sauntered in and looked around, hoping to spot the young Black woman.

There were only a couple of customers in the Laundromat. A heavyset lady in a housedress and pink curlers was loading a washing machine on one side while a tiny woman on the other side watched her dryer spin and tumble with such intensity that Nate wondered what drugs she had been taking. Not his problem. He was here for Aisha.

Since she wasn't out with the patrons, Nate glanced around again, this time noting that there was a flimsy-looking wooden door on the far side of the dryers. No doubt the office. If she was at work today, that was where she would be.

He nodded to the woman in curlers, excused himself as he walked between the staring woman and the dryers, then knocked quickly on the door. "Aisha Reid?" he asked as he tested the knob. It was open. So he turned the handle and looked inside.

A homemade table stretched the entire length of the back wall, such as it was. The room itself was barely five foot square. A small microwave sat on the table along with a water bottle, the refillable kind, and an open textbook. A notebook and pen rested nearby. A couple of folding chairs leaned against one wall, with a third in place at the makeshift table.

"You can't be in there," a confident female voice snapped behind him.

He turned around to face a sturdy-looking Black woman wearing cornrow braids with stacks of beads that clacked together when she moved. "Aisha Reid?"

She frowned at him. "Who wants to know?"

# The Secrets We Keep

For a moment, he thought about telling her he was with the police, but instead he took his chances with a different explanation. "Nathan Fisher. I'm a friend of Albie Gingerich's sister. Her name is—"

"Rachel," Aisha finished for him. "Yeah. I know her."

"Did you also know that she doesn't believe that Albie killed himself?"

She shook her head, the beads clicking together. "I don't know anyone who believes that tale."

Nate was beginning to think the police were the only ones who had bought that theory. Out of convenience or something more sinister?

"I've heard that your brother may have some information about the night Albie died."

"He might. He might not." Aisha shrugged.

"I'm trying to get in touch with him to see, but it seems that he's left town."

She frowned at him, as if trying to understand the enigma that was before her. "He's not hiding or anything. Like the rest of the free world, he has a phone."

"And you're going to give me his number?" It was almost a question.

A full three seconds she studied him. Nate could tell she was weighing the benefits and consequences. Trying to figure out who he was and if he could be trusted. Her gaze started at the gash at his hairline, ran down his faded blue Wranglers, and landed on his boots. Finally she said, "How about this . . . you leave me your number and what you want. I'll call him in a bit and give him that information. He can decide."

He nodded toward the notebook. "Can I get a piece of paper?"

She moved past him and into the room, tearing a blank sheet out of the notebook and handing it to him along with a pen.

**187**

Nate nodded his thanks, then turned to the nearest washing machine. It was empty, the lid up proving its availability. He closed it, then used it as a desk to write a short note about his involvement with Albie. He added his phone number at the bottom. He handed the paper back to Aisha. "Day or night. Call me anytime."

She nodded but didn't look at the words he had written. She only came out of the little room to reopen the washer and give him a pointed look. She didn't trust him. Hell, as far as he could tell, she didn't *like* him at all.

"One more thing," Nate said. "You know anyone named Jay Anderson?"

She shook her head, her braids swinging with the motion.

"Ever hear Keylan mention his name?"

"Not that I recall." She might not like Nate, but he could see she was telling the truth,

"You're in school?" he asked, nodding toward the small study station she had set up in the tiny office.

"I don't want to work at a Laundromat for the rest of my life."

He gave a small nod of understanding. "I appreciate you talking to your brother for me." For some reason he was reluctant to walk away with her still eyeing him like a mouse watched a hawk.

"Yeah, no problem."

"I'm sure you've heard the rumors running around town."

Her gaze turned sharp. "Some of them are mean spirited."

"In a small town they usually are."

She nodded.

"I'm just trying to get to the truth. Why Albie died and if anyone killed him."

*I've never seen a skull fracture commit suicide.*

"What are you, a cop or something?" This time she did look at the paper, her dark eyes quickly scanning his message.

# The Secrets We Keep

"Or something," was all Nate said before dipping his head to her and starting for the door.

He swung himself up into his truck and cranked the engine. The air blew too warm for a moment before the cool started. He just sat there, thinking. Rachel didn't want him there. She had come right out and told him. He had overstayed his welcome. But he would like to talk to Keylan. He could do that from anywhere. Then what?

What difference did it all make?

The crux of it all lay with the coroner. If she could pinpoint the exact cause of death. It was a long shot. After days buried, with no embalming . . . she might not be able to tell them anything other than the fact that he was dead. Only time would tell. And time was something he had a lot of. But he didn't necessarily want to spend it in a cheap motel in a small town in Mississippi. A small town haunted with memories of the past.

He needed to get out while the getting was good.

Nate put the truck into gear and backed out of the Laundromat parking lot.

He would head back to the hotel, finish what he started, and leave in the morning. Another day wasted in Cedar Creek. As he drove his truck through town, he passed the Boondock Grill, briefly noting that an unmarked sheriff's car was parked to one side. He knew that car.

Before he could think better of it, he whipped into a nearby parking space, parked, and got out.

Nate stepped inside, pulling off his sunglasses and running one of the arms through the neck of his T-shirt. He blinked a couple of times to allow his eyes to adjust to the dim light.

As usual, the Grill was filled almost to capacity. When you only had a handful of tables, that happened more often than not, but most folks grabbed their food and left. It was a booming place.

Today Chance Longacre and his cronies weren't around, but Nate did a quick sweep of the tables, and there was the man he had come to see.

Shane Johnson sat at a table alone. Perfect. Shane's concentration was centered on his phone as he scrolled the screen, obviously reading. He hadn't spotted Nate yet. Even more perfect.

But the waitress had, and she motioned for him to sit. It was the same girl he had talked to just a couple of days before. He pointed to the table where Shane dined alone. She nodded and pantomimed drinking. He nodded once more and wound his way through the tiny eatery.

"Fancy meeting you here," he quipped as he pulled out the chair opposite his onetime friend and sat down with a decisive motion.

Shane looked up, obviously startled but covering it well as he flipped his phone over, hiding the screen from view. The action was not lost on Nate. Had he been looking at something to do with the case or merely trawling through Instagram posts from friends?

"I hope the other guy took the worst of it." He shot a pointed glance at Nate's head. "I almost didn't recognize you without your hat."

Nate raised gentle fingers and lightly brushed the laceration on his head. "Yeah. About that."

Shane sat back, obviously interested. "About what?"

"Someone broke into my motel room two nights ago."

"That's something else. How come I didn't see a report about it?"

"You look at every report that comes into the office?"

Shane shrugged. "It's a small town."

And if he hadn't known for sure that Nate hadn't reported it, he did now. "Nah," Nate said, pretending to brush it off. "It's probably just kids being kids." He waited for Shane's reaction. He wasn't disappointed.

## The Secrets We Keep

"Small towns have a very delicate ecosystem," Shane started. "It doesn't take much to disrupt them."

"And that's what this is about, not disrupting the ecosystem?" He resisted the urge to put the last word in air quotes.

"Chance and his buddies claim they had nothing to do with the boy's death. There's no concrete evidence that says otherwise. As far as I can see, this case is closed."

"About that—" Nate sat back as the waitress brought over a glass of tea.

"Unsweet tea." She slid the drink in front of him. "I hope the other guy looks worse," she said with a nod at his forehead.

"I wish I could say that," Nate replied, directing his answer at Shane and not the little blonde. "But I was ambushed."

She whistled under her breath. "Sorry to hear that. You eating today?"

"Not today." If he kept on with the green tomatoes, he would be completely hooked and unable to leave Mississippi for a long, long time.

"Let me know if you change your mind." She nodded at them both, then turned and made her way over to the kitchen.

"You think I had something to do with this?" Shane eyed him warily.

"I think it's a possibility. I had the journal, and then I got clobbered. Now I don't have it anymore. So, who would want the journal bad enough to attack me for it?" He pushed aside the thought that the man who had jumped him from behind was Amish. It could have been anyone wearing an Amish hat, trying to make it look like a Plain person was responsible. Or perhaps it had all been a trick of the lighting. It had all happened so fast.

"You don't have the journal?"

191

Nate watched Shane closely, looking for signs of deceit. It seemed his revelation had surprised the other man. Shane looked genuinely shocked. He might be acting, but Nate had a feeling he wasn't. He truly hadn't expected that to be the case, and he had a feeling the man across from the table from him knew more than he was letting on.

"You mean you took it from me, and someone took it from you?"

"That's exactly what I mean."

He waited for Shane to say more, but the detective just closed his eyes and shook his head. "Great."

"You say you know nothing about it, but if you are trying to get Chance Longacre off by stealing the journal . . ." He let his words trail off.

"You ever know me to cheat at baseball?" Shane asked suddenly.

Nate shook his head. That was one thing he did know about Shane Johnson.

*Baseball is life,* they used to say. Everything and more.

"Baseball is life," Shane said, as if he had plucked the thought right from Nate's head. "I wouldn't cheat at baseball, and I wouldn't cheat at life."

Nate had no choice but to believe him. He felt the same. And he felt that old connection with Shane burgeon once more. So who?

"Maybe Chance did it thinking that the journal might implicate him."

"That would only be a motive if he were guilty," Shane said.

"Maybe. Maybe not. He's got a reputation that could be damaging even if he is innocent. Which, as far as I'm concerned, is still up for debate."

# The Secrets We Keep

"It wasn't him," Shane said soundly, and that connection slipped a bit. Had Nate's onetime, long-ago friend fallen prey to the politics of the small town?

"Even after everything that was recorded in the journal?" At least the parts they had gotten to study. Nate wasn't convinced there wasn't more in the journal that could have shed better light on the case. And then those missing pages . . .

Shane looked from side to side, then leaned toward him, doing his best to keep their conversation private in such a public place. "Listen." His voice turned solemn and quiet. "Chance might be a shit head, but he's not stupid. He's got his future mapped out for him. Harassing an Amish kid for being different or gay or whatever is one thing. Killing him is another. He doesn't have the stomach for it."

One thing Nate knew for certain: Killing changed a man. Even if everyone around him said it was justified. A good job. How could death be considered good?

"You want to file a report?" Shane leaned back and inclined his head toward Nate, his gaze fixed on the nasty-looking cut.

"No." He just wanted to find the journal. And as much as he thought he might be onto something talking to Shane, it seemed a dead end.

Nate stood and tossed a fiver down for the waitress. He thought once about asking Shane if he knew who Jay Anderson was, then decided not to tip his hand for the time being. Shane had looked through the journal. He might be looking for him as well. It was too early to be giving too much away. He waited a heartbeat more, then he rapped his knuckles against the chipped laminate tabletop and turned toward the door.

The heat hit him like a brick wall, the humidity already oppressive. He looked up at the sky as the rain clouds started to gather.

Tomorrow. He'd head home tomorrow. He'd text Bree and let her know, though with so many false alarms in that arena he wasn't sure she'd believe him until he pulled into the parking lot and asked for his cat food back.

He swung himself into the cab of the Chevy and cranked the engine, turning the air up a notch, as the heat had followed him in. He tossed his cell phone onto the seat next to him as a chime rang out.

*I hear u want to talk to me*

*Keylan Reid?* Nate texted in return. His heart kicking up a notch.

*Thats me*

\* \* \*

Rachel bit back a sigh as she pulled into the drive later that afternoon. Her normally chatty children were almost asleep, having run out all their energy playing at the picnic. Kate felt she was too old for a nap, but at this point, Rachel felt they could all use one. It had been a long and trying day. She still believed something was bothering Martha, though she hadn't been able to get her cousin to admit anything was wrong.

Maybe it was her. Maybe she, Rachel, was the problem. She had been out of sorts since she had found out that Nathan was back in town. But everything would return to normal when he left. Well, as normal as it could be with her husband missing, her brother-in-law living in her house, and her brother dead and being chopped to pieces at that very moment.

The thought was chilling. As was the sight before her. Another buggy was already parked in the drive. She knew the carriage with the scratch down one side. It belonged to the bishop. He claimed that the scrape had come from an *Englisch* kid being destructive, harassing the Amish as some were prone to do. Rachel had no cause

# The Secrets We Keep

not to believe the bishop, but for some reason she didn't. It could have been from the misleading light that shone in his eyes when he told the story. He didn't seem to care much for outsiders. True, their community was very closed and close knit. They didn't fraternize overly with the *Englisch* surrounding them. The Amish kept to themselves. They sold the outsiders jellies and potholders, smiled and thanked them, but they kept their private business private.

She chanced a small glance at him as he waited on the porch as if he knew no one was home but that she would be returning soon. His expression was pleasantly neutral but one that she had seen before. She would like to think that it was comforting, but she had seen him turn from calm and collected to almost out of control in the span of two heartbeats. It wasn't something that she had seen more than once, but to know that it existed at all was alarming. He was their undisputed leader, chosen by God, their bishop, and he would remain so until the day he died. Which, considering the fact that he was barely past middle age, would be a long, long time. Just one other concerning thing about Jacob Yoder.

Why was he there? What in the world could he want?

The question left her with a queasy feeling in the pit of her stomach. Surely they hadn't found Freeman . . .

Her hands began to shake.

No. She couldn't get her hopes up for that. She couldn't let herself believe that Kate's prayers had been answered, because if wasn't the truth, the letdown might be more than she could handle today.

She pulled in another deep breath and did her best to control her roller-coaster emotions. She would need her head about her if her next conversation involved Jacob Yoder. And it seemed it would.

She gave him a small wave, then climbed down from the buggy. She helped Amelie and Kate down and pointed them toward the house. "Go on inside," she said with a small nudge.

"Why's the bishop here?" Kate asked. She was rubbing her eyes and doing her best to stay awake. Rachel had the feeling she had fallen asleep before they had stopped. Poor baby.

"I'm not sure, but I do know that he's here to see the adults."

"Miri?" Kate asked.

Rachel shook her head. Sometimes her child was simply too inquisitive. "No, not Miri, I don't think. Just me or Dawdi." *Please let it be Dawdi. Please let it be Dawdi.* But there was something in Jacob's eyes that said otherwise.

She understood then it must have something to do with Nathan being back and her going over there.

She had been so careful not to park her buggy near the motel where he was staying. She had walked blocks in order to hide her true destination. Yesterday when Leroy knocked on Nathan's door, she had hid in the shower. That was a close enough call to warn her off any more repeat visits. But it seemed she hadn't been careful enough.

"Rachel." Jacob nodded at her, all business as she steered her girls into the house and went back to fetch her sister.

She nodded in return but didn't say anything else. Her throat was clogged with fear, apprehension, and a little bit of hope.

The man patiently hovered as she pushed her sister into the house, the girls just barely inside the door.

"May I come in?" Jacob asked.

She wanted to tell him no, but she knew it was time to go ahead and get it over with. Whatever had brought him out here today would keep, but it would only fester. This way was better. "Of course," she said, forcing a smile. "Let me get everyone settled, and then I can make us some coffee."

He nodded once and headed for the kitchen table. He had been to their house enough times he knew his way around. She

# The Secrets We Keep

could hear the chair scrape against the laminate floor as he found himself a seat.

Rachel's hands shook as she nudged her daughters toward the stairs. "Go into your room and stay there, please." Her tone brooked no argument, and thankfully the girls were too tired from the day they had had to protest. Once they disappeared up the landing, Rachel turned her attention to her sister.

"Okay, my girl," she said to her clapping sibling. "It's time to face the music." She pushed her sister's wheelchair into her room and stopped it in front of the poster on the wall. It was one of the few decorations Miri had, but more than merely decor, it served to calm her sister. Miri loved the poster and could stare at it for hours. When she was already exhausted from a busy day, it was the perfect way to settle her down for the evening. It would also serve as the means for Rachel to be able to talk to the bishop without too many interruptions. She hoped, anyway.

She set the brake on Miri's chair. "I'll be back in before supper," she told her.

Straightening, she met the eyes of the kitten in the poster. Larger than life, the cat had one set of claws dug into a small tree branch. The attached paw was cupped around the little branch, while the other three legs appeared to be useless, sticking out at odd angles. The kitty's eyes were wide, its mouth dangling open. The caption to one side said *Hang in there, baby*.

*Hang in there, baby* was right. Good advice if she could manage to take it.

She shook her head at herself, then pulled on the sides of her apron and made her way back into the kitchen where the bishop waited. She should go out and see to the gelding, but he could hold on for a bit. She needed to get this over and done with as soon as possible.

197

"Now," she said brightly as she walked in, as if this—talking to the bishop unexpectedly about unknown matters that most probably had something to do with Nate Fisher's return to Cedar Creek—was at the top of the Things She Wanted to Be Doing list instead of at the bottom. If it was even on the list at all. But there was no avoiding it. "How about that coffee?"

"Sit down, Rachel."

The time for niceties was over.

Rachel perched on the edge of the chair closest to her and gave him her full attention. She didn't know what she wanted him to say. Freeman? Nathan? Something else? *Dear Lord, please don't let it have anything to do with Miri and Adult Protective Services.*

She pushed that last thought away. They wouldn't go to the bishop first. They would be beating on her door themselves. Which left Nathan or Freeman.

"There's been some talk around these last couple of days."

She nodded dumbly. There was always talk, and she was just ready for him to get to the point. Her nerves were frayed and frazzled.

"He made his choices, Rachel. I thought that you had made yours."

"I have," she whispered, somewhat relieved that they were talking about Nathan. This way she could go on pretending there was a measure of hope of her husband returning to their community. Of him being alive.

"Then let him go."

She wanted to protest that she hadn't broken any of the written rules about his *Meidung*. She hadn't eaten with Nathan or done any business with him. They hadn't shared a table or ridden in a car or even a buggy together. But she knew better than to protest against the bishop's rules. He was stricter than most when someone left their community. She secretly believed he didn't like it when

# The Secrets We Keep

someone stayed with their Amish faith but left Mississippi for another district in another state.

"He's helping me find out who really killed Albie," she confessed instead. But once the words were out of her mouth, she wished she could call them back.

Jacob sat back a little straighter in his seat, making his large middle stick out ever farther. His normally flushed cheeks turned even redder, and his eyes flashed with a fire that she couldn't identify.

She shouldn't have said anything. She shouldn't have said anything, but now it was too late.

"You need to let that go too."

She didn't know how to respond to that without lying, so she said nothing at all.

"I know you have been meddling in police affairs. You have them digging around trying to prove that Albie died by other than his own hand. I would love nothing more than for there to be different explanation, but there's nothing. All you are doing is bringing heartbreak onto yourself. It's time to stop."

Tears were running down Rachel's face. She hated when she cried, and she couldn't stop them. Why couldn't she be stronger? Why couldn't she hide her emotions better?

She wanted to jump to her feet and tell the man he was wrong. He was wrong for thinking ill of her brother, he was wrong for coming there and accusing her even without actually accusing her. And he was wrong for not trusting Nathan. Nathan would get to the bottom of it, he would. But she could tell the bishop none of these things, and he knew it. So her tears of frustration continued to fall. Helpless. To be Amish and a woman, there were times when she felt so powerless. Like now.

Jacob stood, the action taking her by surprise, and he was halfway to the door when she realized he must have read her tears of frustration as tears of acceptance. He was just arrogant enough to not make her say the words back to him. He had told her, and now it was on her to follow through. But how could he truly expect that of her?

Which made her wonder all the more if the bishop knew things about that night that neither he nor her father had told her.

\* \* \*

Nate was all thumbs when it came to texting, but he knew it was the preferred form of communication in this electronic age. And yet . . .

*Call me at this number. want to talk about Albie G*

Nate hated the thought of alienating the boy right off the bat, but he would rather have a conversation with words, not just letters.

He breathed a sigh of relief when his phone rang through the truck speakers.

"Fisher," he said into the line.

"Keylan Reid."

"Mr. Reid," Nate started. "I'm very glad you called. I don't know what all your sister told you."

"Enough," he said. "Enough that I figured I should call."

"Can you tell me about the night Albie died?"

The line grew quiet, then a heavy sigh sounded. "I didn't know he was dead until a few days later. Aisha told me."

"You and he were going to leave Cedar Creek?"

"I had been saving up money for a car. We said that as soon as we could, we were going to drive that car as far away from there as we could. Till we ran out of gas or road."

Nate could understand that sentiment. He wondered how far Keylan had gotten.

"I'm just trying to put together all the events of the night. Can you tell me, start to finish?" Nate leaned over and started digging

## The Secrets We Keep

through the glove box for a notebook. He always had pen and paper around, just not forever handy. He found a small notebook under a smashed box of tissues that he was certain Bree had left. There was a pen in the center console. Thankfully, Keylan took a moment to gather his thoughts, and Nate was ready when he began to speak.

"We started off at the Grill."

Seemed logical enough. And he had already verified that through Casey the waitress. She had told him during his first visit to the Grill that Keylan and Albie seemed to be planning something that night.

"We were just eating, minding our own business, when Chance and his buddies came in. Chance Longacre," he explained.

"I've heard of him."

"They just couldn't resist the opportunity to start something with us, you know?"

"What about Jay Anderson? You see him around anywhere?"

"I don't know any Jay Anderson." His answer was sure and succinct, even if his tone was a little perplexed. Nate had no cause not to believe him. Jay Anderson was still a dead end.

"Okay, let's back up a second. What were you and Albie talking about in the Grill that night?"

There was another long pause. Long enough that Nate thought perhaps the call had dropped. Then Keylan finally spoke. "I wanted to leave. Then. That night. I'd saved enough and managed to get a car. I was ready to go."

"That night," Nate clarified.

"Just as soon as we finished eating."

That was something new. And something that might have been recorded on those final missing pages of Albie's journal. Wherever they were.

201

## Amy Lillard

"But?" Nate prompted.

"Albie was a little pressured, I guess. He wanted a day or two more. He wanted to talk to his family."

"About leaving?"

"I think he just wanted to spend a little more time with them. It was different for him, you know. I can come back. I can call. I can talk to my sister anytime I want. But with the Amish . . ."

"I'm aware," Nate said shortly.

"He was going to miss them."

"So what happened to change his mind about leaving?"

"A lot."

Nate waited patiently for him to continue. It was an investigative trick he'd learned long ago: Wait it out.

"I guess Chance and his buddies had been drinking a little. Maybe a lot. I don't know. But when we left, they followed us."

"What'd you do then?"

"I drove around for a while, trying to get them to quit, but finally I pulled over at the park. I already told all this to the other guy."

"Shane Johnson?"

"Yeah, something like that."

Good to know Shane was truly on the case. Hopefully he had asked all the right questions to get to the truth. "Why?" Nate asked. "Why did you pull over at the park?"

"We'd had enough. Sometimes you have to make a stand even if you know it's not going to go too good."

"Tell me about that."

"I was hoping that we could talk to them, you know, buddy up. But they just ended up beating the crap out of us. Albie took the worst of it. He just wouldn't stop fighting back."

"Yeah?" That was another something he hadn't known. He'd pictured Albie as a direct extension of how he had been when Nate

## The Secrets We Keep

knew him. A sweet child. Mild mannered, like most Amish, and cordial. Nate hadn't known about this fighting side. But Nate supposed some men developed it whether they intended to or not. Especially with people like Chance Longacre there to lead the way.

"I think something snapped in him. He wasn't going to back down no matter what."

That didn't compute with the suicide theory. A person who was willing to fight to the end wouldn't bring that end on himself. Of course, it also went against everything most considered true about the Amish. But Nate had grown up in the community. It wasn't as cut and dried as the outside world believed. Amish were Amish, but they were also human. When human beings were involved, anything could happen.

"Finally, Chance and them got tired, I guess, and left."

"Tell me what you remember about Albie's injuries," Nate nudged.

"Typical," Keylan cryptically replied. "Busted lip, black eye. Maybe even a cracked rib or two."

"Head injuries?"

"Other than the ones to his face?" Keylan asked.

"Right. Did they hit him with any sort of object other than their fists or feet?"

Keylan stopped, and Nate had to wonder if he was trying to remember or deciding on what he really wanted to tell Nate. "Why are you asking me all this again?"

"I'm a friend of Albie's sister. She doesn't believe that he killed himself. I'm looking into it for her."

The young man seemed to mull that over for a second. "They didn't hit him with anything like a bat or a stick or tire iron. But he was busted up. And done."

"What do you mean by that?"

"By the time they left the park, Albie had decided that we needed to leave that night. But he said he needed to go home and get his bag and his money. There was something he wanted to do with his dog."

"The heeler?" Nate asked.

"Yep, that's the one. He was breeding puppies to save up money. I figured he wanted to say goodbye to his sister and his dad."

"What did you do while he did this?"

"I cleaned myself up in the gas station bathroom, filled up the car, and waited for him down the road about two miles from his house."

Nate turned this information over, looking for holes. "You said Chance and his cronies left the park. Do you believe they followed you after that?"

"I don't know. I dropped Albie off at the end of the road to his house. His dad would always get upset when I came over, so we had a meeting place set up. That way Samuel wouldn't see who he was going with."

"He didn't want you around? Albie's dad."

"No."

"Because you're *Englisch*? Black? Gay?"

"I don't know. Maybe all of them."

"What about Albie?" Nate didn't have to finish the question for Keylan to understand.

"You know the answer to that."

"I just want your take on it."

"Then, yes. Albie was gay. It's not easy being gay in an Amish community like Cedar Creek."

# The Secrets We Keep

As far as Nate could tell, it wasn't easy being gay in their small town no matter what your religion.

"So you left Albie alone for a while." Long enough that Chance could have circled back if he had known where the two were going. It was a stretch but entirely possible.

"He didn't kill himself." The words were quietly, intensely spoken.

"I don't believe he did either. But from the time you dropped him off until the time his family found him, he sustained a possible fatal head injury as well as being hung."

It wasn't common knowledge, and Nate could hear Keylan's sharp intake of breath as he digested the news. "His head? How did he hit his head?"

"I was hoping you would tell me."

"I don't know, man. I waited where I said I was going to be for two hours, and he never showed."

"So you left."

"I couldn't swing by his house and knock on the door, now, could I?"

"Then the question remains: How did he get such a devastating injury?"

He could almost hear Keylan shake his head. "I have no idea. Maybe you should talk to the people in that house."

**205**

# Chapter Thirteen

The people in the house. Samuel. Rachel.

Samuel.

Twelve years was a long time. People changed. He only knew the Samuel Gingerich of twelve years ago. Even then Nate hadn't known him well.

Nate was fairly certain that Samuel had held a grudge against him since he had walked away and left his daughter heartbroken.

But he didn't know for certain. Maybe Samuel had mellowed in the years that had passed. Maybe he had hardened.

Maybe he didn't care about that at all.

But had Samuel known his son was gay? Had he known the boy was planning on leaving everything he knew behind?

His swirling thoughts kept bringing him round to the same result: Samuel Gingerich was an Amish man, raised in the church to turn the other cheek. Could it be that Chance Longacre and his buddies, having too much to drink and hyped up more than usual, had followed the boys and retargeted Albie that night? Perhaps Samuel knew more than he was saying. Perhaps he had turned the other cheek, and his boy had paid the price.

It wasn't a conclusion Nate could get behind one hundred percent, but it nagged at him like a broken tooth.

# The Secrets We Keep

And there wasn't one thing he was going to do about it. Shane was a good detective. He had tracked down Keylan. He would figure it out. Nate needed to let it go and get out of town. Let them figure out their problems themselves. He had enough of his own to worry about.

Tomorrow. It had become his mantra, but now it had all come to an end. Tomorrow he was heading back to Tulsa. When he crossed the Mississippi River, he would text Bree and let her know he was on his way. But until then . . .

He had an apology to make.

Nate turned his truck around and headed back out of town. He shouldn't take the chance that her father wouldn't be home. That she would be home. That she would even talk to him. But he couldn't leave it like this. Not again. He wanted to clear the air. Once and for all. He would be leaving, and he had no reason for coming back. Ever. When the time came that his mother passed, he wouldn't be welcome. He knew that. He had lived through that cold welcome twice now—first with Mattie and now his father. He couldn't go through it again. It wasn't worth it. It just heaped insult on injury and did nothing for the grieving process.

Not that he was grieving for his father much.

Then why had he come back?

His father had cut him off without a word. Nate had left, and as far as Karl Fisher had been concerned, his young son was dead.

So why had Nate come back?

Two reasons, he supposed. Two reasons other than that he had too much time on his hands after "the incident." And those two reasons? Rachel and his mother.

He had held the hope that maybe he could somehow mend fences with his *mamm*.

But it seemed that his brother had picked up the mantle of hate that his father had carved and was determined to carry it

**207**

through. There would be no reconciliation with his mother if Leroy had anything to say about it. And yet Leroy had been the one to call Nate to let him know about their *dat*.

And Rachel. There would be no reunion for the two of them. No rekindling there. She was married. She was Amish. Too much stood in her way. But he had gotten to see her again. And for that he was grateful. Now he would apologize and be on his way. He'd leave them to their lives, let the dust settle so they could return to normal. He was going back to pick up the pieces of what remained of his life and start over once more. He was getting good at new beginnings, even when what he truly wanted was something he had left behind so long ago.

He pulled his truck into the narrow, packed dirt drive and came to a stop close to the house.

Everything looked the same. As if twelve years hadn't passed. As if Mattie weren't dead, his father were still alive, and Rachel were getting ready to go on a picnic with him.

And a young man in Tulsa hadn't lost his life at Nate's hands.

He shoved the gearshift into park and cut the engine. He had barely gotten out of the truck and started for the house when she came out onto the porch. She looked just as tired and angry as she had the last time he saw her. Maybe even more so.

"You can't come here." The words were hissed at him urgently as she looked around. "If Dat gets home. Or Daniel comes by . . ." She shook her head.

"I'm not here to stay. I . . ." He couldn't finish. Suddenly his words were gone, and his eyes stung. He cleared his throat and tried again. "I'm leaving in the morning."

She leaned back and crossed her arms, waiting for him to continue. At least he had that.

"I can't leave things like they were the other night." Him shoving her in the shower and pulling her out only when his brother had

# The Secrets We Keep

left. "I came to say that I'm sorry for treating you that way. But it was for you. Not for me. If my brother had seen you—"

She seemed to wilt before his eyes. All the starch went out of her posture and her expression softened. "I know that. That wasn't why I was angry."

He waited for her to continue.

"Leroy coming by . . . having to hide, showed me that what we were doing was wrong. Then the bishop . . . you're shunned, and—" She shook her head. "I can't keep going on like this, Nathan."

He wasn't sure what all she meant. Just the sneaking around? More? Or was he just reading more into it because he wanted there to be more? More, more, more. He pushed the thought away. There was no use going down that road.

He swallowed hard. "I'm leaving tomorrow. I just wanted you to know."

"What about the coroner's report?"

"Shane will take care of it. He's a good cop." He might be in Walker's back pocket, but he couldn't argue with an official report from the medical examiner's office.

"I don't know him. What if he gets the report and tries to bury it?"

*Tries to bury it?* "Have you been on the internet again?" He tried to make light of the words, but they just sounded tired.

"I have to have something to do at the library while Miri is at story time."

Nate grunted. "I don't think Shane will bury it."

"Those boys will get away with it." Tears filled her beautiful green eyes.

"We don't know that for certain."

"I do."

This was all a bad idea. Too many big names in a small town were involved. "Whatever happens, it won't bring Albie back."

The moment hung suspended between them, the truth weighing heavy on them both.

She should never have started this. He should never have come here. They both should have left well enough alone.

"Your head . . ." Her quietly spoken words took him off guard.

"It's healing." He did his best to shrug it off. Just another scar to mark the time. And now it was time to leave. "Goodbye, Rachel." The words nearly stuck in his throat. He turned away. Time to go. Past time to go.

"I didn't think you would walk away from this."

He stopped, turned back around, even though he told himself not to. He wanted to protest, but doing so would just prolong the inevitable. "There's nothing to walk away from." He said the words though he knew they weren't the truth. There was nothing and *everything* to walk away from. Starting, but not ending, with the woman in front of him.

"I asked for your help."

"And I gave you what I could. The ball's rolling. I don't have any jurisdiction here. I'm just a cop from another state poking my nose where it doesn't belong." Something he should have remembered a long time ago.

He started to leave once more. He couldn't tell her goodbye again. He just couldn't say the word knowing he would never see her again.

"I have them."

Her quietly spoken revelation stopped him in his tracks. Despite everything telling him once more to leave it alone, he turned back to face her. "You have what?"

"The journal pages. I have them."

"Why are you telling me this now, Rach?" Was she determined to forever keep him on a string?

"Jay Anderson. There's more about him in them."

# The Secrets We Keep

There was that part of him that just wanted to walk away . . . *needed* to get the hell out of here. And then there was the other part . . .

"Meet me at the park tomorrow. At lunchtime."

"I can't do that. I'm going home in the morning."

"Nathan, please."

"Give them to Shane Johnson. He's the detective working the case. He'll know what to do with the information."

"I don't want to give them to Shane. I want to give them to you."

"Why now?" Because he was leaving? Because she couldn't stand to see him go? Because she was bound and determined to blow their tiny town apart?

She didn't answer. Just crossed her arms and looked to one side as if she couldn't stand to see him any longer.

"Rach . . ."

"Please, Nathan," she beseeched. "Please."

"Lunchtime?" He was a fool. No two ways about it.

"*Danki,*" she whispered.

He didn't reply, just walked stiff legged back to his truck and swung himself into the cab. He was more than a fool. But it seemed there was no stopping now.

"You can't tell my *dat,*" she said the following afternoon as she pulled the ratty pages from her bag. It appeared she had read them many times since she ripped them out of the journal.

Nate took them from her and rubbed his eyes, which were filled with grit after a near-sleepless night. He had fallen into a fitful sleep sometime after one, only to wake up near dawn in a cold sweat. He'd been dreaming about the kid again. Damon Gary. In his dream, he chased him down the same alleyway, turning corners with his gun drawn, though in reality it hadn't been like that at all. But the dream was as vivid as the day had been, Nate running behind him and the boy doing everything possible to get away. Then Nate rounded a corner and there he stood, hand raised, with a bright-red water gun pointed at Nate. In the way of dreams, a bright-green dot of light lit on Nate's chest. A laser sight. The boy was going to shoot Nate. Nate's gun was no longer in his hand, and he reached to draw it once more. The boy had the upper hand, and yet somehow Nate managed to pull his gun and fire. That was when he woke up. Sweating. Panting. Wishing forever he could take it all back.

He glanced at the papers and rubbed his chest. That spot in his dream where the laser sight had marked him. "Why now, Rachel?" His voice sounded tired.

"I didn't want everyone to know."

So they held proof that Albie was gay. Proof written in his own hand. "It's not really much of a secret."

"If Dat found out . . ." She couldn't finish.

"Albie's gone," Nate started. "It's not time to drag all this out." But the advice was futile. He had grown up in the community. He knew what the culture was like. They might not allow Albie to be reburied in the cemetery even if the coroner determined that he had not committed suicide. This abomination was equally serious. Only a confession in front of the church could wipe it clean, and it was too late for that now.

"Just read them, please."

There had only been a couple of times in their lives that he denied her. Now was not one of them. He started to read.

*Dear Rachel,*

*I told Keylan to pick me up at the end of the road tonight. We're leaving. I'll miss you something terrible, but I know if I stay they'll find out. And if they find out, they'll send me away.*

*I've tried. It's not like I haven't tried. And I've prayed, but nothing has changed. I don't want to feel this way, but I can't seem to stop. Keylan tells me that if we leave, go west and just keep driving, there are towns, big cities that don't care if we go against the grain. I can't imagine that being true. I'm scared. Not to leave, but that it won't be true. That we'll be just as persecuted there as we are here. And we'll be without our families to help us. But I suppose, no I know, it's a chance I have to take. After tonight, especially. Chance Longacre is at it again. I can't take much more.*

*I need you to do something for me. I sold a puppy to a man named Jay Anderson. He'll be by once they're born. I told him he could have the pick of the litter. I need the money to start over. The rest of the puppies you can sell or whatever. Maybe the money will help ease the betrayal of my leaving.*

*I'm also leaving this journal for you. I hope it helps you understand. I know we'll probably never see each other again. But I'll try to write you from time to time. Maybe Dat won't notice.*

*Tell Amelie and Kate that I love them and I always will. Same to you and even Dat though I know he'll never speak my name again.*

*Always,*
*Albie*

Nate scrubbed at his eyes once more. He'd had his share of gay friends since he left. He'd heard about their troubles growing up and how they had struggled to be accepted. And he knew that society as a whole was now more supportive than it had been in the past. The same could not be said of Cedar Creek. Not once in all

# Amy Lillard

that time had he thought about anyone he knew back in his small Amish community who might be struggling with such an identity, magnified by an unyielding set of rules that had no room for change.

"There's more." Rachel handed him another small stack of papers.

He took them without saying a word. What more could be said? Instead of reading them, he glanced out to the swings where Amelie and Kate were playing, blissfully unaware of the heartache so close to them.

Rachel's daughters. He didn't know them at all. Hadn't spent any time with the older one. But she seemed as solemn as Kate was outgoing. They were the future. A future he would never share with Rachel.

"Are you going to read them?" Rachel's voice shook. She was afraid. Afraid he was upset with her. But he couldn't be, not after everything he had put her through.

"You know these pages won't change anything."

"I'm just trying to understand."

He shook his head. "From this side, there's no understanding. Just acceptance. You don't live—Albie didn't live—where acceptance is an option."

"But we could have sent him to counseling—"

"It's not that simple," he said. That was the first thing he had learned in the *Englisch* world—everything was complicated. The outside world was full of layers and shades of gray. The Amish world where he had lived was painted solid black and white. Sin and not sin. Accepted and not accepted. The biggest problem was, not all of it had anything to do with what was really in the Bible.

"But it could be," she protested. "If he hadn't started to run away—"

# The Secrets We Keep

Nate shook his head again. "He couldn't stay here," he said simply. "Not if he wanted to live the life he wanted to live. He felt compelled to live."

"I don't understand."

He wasn't sure he could explain it in any words she could comprehend, but her eyes begged him to help. What was a man to do?

"In the *Englisch* world, people believe that a person is born . . . that way. It's not a choice they make. That God created them with this . . ." He couldn't finish. Didn't know how.

She was already shaking her head before he stopped speaking. "God doesn't do things like that."

Honestly, sometimes he was shocked at the things God was and wasn't capable of doing. But he knew he had seen the worst of it all. Death, murder, betrayal, abuse of every type imaginable. Tulsa wasn't a huge metropolis, but it was big enough to support its fair share of crime. "I'm just telling you so you'll know. If Albie had gotten out, he wouldn't have had to change in order to fit in. He would have been accepted. By most people, anyway."

"That would have been the same if he had gone to the counseling."

"Have you ever known anyone to go someplace like that and come back truly changed?"

"There was this one guy in Adamsville. He went away for some time. Then he came back and got married."

"And he's living happily?" Nate asked.

"He killed himself last year. Everyone said it was a hunting accident, but it just didn't make sense. How he was shot with his own rifle."

It was easier for the church to believe the lie than accept the truth: Their counseling was ineffective at best, destructive at worst.

Nate turned back to the pages he still held.

*I'm tired. So tired of pretending. So tired of being different. So tired of hiding everything I feel. I'm tired of lying to my family. If Dat were to ever find out . . .*

*I write this and then I feel selfish. It isn't about me. Or at least it shouldn't be. And yet it is. How can I go on like this? I'm so confused my head is spinning. Maybe those boys are right. Maybe I am not fit to walk the earth.*

"Jesus." Nate resisted the urge to crumple the papers and destroy the words.

*No. They don't get to decide. If that's truly the case, then they'll have to come get me. I can't be all bad. "Jesus loves me. This I know."*

*But does He love me even though I am like this? Or does He hate me for my sinful thoughts?*

*Keylan says there are places where people don't care that we're different. It sounds better than heaven, and I'm almost afraid that they don't exist. Or that I'll leave and never find one.*

Nate didn't want to read any more. So far there was nothing to implicate Chance and his buddies further. Jay Anderson was a customer, perhaps still a suspect, but it wasn't likely. Without some sort of tangible evidence, the DA would never file charges. No matter what the coroner's report stated. It was an uphill battle. Yet Nate supposed if they could prove that Albie had died from the head wound, then at least they would be able to get a leg up.

*I've never seen a fractured skull commit suicide.*

Nate had talked to Chance. He might be a punk and a bully, but Nate didn't get the impression that he was a killer. Unless you were

The Secrets We Keep

a killer, murder would eat at your gut until there was nothing left. Nate's was considered a justifiable homicide. Yet there was a hole in him that he was beginning to accept would never be filled again.

"Rachel, it's very likely that Chance and his group of friends had nothing to do with Albie's death." And if that was the case, it could be that an Amish kid who would never fit in where he was born had decided that leaving was too hard and had taken the only way out he could see.

Yet Nate couldn't say those words to her. He couldn't say them and watch those meadow-green eyes fill with tears over the loss of her beloved sibling.

"I need to know the truth," she stubbornly said.

"The truth is there's no evidence here," Nate said. "Without evidence, they won't arrest anyone. That's the law."

She bit her lip, then smiled, a forced upward curve of the corners of her mouth. She waved to the girls, who were wagging their hands at her and making silly faces.

Sometimes Nate wished he could go back to an age like theirs, when the worst fear he had was not getting dessert because he got into trouble at school. He hadn't appreciated that time enough while it was happening. If he could go back, he would take the time to enjoy life more. The little things. That was one thing he had learned straightaway. The little things soon became the big things a person wished they could hold on to.

"I understand." She said the words, but her voice was choked. She wanted better for her brother. He couldn't find fault with her in that.

They sat in silence for a moment, watching her girls play. Both of them had moved from the swing over to the slide. Apparently Amelie had stopped at the top of the largest slide in the park, keeping Kate from going down ahead of her. Nate could remember standing in that very same spot once upon a time. He and his siblings didn't get to play on slides very often, and it hadn't looked that tall when he'd started out. But by the time he got to the top, he had changed his mind, and a crowd of boys behind him jeered for him to just "go already." Peer pressure had him finally closing his eyes and making the long scary journey down the slide.

Everyone thought that since he was a cop, he had been born brave and fearless. He was neither. He was cautious to a fault. Which made the boy's death all the more perplexing. Nate wasn't the kind to pull his sidearm. He wasn't the kind to jump the gun, so to speak. He was careful and thoughtful. But when push had come to shove, he had shown his true colors.

Damon Gary had been holding a gun. A black water pistol—not a red one like in his dream—that from the distance between them, Nate hadn't been able to tell wasn't the real deal. He'd yelled for the boy to drop it. Instead he had raised it, and the rest was history.

Some guys in the office had called it suicide by cop. Nate wasn't sure what it was for Damon Gary other than death. And Nate was left to pick up the pieces of his psyche and try his best to put it all back together again. Humpty Dumpty on a personal level.

Finally Amelie made her way down the slide. She finished triumphantly and ran back around for another turn before her sister even reached the bottom.

"You're leaving tomorrow." It was a statement. Rachel didn't even look at him when she said it.

"I've got to go sometime." Even with all the heartache that had followed him here, he was reluctant and anxious about going home all in the same moment.

"Do you?"

*You don't have to go home, but you can't stay here.*

"Yes." But the word wasn't as confidently spoken as he would have liked.

# The Secrets We Keep

"I suppose you need to get back to work."

"Yeah." He nearly choked on the lie.

He should have never stayed. He shouldn't have agreed to help her. But as always, he was a fool where Rachel was concerned.

"Did you see me? Did you see me, Mamm?" Amelie came running up, cheeks pink and breath heaving through her wide smile. "I did it. Kate said I was scared, but I wasn't. I just wanted to make sure before I went."

"I know, *liebschdi*." Rachel smoothed one side of her daughter's prayer covering. The tears he'd thought he heard in her voice were gone, if they had ever been there at all.

Maybe it was all just wishful thinking. That one day the two of them could start again right where they'd left off. When he had gone to play baseball. Or four years later when he had returned for Mattie's funeral. Either would work as long as he could have her.

"I'm going to go do it again," Amelie gushed. "Watch me."

"I'm watching," Rachel assured her.

Amelie took off running back across the playground.

Nate stood. "I should be going." Sitting here watching her children play, waiting beside her—it was too much like family. But those weren't their children. They were *hers*. With someone else. Nate had left, and life had gone on without him. She'd gotten married. She'd chosen another.

"Okay."

His heart sank at the word. What had he expected? That she would beg him to stay? He had been threatening to leave since he'd set foot in Mississippi. Now the time was really here, why was it so hard to leave?

Because it wasn't just Cedar Creek, but Rachel's side. He'd spent one night with her again, and he felt like he was eighteen all over again.

Throat tight, legs stiff, he made his way across the parking lot to his truck.

"You know, you're a hard man to track down."

Nate shrugged at Shane. "I take it this isn't a social call." He didn't invite him into the room. Whatever needed to be said could be said right there on the walkway.

"Saw you at the park this afternoon," Shane started.

Nate only shrugged again. He still hadn't figured out if Shane was on the level with this case or a puppet for the sheriff—and in turn the senator.

"You were seated on a bench next to Rachel Hostetler. I didn't recognize what I was seeing right away, but then when I got back to the office, I realized that you were reading the journal pages."

Nate started to speak, but Shane held up his hand to stay the words.

"Don't deny it. Just hand them over."

"I'm not giving you anything." He couldn't even if he wanted to. He didn't have them.

"Nate, we go way back, but I've got a lot of pressure on me with this case. Hand them over, or I'll have to arrest you for obstruction of justice."

"I don't have them, and even if I did, you would never be able to make that stick. There was nothing in them you need to know."

"I need to be the judge of that." Shane turned and started for his truck.

"Shane," Nate called after the man.

The detective turned, hand on the door handle of his service vehicle.

"Leave it," Nate quietly commanded. "What's in there will only bring heartache if the community finds out. He was persecuted and hanged because he was Amish. That's enough of a hate crime. It doesn't have to be about anything more."

Shane stopped, seemed to think about it a moment. "That's all it said?"

Nate raised three fingers. "Scout's honor."

"I don't recall you ever being a Scout," Shane said with a small quirk of his head.

"No good will come of those pages being made public."

Shane pressed his lips together and eyed Nate with a calculated precision. "I better not regret this," he said before swinging himself up into his truck.

Funny . . . Nate was thinking the same thing.

That evening while Nate was lounging on his bed, trying to pretend he wasn't bored, anxious, and generally out of sorts, his phone dinged.

He picked it up from its place just within reach. He only had to move his hand in order to grab it and view the screen.

*Out of cat food*

Bree.

Satchel needed food. Good thing he was going home the next day.

He texted back: *Be home tomorrow. Pay you back.*

About the time he returned the phone to its original place and turned his attention back to the rerun of *Gunsmoke* he was watching, it rang.

For a moment he contemplated not answering. But his conscience got the better of him, and he thumbed it open.

"Hi," he said, hoping he sounded normal. Nothing felt normal these days. He walked around conspicuous and stiff, like he was too big for his skin. Like everyone was watching. Like everyone knew. What, he wasn't sure, but they knew.

"Hi yourself, stranger." Her voice was like a piece of him that had gotten lost and suddenly turned up again. "Just wanted to touch base," she continued.

"Yeah? Don't trust me to make good on the cat food?"

She chuckled, the sound like smooth whiskey and warm honey. "Not quite. It's just that—" Her tone changed. "You're not coming home, are you?"

Nate pushed himself up in the bed, banging the back of his head against the headboard in his surprise. "What? Of course I am. I said I'd be home tomorrow." Now why did he sound like he was defending himself to a jealous wife or girlfriend? Bree was neither. On-again, off-again lover, yes. But no more than that.

"Nate. We've known each other too long for you to start lying to me now."

He shook his head, even though she couldn't see him. "I'm not lying. Tomorrow I'm out of here."

"How many times have you said that to me since you've been gone?"

He didn't answer. It was rhetorical, right?

"I'm not trying to pin you down, just . . . well, I wonder if maybe you should rethink a few things."

"Like?"

"Like whatever it is that's holding you there," she said on a sigh. "But I wanted to let you know that I've got Satchel whenever you do come back for however long. He'll be here. And you don't have to pay me back for the cat food." This time there was the hint of a smile in her voice.

## The Secrets We Keep

"I'm coming back," he said again, though this time he wondered who he was trying to convince. "I'm in a motel. I can't stay here indefinitely." Plus he'd worn out his welcome with just about everyone in town.

"So find an Airbnb."

"I don't even know how to start doing that."

"On the app usually. That's where most people start. Here, 46B Peach Tree Lane. There's an apartment for rent. Fully furnished. Weekly rates. Oh, pet friendly."

"Bree."

"Nate. Look, we've always told each other the truth," she said. It was the hallmark of their nonrelationship. "So I'm telling you the truth now. Whatever is there that's pulling at you, work through that, then see how you feel about coming back here for good."

# Chapter Fourteen

～

Leave it to Bree to find the tiniest garage apartment for rent in the whole of Pontotoc County.

"My grandmother converted this apartment years ago," the owner said, waving a hand. Lorie Atwood was a middle-aged beauty queen come back home to stay only to find nothing was the same. He could feel her on that one. "She wanted to make some money, but she didn't want her car out in the weather, so she only used half the space. But it does have a full kitchen and a full bath, tub and shower. And we're right in town, so that's good. There's a carport where you can park your car, just make sure you stay all the way to the right. I park on the left." She smiled, and that beauty queen beam had retained its power. "Momaw's car is still in the garage."

She had told him how she had come back to Pontotoc to live after her divorce. She had moved in with her grandmother to help them both with expenses, and then her momaw had passed.

"No problem." He smiled back at her, feeling more like himself than he had since he had set foot in Mississippi. She wasn't a part of his past. She held no ghosts for him, no memories, no bad feelings, no hurt or betrayal.

"Okay." She handed him a set of keys. "Back door, front door, side gate if you need in the backyard for anything. I just ask that

## The Secrets We Keep

you be careful when you go back there. My dog may be out there, and she likes to escape. Unfortunately, she's good at it."

"Breed?"

"Two hundred percent mutt, all small variety. She's about eight pounds and very agile."

"Noted," he said with another smile in her direction. Maybe this wasn't such a bad idea. He needed a break. He had come here for a break, a diversion. But instead the cop work had followed him. Now truly it was only a matter of waiting on the coroner's report. In the meantime, he would debrief. Maybe try his mother one more time. He was nothing if not a glutton for punishment. And Rachel. Well, that ship had sailed. They both knew it.

But the one in front of him . . .

"Hey, listen," Lorie said, as if the thought had just occurred to her. Somehow he figured she'd been mulling it over since he got there. "I've not mastered cooking for one, and I always end up with more leftovers than I can eat. Would you like to come to supper tonight? I'm making spaghetti."

For the first time in a long while, Nate's spirit lightened just a bit. "I love spaghetti."

\* \* \*

"One more thing."

At the bishop's words, everyone stopped. Church was over, and it was time to go outside, set up the benches for the meal, and start serving. Rachel turned toward Jacob. It had been a particularly long sermon today. She hated that she thought so. There had been a time when she enjoyed church, loved everything from the singing to the foot washing that occurred twice a year. But lately she felt more and more restless. It all went back to Albie's death, then the return of Nathan Fisher to Cedar Creek.

"Rachel Hostetler."

She stiffened at the sound of her name.

"You have been seen out with Nathan Fisher, and you know that he is under the *Bann*."

She opened her mouth to protest, plead her case. She hadn't ridden in a car with him. She hadn't accepted money from him or sat at the same table and shared a meal. But she knew the bishop didn't want to hear her excuses. That was the reason he had started this conversation in front of the entire congregation instead of giving her a private moment to think about and begin to change her actions.

The bishop raised one hand. "Nathan made his choices, just as you have made yours. We would hope that by placing him under the *Bann* and restricting his activities, he would have eventually returned to the fold. To date, we know he has not, nor does he appear to have any intention of doing so. It's too dangerous for those of us who follow God's plan to fellowship with those who have strayed."

She gave a stiff nod. What else could she do? She needed to stay away from Nathan Fisher, and now everyone in the church knew so as well.

The women made their way out to start arranging the food while the men moved the church benches outside. The bishop caught her before she could follow behind.

"It's for your own good," he said.

There was something in the tilt of his head or his smug attitude, that he really knew what was best for her . . .

There had been a time when she believed with all her heart that the church and the elders had her best interests in mind. But that was before her heart was broken so many times she had lost count.

She nodded instead of speaking, not trusting her voice to say what should be said rather than what she defiantly wanted to say. Then without a word, she walked out the door of the house.

## The Secrets We Keep

Church was at the deacon's this week. Rachel liked Rudy Fisher. He was an uncle of Nathan's. Or maybe it was a cousin. Anyway, Rudy had the same temperament as Nathan, easygoing, caring, all around a good man. Nathan had just made poor choices as far as the church was concerned.

And yet he seemed to call to her heart every time he was near.

Normally the women were chatty as they worked, talking about happenings in their community and those surrounding their church district, but today they were all strangely quiet. Rachel knew that if she hadn't been there, she would have been the talk of the afternoon.

She went about her work without looking up, without engaging with any of them. To say something now would just lead to questions and judgments, and she wasn't up for that. She hadn't done anything wrong. Not really. And everything that she had done had been to help Albie or Nate. She wasn't about to defend it. No, that wasn't right. She would defend her choices. She had made fine choices. She just didn't want to *have* to defend them. For doing so would almost be an admission of guilt.

"Don't worry about them."

Rachel nearly jumped out of her skin as a quiet voice sounded next to her.

"*Danki*, Martha." She appreciated her cousin's support, but in case anyone was listening in . . . "I know better than to be persuaded to go against the *Ordnung*."

Martha nodded. She might be young, but she understood how things were expected to be in a church such as theirs. "*Jah*. Of course."

Everything Rachel had done had been out of love, caring, and kindness. She was trying to find out the truth about her brother's death, and that had caused Nate to be injured. She wouldn't have been able to live with herself if something worse had happened to him that night. Plus she had the heart-sinking suspicion that her father was the one responsible for the attack. He might not have done it himself, but she wouldn't put it past him to get Daniel to do something like that.

She'd had to let Nate read the pages that she had torn out. But she couldn't allow just anyone to read them. She had to do what she could to save as much as possible of her brother's reputation. She couldn't have him viewed differently just because he'd made a few bad choices without weighing all the consequences.

And all of it . . . She would do it all again in a heartbeat.

\* \* \*

Nate had to admit that the Airbnb idea was a good one. The apartment was not much bigger than the motel room, but somehow it seemed homier. Maybe it was the cozy touches that Lorie had placed around the small space. A tiny houseplant perched on a stool in front of the only window in the place. If Satchel were there, he would eat the unsuspecting greenery straight to the dirt. A tiny, cream-colored love seat sat in front of what used to be the garage door. A pillow covered with the old state flag rested in one corner of it, and another with the new state flag sat in the other. A too-large-for-the-room braided rug took up most of the space on the sealed concrete floor and reached almost into what would be considered the "kitchen": a line of appliances and a small stretch of counter space. The TV was mounted above a waist-high bookshelf filled with novels and DVDs. Pale-green walls, a few wooden accents, and an old ladder upcycled into a quilt rack completed the look. The bed and bath were more of the same. Home for now.

He'd had a good time last night getting to know his new landlady, though she made him swear he wouldn't call her that. She did

# The Secrets We Keep

make some mean spaghetti, and she was serious when she said she couldn't cook for one. There was enough food for an army, and she made Nate promise that he would come back Monday night for leftovers. She was easy to be with, beautiful, smart, and kind, but he had resisted her flirting. He had no idea how long he was going to be in town, and he wasn't quite the love 'em and leave 'em type. No matter how willing the participant.

For now, he needed to stop patting himself on the back for his resolve and figure out what he was going to do for lunch. He knew that if he knocked on Lorie's door, whatever she had, she would share, but he really needed to keep his distance. He grabbed his hat off the table by the door and started out of the tiny apartment.

Thankfully, his head had stopped throbbing. Even though it was still a little uncomfortable to wear his hat, he felt vulnerable without it. It was a part of him. At one time he would have said like his gun and his badge, but they didn't hold the same appeal for him these days.

He locked the door and headed up the street. They were only two blocks from the main thoroughfare in town. He could make his way to the Grill and be back in no time at all.

Then, after he ate, he planned to make a quick trip out to Rachel's house. He would leave her a note explaining that he was staying for a while. He couldn't say how long because he didn't know. Maybe he would wait until the coroner's results came back. Maybe not. That was something yet to be determined.

The only thing set in stone was the fact that he was a chicken-shit for waiting until Sunday—church Sunday—to contact her. But he needed some distance, as much as he could grab.

His footsteps slowed as he neared the darkened restaurant. They were closed on Sunday. He'd forgotten in his time away. The next best place was the burger joint at the end of the same building. They sold their fair share of cheeseburgers and fries, but their main staple was ice cream. Small batch, hand churned, all natural.

Unable to resist that temptation, he ordered a chocolate malt to go with his meal. He hated that it reminded him of Rachel. It was being back in town that was doing it, making everything about her once again. He'd had a chocolate malt a hundred times since he left and never thought about her even once. Okay, maybe not a hundred, but enough times that this one shouldn't matter, shouldn't make him think of anything other than how much extra gym time he would have to put in.

He paid the young girl behind the counter, grabbed the brown paper sack that contained his food, and started for the door.

Just as he got there, Chance Longacre sauntered in. He looked up, saw Nate, and held the door for him.

"Do you have a minute?" Chance asked.

Nate stopped, taken aback by the unexpected question. He gestured with his food. "Just heading back to eat."

Chance cleared his throat. "It won't take but a second."

Nate nodded and stepped out of the tiny bistro. "What's up?"

The young man shoved his hands into his pockets and shot Nate a sheepish grin. "I know you think I had something to do with that boy killing himself. But I swear I didn't. We didn't."

For the first time since Nate had run into the teen, he noticed that his cronies weren't right behind him. "You did beat him up, though."

Chance had the decency to turn red from embarrassment. "I'm not proud of it, but Dad sat me down and talked to me. I'm working on getting myself together. If I want Ole Miss and Ole Miss Law, I've got to make sure I stay out of trouble."

Nate could only hope it was the truth. Or was Chance telling him this to cover his tracks and keep himself out of further trouble?

# The Secrets We Keep

It sounded to Nate like if something bad were to come of this, his father might not get him out of it.

"I know I shouldn't have hazed him, but—" He shook his head. "No buts. I shouldn't have hazed him. Still, I would never have killed him. Someone else did that. And if you want me to swear to it, I'll place my hand on as many Bibles as you can stack up. Or a lie detector test. I'll take one of those. Because I promise you, I had nothing to do with it."

\* \* \*

Rachel could feel the anger coming off her father as they rode home that afternoon. A red heat seemed to hover around him. He hadn't said one word in the hour they had been traveling.

The girls played some clapping game in the back, with Miri clapping along in her offbeat way, laughing at everything and nothing at all. Their chanting song filled up the empty space but almost echoed back in the cavern that separated the family.

It had been the most uncomfortable after-church meal Rachel had ever endured. Even including the one after Freeman had disappeared along with Daniel's wife. Everyone suspected that they had run off together. But Rachel knew better. Her Freeman was nothing if not a good man. He had proved that to her many times over since their wedding. She had been jilted and shamed when Nathan chose to leave the church and their community behind. It was Freeman who had helped her pick up the pieces. How she wished he were here now. Then again, if he were, no one would be whispering about her and Nathan Fisher.

"I swear to you, girl," her father said, his teeth clenched as he talked through them, "if you weren't already married . . ." He shook his head. "It's shameful. That's what it is." He didn't yell.

He didn't scream or pitch any type of fit like he was prone to do. That in itself made his dressing down even worse.

"I meant no harm. It was all for Albie." She bit back the tears that stung her eyes. What was that *Englisch* saying? *No good deed goes unpunished.* She had always thought it a very negative outlook, but it seemed to fit here like a hand in a glove.

He swung on her then, turning to face her with such speed that she thought he might strike her.

She flinched.

"Was it now?" he snapped. "Are you sure about that? All for Albie." He scoffed.

It had started out that way, but Nathan seemed to hold some power over her. When he was near, she lost herself and melded with him. Then it all became about him. It had been her downfall more than once since she'd fallen for him. But she was an adult now. She didn't have to give in to those feelings. They weren't real. Once upon a time she had thought she was in love with him. And he with her. But it couldn't have been true. Love didn't hurt this bad. Love didn't willingly leave. Love didn't walk away.

"I'm sorry, Dat." And she was. Sorrier than she had ever been. Albie was gone. She was practically shunned herself. The damage was already done. All she could do now was work toward forgiveness.

He must have heard the sincerity in her words. His posture softened just a bit, and his grip loosened on the reins. "You've got to be more careful, Rachel. He left and he's not coming back."

"He's stayed because I asked him to."

Her father shook his head. "He has other reasons."

"What do you mean?"

"I've heard stories. I don't know how they got around, but they're saying that he killed somebody." Her father shook his head. "I can't imagine it. He didn't grow up that way. It just goes to

## The Secrets We Keep

show how quickly the world can corrupt. He wasn't a bad kid, but he turned out to be a bad man."

Her stomach sank at the words. He wasn't a bad man, but she couldn't protest. She couldn't fight what she didn't know. She thought he was a good man because she wanted him to be a good man. She needed him to be.

Samuel turned the buggy into the short lane that led to their house. It was hidden a little behind a line of trees that had been planted to stop the soil from eroding. Most of the houses in the area had a shop where they sold different items—potholders, candles, and canned goods. Once upon a time she'd had one as well, but after Miri took such a turn and Freeman disappeared, it seemed that she couldn't keep up with it all. It sat empty, just on the other side of those trees and in front of the house itself. The barn sat off to the other side, and that was where her father was headed.

He stopped their carriage and waited for her to get down. At least he didn't say more as she went around to get Miri from the back. Her girls clamored down and raced into the barn to check on the new puppies. They had just opened their eyes and were starting to stumble around in the barn like little drunken balls of fur. She was going to have to do something to keep them out of the main barn so they didn't accidentally get stepped on. She planned on selling them for seventy-five dollars each. The money was greatly needed, as always, and she hoped the contribution would take some of the strain off her father's shoulders.

She unstrapped Miri and eased her sister out of the back of their special carriage. Her father was there waiting. She was surprised to see him. She thought he had gone into the barn with the horse already, but he stood there watching her.

"What?" she finally asked, hoping her voice didn't sound as urgent and impatient as she felt.

# Amy Lillard

"I meant what I said." He sent her a disapproving frown. It had worked on her when she was younger. He would scowl, and she would scurry to do whatever it was he wanted. But now . . .

"*Jah*, Dat."

He reached out a hand to stop her from taking her sister into the house.

She looked from his fingers up into his face, not defiant, but holding fast for certain.

"I'm telling you for your own good. Stay away from him. Nathan Fisher is nothing but trouble."

# Chapter Fifteen

"Kate, quit wagging that puppy around. He's too little to be held so much," Rachel called from the porch.

"I didn't do it," Kate protested with a slight rise in her chin. "He came out here by hisself. I was taking him back."

Rachel didn't know whether to believe her daughter or not but decided it was in everyone's best interest if she played along for now. "Hold him easy," she told her daughter. "And take him back in with the rest. In a week or two you can bring them out to play, understand?"

"That's forever from now."

"Do it, Kate."

"*Jah*, Mamm."

Rachel waited a heartbeat more to make sure her daughter was going to comply without any further protest, then let herself back into the house. The screen door closed behind her just as her guest spoke.

"You're going to have to take her in hand, Rachel Hostetler." Lydie shook her head. "I'm telling you for your own good. She's going to be a handful if you don't start now."

Rachel forced a smile. Kate was already a handful. But it seemed everyone was jumping in to tell her what was "for her own good." Any minute now she supposed Daniel would come strolling in telling her what was for her own good as well.

"She's a good girl," Rachel told her neighbor as she picked up the pile of mail she had just brought into the house moments before Lydie came over. Hopefully the words held a note that would forestall further comment.

Her fingers trembled as she came across an unpostmarked envelope bearing her name in a familiar scrawl. Nathan.

"I have to tell you that I wasn't surprised that Jacob said what he said yesterday," Lydie started.

This was clearly the real reason for her visit.

Nathan's missive would have to wait. She tucked it into the pocket of her apron, then eased down in the seat across from Lydie. She had known this confrontation was coming. Lydie had been like a mother to her all these years, since her own mother had died. Most times Rachel appreciated the advice, but today she was feeling a little too frazzled to accept unsolicited comments with aplomb and grace. And yet what choice did she have?

"*Jah*, well . . ." It wasn't quite an adequate response, but it would have to do for now. It was all she had.

Lydie reached across the table and took one of Rachel's hands into her own gnarled ones. She squeezed reassuringly, prompting Rachel to look up and meet her steady blue gaze.

"We have all loved and lost," she started, surprising Rachel with the words. "But we have to move on."

"*Jah*," Rachel whispered in return. She hadn't thought about Lydie and her life before she moved into the house next to the Gingeriches ten years ago. The woman had been widowed long before she moved to Mississippi from Ohio, but other than knowing that fact, Rachel hadn't contemplated her life in the other state. "I pray every night that he will return," she said. She prayed even

# The Secrets We Keep

though she knew deep in her heart of hearts that Freeman Hostetler was gone from this earth.

"I'm not talking about Freeman," Lydie gently explained before releasing Rachel's hand. "Love can heal all wounds just like they say. Yet when it's pointed in the wrong direction, it can tear apart families and ruin lives if it's allowed to have its head."

At those words, the envelope in her pocket seemed to burn through to her skin.

"You're young. You have so much of life ahead of you. Don't let misplaced feelings ruin your future."

Rachel sighed as she turned her buggy down the short lane that led to the house. She had taken the girls and Miri into town to buy a few things at Walmart, and the trip had worn on her. It was always an ordeal to take both girls and her disabled sister into a store, but she couldn't ask Lydie to watch them again. This was her cross to bear.

Everything was starting to rub her wrong. She just needed a few minutes of peace and quiet. What she wouldn't give to be able to go down to the creek behind her house. The one where she and Nathan used to meet. What she wouldn't give to lie on those banks next to him and let the world fall away. Just for an hour or two. She wouldn't trade her life for anything. It was hers and hers alone, but sometimes the pressures and responsibilities became more of a burden than a blessing. In those times she usually went to prayer. But that would have to wait for a bit, she thought as she pulled her buggy to a stop in front of the house. For now she was just glad to be back home.

Lydie's advice had haunted her all through the evening and into her sleepless night. It was well after midnight when she finally rose and read what Nathan had delivered to her. He was staying in Cedar Creek. He hadn't said for how long or why. But knowing that he was near made her heart feel a little more content.

And she knew then. That was exactly what she was doing. She was in danger of letting misplaced love ruin her future.

She had been called out by the bishop for such behavior. And because he was the bioship . . . well, that made it as good as truth in the eyes of their district. She would have to be more careful from now on.

No, she needed to stay away from Nathan Fisher. It was as simple as that. She set the brake on the buggy but stilled as she noticed the barn door was open.

Had she left it that way?

Her father had gotten up before her and headed over to help Daniel with one thing or another. It couldn't have been him. Maybe one of the girls had snuck into the barn to look at the puppies before they left.

But she would have noticed that. Surely.

"Kate, Amelie," she started, "did either one of you go into the barn before we left?"

"No, Mamm," they said together.

There went that theory.

Rachel rested the reins in her lap and took a moment to think. Was there someone in the barn?

She almost shook her head at herself. She was starting to get paranoid. But who could blame her? The tranquil life she lived in Cedar Creek was not so tranquil these days. She wanted to brush off her worry and concerns, but something said she should take them seriously. She had to.

"Are we getting out?" Kate demanded.

# The Secrets We Keep

"Amelie, you and your sister need to stay in the buggy. Do you hear me?"

"What's wrong?" Amelie asked, immediately anxious and frowning.

"Nothing you need to be concerned about. But stay here." She climbed down from the carriage. She would take just a quick look-see into the barn. There wouldn't be anything odd inside, and that would be that. She could go on with the rest of her day.

But she found her steps slowing the closer she got to the open door. The hairs on the back of her neck were standing on end, and each inch she drew closer to the barn made her heart beat faster in her chest.

It was nothing, she told herself, even as she kept her guard high. It had to be nothing. She was overreacting. She could laugh about it later. The next time Lydie came over for coffee and milk-soaked cookies, she could tell her friend all about the time she thought someone had broken into her barn.

Her hand trembled as she reached the partially open door and pushed it open a little farther. She craned her head inside, wishing Nathan were there with his police gun so he could protect them all. If someone was inside, what was she going to do?

Suddenly she wished she had grabbed a stick of firewood for protection, but how would that look to her girls? The Amish were pacifists. They didn't go around knocking people on the head with firewood. Even when they broke into their barn.

Rachel eased inside, wondering whether or not to call out. What if it was her father? What if he had come back from Daniel's on foot to get something from the barn? Or Daniel himself? He was always lurking around, and though he made her uncomfortable more times than not, he wasn't dangerous. At least he had not yet proven himself to be so.

239

"Hello?" she called, her voice rusty and frog-like in the cool, dim light of the barn's interior.

"There you are."

Rachel nearly jumped out of her skin as a woman appeared at the end of the row of stalls. She was unidentifiable in the darkness, but Rachel could see that she held one of the puppies in her arms. Maybe not friend or foe, but a neutral party. A customer.

She sucked in a deep breath to calm her racing pulse and did her best to get her fear under control. "They're not ready to go yet." She was almost reluctant to sell the dogs at all. Her family could use the money, but it was the last thing she had of her brother.

"This one's mine," the woman boldly stated. She walked nearer, and before Rachel could answer, she recognized her.

"What are you doing here?"

Judith Preston stepped closer, her smile gleaming proudly. "I just came to check on my puppy."

Rachel shook her head. "I'm not selling you a dog."

Albie had had more than one run-in with the woman, the last being trouble over the stud fee for a previous litter. Judith had bred a few blue heelers herself, though she was more interested in studding out her own dog for pups that she could turn around and sell at a profit. Easy money for her.

Daisy, Albie's prized bitch, was almost ready to retire, and the last litter of puppies she'd whelped, studded by Judith's male, had only one living female, a beautiful girl named Susie. Albie needed her in order to continue his business. But Judith decided she wanted the same pup for her stud fee. That was something that Rachel hadn't even tried to understand; more often than not, Judith seemed to be antagonistic for the sake of being antagonistic.

## The Secrets We Keep

In order to keep the pup for himself, Albie had ended up having to pay Judith twice what the dog would have sold for in order to appease her and make up for the stud fee. He had made almost no money off the transaction. Though he seemed to let the trouble roll off his back like water from a duck, it had left a bad taste in Rachel's mouth.

Judith smiled and continued to stroke the puppy's back. Soon they would start to gain their color, adding gray and red to their predominantly white coat. "I don't need you to sell me a dog. I already own this one."

Rachel shook her head. "What are you talking about?"

The smile widened until it appeared triumphant. "Albie came to me before he died and wanted to sell me one of the pups."

"They weren't even born yet."

"Yes," she agreed. "But it seemed he was desperate for some money."

Perhaps that explained the wad of twenties she had found in his bag.

"Pick of the litter goes to a man named Jay Anderson."

Judith threw back her head and laughed. She *laughed*. "Sweetheart, I *am* Jay Anderson."

"No. Albie said he was a man."

"Sort of, I guess."

She wasn't making any sense.

"The person claiming to be Jay Anderson that your brother met was a man. My cousin, Richard. He paid Albie for a dog under my name."

"You're not Jay Anderson." Rachel's voice shook as her confidence slipped.

"J for Judith, and Anderson is my maiden name."

241

Rachel closed her eyes and took a deep breath. This couldn't be happening, and yet it was. Albie had told her in those final pages that Jay Anderson was to get first pick of the litter. And if Judith was Jay Anderson . . .

She opened her eyes again, resigned but firm. "I'll need to see your bill of sale."

"Of course. I don't have it with me right now. I was just coming to—"

*Stake my claim.*

"—check out the merchandise."

"Of course," Rachel said quietly in return. What more could she do? If the woman had a bill of sale and if Albie had already been given the money . . .

"This one is mine." Judith handed the tiny puppy to Rachel, then with a smile that had turned from triumphant to evil, she swept from the barn.

\* \* \*

"I take it we have guests tonight." Rachel stood at the sink and looked out over the yard as her father came in the back door. Her brother-in-law Daniel and his cousin James Miller were both working on a diesel engine that had once been Freeman's. They must have brought it there from the other house, the one that Rachel had shared with her family before Freeman disappeared.

"*Jah.*" Her father's answer was firm and suffered no reply from her. He knew how she felt about both Daniel and James, but he seemed to have them on some sort of tether.

Rachel only nodded. She knew better than to raise any sort of protest. It wasn't worth the fallout. Instead she went to the pantry and took out another package of pasta for tonight's supper. The meat portion would be stretched thin, but she would add some

# The Secrets We Keep

bread and another vegetable, and surely that would see them through. There would be no leftovers for tomorrow's lunch, so she pulled a package of lunch meat from the freezer and placed it in the propane-powered fridge to thaw. Soon it would be entirely too hot to run the stove during the day and they would be eating sandwiches practically every meal. She had wanted a warm offering while she could have it, but it seemed that idea had been tossed out the window.

She sighed at herself. She was being overly dramatic, but it had been that sort of day, and it looked as if the drama was going to continue on into the evening.

Dutifully, Amelie and Kate helped her set the table as the *yumasetti* bubbled inside the oven. The traditional Amish casserole was always a hit with her girls and was a good meal to stretch if one had to. So at least that was a blessing. And she needed all the blessing reminders she could get as the men stomped into the house and prepared to eat.

After their silent prayer, the men served up their helpings of the casserole. Rachel made Kate a plate and then one for Miri. Amelie helped herself as Rachel stirred Miri's portion to cool it. As usual, Rachel would be eating after everyone else, but such was life. She couldn't remember a time when she had eaten at the same time as the rest of her family.

"At least we got my engine running," Daniel said, biting into one of the buttery yeast rolls Rachel had made that afternoon. She had made extra so they would have plenty for a couple of days. That always took some of her workload off, preparing food in advance, but it seemed all of today's efforts were for naught.

*Freeman's engine,* she thought. Then she reined in her attitude. It did no good to remind her father that Freeman's property was truly hers and he shouldn't be going around giving it away, but her father didn't see it that way. He had taken her in when her husband had disappeared, and she should be grateful.

And she was. But she had a feeling her father believed she had done something or been lacking in some way that caused her husband to leave her. It was a stigma that she bore in her community. Just one more cross to bear.

Like her husband and helpmate being gone wasn't enough.

"Good," her father said. "You may need it when it comes time to set that new driveway."

A new driveway. A new well. What else was Daniel doing at her farm?

"Good thing you got the other well back in action," James said. He looked around to see if Rachel was paying him any mind.

She was feeding Miri, doing her best to keep her sister as clean as possible. Sometimes that was an unattainable feat. Her sister was spastic and unable to sit still in her chair, one of the main reasons she was restrained in her seat. It was a terrible sight, but unavoidable all the same. Still, Miri seemed happy. Always happy.

Sometimes Rachel wished she could have a bit of that pure, innocent joy for herself.

James caught her gaze, and Rachel forced a smile. He turned back to his plate as if he hadn't looked at her like *that*.

She had been avoiding eye contact with him ever since they sat down to eat. Something about the way he looked at her made the skin on Rachel's arms itch. She shifted in her seat and resisted the urge to smooth a hand down the goose bumps his gaze caused. Not good goose bumps but creepy ones. Ones that made her want to run from the room.

"I just wish I could have done more," Daniel was saying.

While she had been collecting herself, the conversation had shifted to a new topic. Thankfully, Kate was quiet this evening.

# The Secrets We Keep

Normally chatty and open, she seemed to turn into Amelie's solemn twin whenever James Miller was around. Just another reason to avoid him. Kate was young and innocent and talkative. She had never met a stranger, and yet she seemed intimidated by his mere presence.

Not that there was anything to cause her to be openly frightened. He wasn't a large man, standing no taller than her *dawdi's* nearly six feet. His red hair was unusual. There was only one other person in their community with red hair, a woman by the name of Marjorie Graber, the preacher's wife. She liked to pinch the cheeks of the little children as they passed by. But again, nothing to be afraid of. Maybe the flaming beard . . .

As a widower, James was entitled to wear a beard, and his was indeed an impressive sort of growth. Thick and full and bright. But Kate was spunkier than that. She wouldn't let something like facial hair deter her from whatever she wanted. No, it had to be something deeper.

"Me too," James added.

Rachel could feel his gaze land on her once again, but she refused to look up from her task of cooling the next bite of Miri's meal.

"Maybe if we could have made a man of him, he wouldn't have—"

Rachel coughed. Loudly. They were talking about Albie, and the last thing she wanted was for them to start discussing suicide in front of her girls.

"You okay?" Daniel asked, his tone caring but his beady eyes calculating.

"Just tiny ears," she said, cutting her gaze toward her daughters.

Both men nodded but continued on. At least now they were being a little more careful about what they said, the words they used.

"Someone should have made a man of him," Daniel lamented.

"I tried," her father said. "I definitely tried."

They continued on like this as Rachel continued to feed her sister. She wanted to protest, but she knew her father would be upset with her if she did. Still, it was hard to listen to them talk about her baby brother as if there had been something wrong with him.

Yet a part of her wondered . . . was there something about Albie's makeup that she had missed? It seemed that everyone around her felt him somehow lacking. There was nothing that she had seen or noticed. As far as she was concerned, he was just Albie.

She hadn't wanted to believe the words that he had written in the journal—unnatural feelings and urges—but now she was starting to wonder. Listening to James and Daniel talk about him made her question everything about her brother that she thought she had known. If his actions were so detestable to the two men sitting at her table, maybe they had tried to do something about it.

Maybe they had tried to toughen him up and it had gotten out of hand. Maybe they had taken it too far. Or maybe he hadn't responded well and things just simply went sideways.

Or maybe she was looking for trouble where there was none. Maybe she was so wound up after everything that she was looking for a murder around every corner. She should do as Nathan instructed. She had to be patient, wait for the coroner's report. Once she had it in hand, she was counting on everything becoming clear. Though what was she going to do if it gave no answers?

# Chapter Sixteen

After everything that had happened, she shouldn't be here. She should leave well enough alone, but the conversation at dinner the night before had played over and over in her head like some twisted omen. She doubted her brother. She doubted herself. But most of all she doubted the two men who had been seated at the table with her.

She couldn't say she liked either of them, but they had never done anything to cause this hostility. She shouldn't come here, running to Nathan, like she had the right to.

And yet here she was.

She parked her buggy in the lot across the street from the motel around the front side, not close to where Nathan's room was located. She traipsed around the block as if she were shopping, then sidled up to his door and knocked.

But there was no answer. Where was he? That was when she noticed that his truck was not parked outside the room like it always had been. He was off somewhere doing something. Not solving her brother's murder, of that she was sure. He'd told her a great deal of police work consisted of waiting on reports from the lab. It was just the way of the times.

But she had wanted to see him. She was insane for coming here. Crazy for thinking she had the right. Lydie had warned her against this very thing, and yet here she was.

She wanted the comfort that only he could give. Just the sound of his voice was like a balm to her soul. She hadn't realized how much she missed him until he was back. All too soon he would be leaving again. Then she didn't know what she would do.

Learn to go on without him. A third time.

"Rachel?" She turned as Nathan pulled his truck into the lot behind her. He had the window rolled down and a confused frown on his face.

She gave him a weak smile. "Hi."

"What are you doing here?"

With a small shrug, she grimaced. "I don't know. I just wanted to talk to you about something."

He gestured toward the passenger's seat. "Hop in."

She should tell him no. She shouldn't be talking to him. And she definitely shouldn't be getting into his pickup truck. Yet that was exactly what she found herself doing.

"Were you out running errands?" she asked, a little breathless as she settled herself into the seat. Why hadn't she asked to go into his room? That would have been safer. As far as someone seeing them together. Someone Amish, that is. She wasn't worried about the *Englischers*, but after her embarrassment at church on Sunday, she was worried about someone Amish finding out that she had been in further contact with Nathan.

"I just happened to be driving by, and I saw you."

"I don't understand."

"I'm not staying there any longer." He started to put the truck into gear, but she shook her head.

248

# The Secrets We Keep

"Can we just sit here for a bit? And talk?" she added.

"Yeah." He left the truck idling in park, then unbuckled his seat belt to turn and face her. "What do you want to talk about?"

So many things had happened since she had seen him, yet she couldn't find the words to tell him about any of them. All she could think about was him sitting within touching distance and how much she had missed him. "Why aren't you staying here now?"

The sudden thought hit her. He had changed his mind and was leaving after all. He was going back to Oklahoma. He had been talking about it since he arrived, but when he left the note in her mailbox, she had thought perhaps it was all a bluff. But if he had given up his motel room . . .

"I got an Airbnb over on Peach Tree Lane."

"Oh." The one syllable was small. She didn't know why his words felt so painful. He had moved, but he hadn't told her where he was. But it wasn't like they should be spending any time together. She shouldn't be in his truck, sitting here with him in broad daylight, bold and brash.

Still, she felt a little better knowing that he wasn't leaving. *Not yet.*

"Rachel?"

"*Jah?*" She pulled herself out of her thoughts and turned her full attention to the man at her side.

"What did you want to talk about?"

*So. Much.*

She wanted to talk about Judith and the mess with the puppies. And church and his *Meidung*. She wanted to tell him everything all at once, but she had to stick with the most important first.

"I think Daniel and James might know more about Albie's death than they are letting on."

"Daniel Hostetler?"

She nodded. "And James Miller."

"Aren't they cousins?" It wasn't a far stretch. Almost everyone in Cedar Creek was related by blood or marriage to almost everyone else. He didn't wait for her to respond before continuing. "Why do you think they know something?"

She shook her head. She didn't want to discuss this. Talking about it made it seem real. And it was something that she didn't want to be real, these variations in her brother's thoughts and behaviors. "They were talking over supper last night," she finally said. "They wanted to toughen him up. Their words. Make a man out of him."

Nathan's expression went stony cold, then turned impassive, as if every emotion he had was drained from him in that moment. "And you think that's what did it?"

"I don't know what I think other than my brother did not kill himself." It was the only thing she knew for a fact, even though to date there was no proof otherwise. That was why she so desperately needed Nathan.

*That's not the only reason.*

She pushed that voice aside and waited for him to respond.

"What are you going to do if it comes back that he died from hanging?"

She shook her head. "I don't know," she whispered. "But I know that part's not true." And no one was going to tell her any different. It wasn't something she was willing to believe.

He seemed to think about it a moment, take it all in and add it to what he already knew. His look turned thoughtful, and his eyes darkened. "I'm not sure what I'm supposed to do about this," he said quietly. "I'm not a cop here. I don't have the authority to go around questioning people."

# The Secrets We Keep

"That's not what I want." Truthfully, she still didn't know what she wanted. She only knew that she trusted Nathan. After everything that had happened between them, she still trusted him.

"What *do* you want?" he asked.

She sucked in a deep breath, but she didn't know the answer. She wanted everything and nothing that he could give her. She wanted peace of mind. Her brother back. Her husband found. She wanted to go back in time and convince Nathan to stay with her eight years ago when he'd come back to Cedar Creek after Mattie died.

But if that wish were to come true, then she wouldn't have her girls, and that was something she couldn't wish for at all.

"Why don't you take your concerns to Shane Johnson?" Nathan asked. Apparently, he had realized how loaded his question had been. "He's the detective on the case."

"I don't know him." She had met him once at the sheriff's office, but she didn't know him. Not like she did Nathan.

"He's a good man."

She didn't care about that. She cared about trust. And she trusted the man seated next to her. "Please, Nathan. Just stop by there and talk to them. See what they are up to."

"I don't know what good it would do."

"I just want to know."

He hesitated for a moment more, and she knew he was looking for a reason to tell her no. But he didn't. He nodded and said, "Okay," and she loved him all the more for it.

"One other thing," she said. She needed to be getting out of his truck before someone saw her inside it. They would think she had been riding around with him instead of just talking. Not that it overly mattered. She was certain the bishop would frown as much on her talking with Nathan as he would anything explicitly stated as *verboten* in the *Ordnung.* "I found out yesterday Jay Anderson is a woman."

\* \* \*

A woman. He hadn't seen that coming. But it made sense now that he was looking back. That was why no one knew who Jay Anderson was. Well, not because she was a woman, but because the name didn't exist on a person in Cedar Creek. Judith Preston was Jay Anderson. That was why there was no Facebook profile, no Instagram presence. Nothing to give a clue as to her true identity. Even Sherlock Holmes wouldn't have been able to deduce that from the clues and information provided.

She was a woman, and she wanted a puppy. Said she had a bill of sale. If she did, there was no fighting it. There was no way to prove whether or not Albie had gotten the money after the receipt was handed to "Jay." There might have been money in his go bag, but there was no telling where it really come from. There was no proof that the man claiming to be "Jay" hadn't roughed Albie up that night in addition to the damage inflicted by Chance and his crew. Injuries that might have brought about his demise.

If Nate was calculating it correctly, Jay Anderson had contacted Albie previously and requested to purchase a puppy from his latest, upcoming litter. The night Albie was killed, he had needed the money. So he had met Jay in person—or rather, Richard, Judith's cousin, posing as Jay—and was paid for the pick of the litter. The puppies hadn't even been born yet, and Albie was selling sight unseen, but he had also trusted his sister to conclude the matter after he was gone. That pointed to Albie's plans of leaving Cedar Creek and not the unthinkable action of suicide.

# The Secrets We Keep

Nate supposed it could be argued that leaving could also mean dying, but one didn't need money to die. That was one thing in life that came without charge.

Rachel had done right in telling Judith that she would have to see the bill of sale before she surrendered any of her brother's prized pups to the woman, but Nate had told her that if Judith did produce the document, Rachel shouldn't argue. Proof was proof.

Rachel didn't seem to like the idea, and he couldn't blame her. From what he could tell, Judith Preston was a real piece of work. One would only hope that she treated the animals she raised better than she did the people she did business with.

Now he was on his way out to the farm that Rachel had shared with Freeman. Nate could tell himself a hundred times that he shouldn't be getting involved. That Rachel's problems were not his responsibility. That he had problems of his own. That he didn't have any jurisdiction here in Mississippi. And yet he found himself pulling into the rutted drive of the property that used to belong to Rachel and Freeman.

That in itself was tough. He could just imagine the big man striding from barn to house, stomping the dirt from his feet, before stepping inside to kiss his wife. He could imagine them watching the girls play in the summer evenings, running and skipping rope under the shade of the large oak tree planted off to one side of the barn.

But he knew this to just be his own imagination. If Freeman had disappeared three years ago, then Kate would have been only a year or so old. There wouldn't have been running and skipping across the yard like in his mind's eye. But the imagination was a very powerful thing. He wondered if Freeman and Rachel had been happy together. If she had truly moved on from him when Nate told her he couldn't return.

253

He hadn't been overly surprised to learn from Sarah that Rachel and Freeman had married. Freeman had been in love with Rachel for about as long as Nate himself had. It was obvious to everyone around them. Yet she'd had eyes only for Nate.

But there were expectations in their community. Get married, have babies, carry on. And that was just what she had done. Only without him. That had been no one's fault but his own.

He slammed the mental door shut on his meandering thoughts and cut the truck's engine. The place appeared deserted, but he knew that looks could be deceiving. Rachel had told him that she had overheard the two of them, James and Daniel, talking about adding a smaller barn and paddock to the back side of the red building. Seemed Daniel thought it might be a good idea to keep a few hogs, and for that they needed to have a separate enclosure, a gestation barn, and a farrowing room. He had brought James in to help him build the structures.

Nate paused for a moment, listening, and he could hear the tap-tap-tap of hammer against nail. He closed his truck door, and the noise stopped. They were around somewhere, and now they knew he was there as well.

As he waited, he let his gaze wander around the property again. The field next to the house was planted with soybeans, as was the land across the gravel road. The spot where the kitchen garden would have been was riddled with weeds as well as the ghosts of tomato stakes and bean poles long past. A clothesline stretched from the front porch to the top eave of the barn, but unlike at the houses he had passed on his way here, no clothes flapped in the early summer breeze.

When Nate was living in Cedar Creek, an elderly widow by the name of Melva Ebersol had washed laundry for bachelors and even families in the area who needed the service. In return they did

## The Secrets We Keep

repairs and such to her property. Perhaps Daniel used her for his own clothes. If she was still alive. Surely she was. Thinking back, she had seemed old at the time, but he understood now that he had reached that age when old became relative.

A wooden frame sat over what Nate supposed was the old well and another on top of what could be the new well site. Rachel had told him there had been a problem with water on the property dating back to even before Freeman disappeared. Well water could be both a blessing and a curse, but it was necessary in order to live "off the grid." The Amish were pros at living off the grid. No electricity, no phones, no water or sewage to tie them to the other houses surrounding them. They relied on each other but weren't tethered with lines and pipes.

"Help you?"

Nate turned his attention to the man coming around the side of the building. He would have known him anywhere. James Miller. James might have filled out a bit and grown a beard, but the years had not dulled the copper of his hair or the malicious glint in his eyes.

"I'm a friend of Rachel's," Nate explained.

James shook his head from side to side. "Not a good one, or you would know that she don't live here no more."

"Nathan Fisher," a second voice drawled, joining the conversation. Nate turned as Daniel Hostetler came around the side of the house.

"Hi, Daniel."

"I'll be," James muttered, almost chastising himself for not recognizing Nate right off.

"I think you should go on ahead and leave," Daniel said. He stopped halfway between the house and where Nate was standing. He crossed his arms and spread his feet out wide, taking a stance that was nothing if not defensive.

255

"Maybe," Nate said. "But I wanted to talk to the two of you about something."

"Something?" Daniel raised one brow in question.

"Albie," Nate said simply, gauging their reaction to the boy's name.

"What about him?" Daniel almost bristled, as if he was expecting more of an accusation to come.

"You know the coroner is doing an autopsy to discover the cause of death."

"*Jah*. Don't know why, though. Everyone knows he killed hisself." Daniel's chin lifted as if he were daring Nate to say more.

James watched the exchange between the two of them, but he offered no comments of his own.

"I guess that will be determined."

Daniel shook his head. "Just wasting everybody's time."

"Did you see him that day?" Nate asked. He was watching every sunbeam and shadow that crossed the man's face.

"The day he died?" Daniel asked. "No."

"What about you?" Nate looked to James to see his reaction.

Caught off guard, the man blustered. "No. No. I don't go over there much."

"Rachel mentioned that you were mentoring him on being a man."

Daniel shrugged. "He was kinda sissy, you know. No, wait. You don't know. Because you left. Kinda like you should do right now." He took a menacing step forward. That was when Nate noticed that the man still held the hammer he had been using to build whatever on the back of his barn.

The move was overtly threatening, but Nate refused to budge. He might not have any jurisdiction in this state, but he wasn't about to be chased off by the likes of Daniel Hostetler. He had known both brothers his entire life. They were about as different as two people in

# The Secrets We Keep

the same family could be. Freeman had always been even keeled, caring. Daniel, not so much. Even when they were teens.

"I'm just asking you a question, whether or not you had seen him the day he died."

Daniel stopped, hammer still in hand, but he didn't come any closer. "I don't remember if I did or not. And if I had, what difference would it have made?"

"None, probably. Unless he said something to you about his plans to leave home."

"He never mentioned anything like that. Don't know why anyone would want to leave." The barb was pointedly aimed at Nate. Daniel knew exactly why Nate had left. Everyone in Cedar Creek did. But it didn't make a difference *why* a person left, only that they had. Nate had gone, but Albie had died before he made the move. That put them in two very distinct categories.

"Everyone's different," Nate said with a one-shoulder shrug. This conversation wasn't going anywhere. He could press the men, but what good would it do? They were mean and petty, but he didn't think they were killers. Both were the kind to pick on those weaker than themselves, but killing would expend too much energy, and frankly, Nate didn't think either had it in them.

"Some more than others," James quipped.

No, they were bullies, but they weren't smart enough to kill someone and then frame it up like that person had committed suicide. Rachel was desperately searching for answers, but there were none here.

"It's been nice talking to you," Nate said. He was reluctant to turn his back on the men. Thankfully, he hadn't gone too far from his truck, and he could back up without raising too many suspicions. Then again, what did he care if the two men knew he didn't trust them? They weren't exactly the salt of the earth, and he was going home . . . soon.

He had only come by here for Rachel. Everything for Rachel.

They stood there, unmoving, as Nate climbed into his truck, started the engine, and backed out of the drive. No, he didn't think they were killers, but they were certainly up to something.

The smell of fresh grass and wildflowers, the feel of the soft ground beneath his feet, the sight of the woman standing across from him. He should never have come here, back to the creek where he and Rachel had spent so much time as kids, as young adults. He should have never accepted her invitation. There were too many memories haunting the place where they used to meet. Yet here he stood looking at her, waiting for her to respond to the information he had given her.

"But—" she started, then broke off, shook her head. He wondered if she too was overcome with the memories the creek bank brought back. All those days growing up. And then one time again when Mattie had died. He had met Rachel here, and she had comforted him in his loss and grief. She had asked him to stay with her, but he had refused. He had asked her to come back with him, but she couldn't. She couldn't leave her sister behind, and she didn't feel she could drag Miri away from everything she had known her entire life. It wasn't fair, the ties that bound them, but what in life truly was?

"I just don't think either one of them had a hand in Albie's death."

For a time, Nate had wondered if Rachel was being overly skeptical about Albie's suicide, but after reading that her brother had received money that night, he had to completely agree with her now. Someone had killed Albie Gingerich. The question was, who?

And why?

Over a puppy? Not likely but still possible. People had been killed for less. But there was more at stake than dog breeding.

# The Secrets We Keep

Maybe he had been killed because he was different? Or Amish? Gay?

Nate knew that Rachel didn't want to believe her brother might have had tendencies that were not "natural." She didn't want to believe he could have been that different at his very core. Mostly because his life would have been so hard. But his life was over now. It was just the two of them, and still she couldn't accept it. So he wouldn't bring it up. No sense in causing her even more pain and grief. The coroner's report would settle the matter—he hoped, anyway—and that would be that.

"Just be patient," he told her, then he immediately regretted the words as tears started to well in those incredible green eyes. "Don't cry. Whatever happens, none of it will bring him back."

"I know." She sniffed and blinked to dash the tears away. Two escaped and ran quickly and silently down her cheeks. "I just—"

"Rachel, listen to me. I think it's time to let this rest. Let the coroner do her job. Even if Albie didn't kill himself, even if someone strung him up in that barn that night, the chances of the police actually finding the culprit will be next to impossible. Evidence has been destroyed. The crime scene was contaminated. There's nothing left to prove a guilty party."

"I just want him moved into the cemetery."

"It may be time to accept that won't happen."

She shook her head. "Nathan—"

He couldn't stand it. There were too many memories haunting him, taunting him. He just wanted to hold her close and let the world fall away. But that wasn't possible either.

"I've got to go."

She took a step toward him.

He took a step back.

"Nathan—"

"Bye, Rachel." Somehow he managed to turn away from her and walk back to his truck.

He managed to get his heart rate back into a normal rhythm as he pulled into the drive at Peach Tree Lane. He remembered to park to one side so that Lorie would be able to get out if she needed to. Not that she went out much at night. She seemed to be something of a homebody, enjoying her house and the comfort she found there.

Nate was just unlocking the side door when Lorie came up.

"I thought I heard you," she said, her smile bright and welcoming. "I just finished cooking some supper, if you'd like to join me."

His gut reaction was to say no, that he wasn't hungry, but that would be a lie. Plus he really didn't need to be alone at the moment. Isolation would just make him stew over the day and Rachel and the last few days, and everything else that had been weighing on him since he left Oklahoma. Since before he left Oklahoma.

"Tacos," she said in a singing kind of voice, doing her best to entice him to join her.

Why shouldn't he? He was single, she was single, and she seemed willing. Or maybe he had been out of the game too long. Maybe.

"Sure." He smiled in return, hoping it didn't look pressed, stressed, or even tainted by his churning thoughts.

"Come on," she said, motioning for him to follow her into the house.

The smell that greeted him was spicy and delicious. He really was hungry. Somehow he had skipped lunch.

Not somehow. He had been too wrapped up in all things Rachel to make time to feed himself. It was pathetic.

"This is quite a spread," he told her, looking at the counter covered with Mexican delights.

# The Secrets We Keep

"I love tacos," she told him. "So I always make more than what I'll eat. That way there will be leftovers."

She wasn't playing. Even with him eating, there would be plenty for the next day. And maybe even the day after that.

Spicy taco meat, refried beans, crunchy and soft shells, lettuce, tomato, sour cream, cheese. Even guacamole.

"Help yourself," she told him, handing him a plate.

Nate dished himself out a couple of tacos, some chips, guacamole, and salsa, then followed Lorie into the dining room. Even when he ate with Bree, they sat in front of the TV, usually chomping Chinese food out of disposable containers while they watched some show or another. But not with Lorie. She cooked, ate at the table, drank out of real glasses. The entire scene was more domestic than he was accustomed to. Part of him craved it, this connection, while another part wanted to run for the hills. He didn't know why. They had enjoyed meals before and there had been no contention. No strain between the two of them. But tonight . . . He told himself that there was nothing to be afraid of, and yet he felt like he was teetering on the edge with no way back up if he fell.

"You're very quiet tonight," Lorie said, taking a drink of her tea and glancing at him from under her lashes. "I mean, more quiet than usual."

He shook his head. "Just a few things on my mind."

"The Amish kid?"

He had told her about Albie and how he had died. He hadn't said much about Rachel, but he could see the light dawn in her eyes when he mentioned her name. Apparently, he was very transparent when it came to his feelings for Rachel Gingerich. Hostetler.

"Yeah," he admitted. "And his sister."

"You know, you kind of lock up when you talk about her."

"I do?" He took a bite of the taco and chewed. He had wanted to act nonchalant, but the food had turned to paste in his mouth, and he couldn't seem to make his jaws work properly. Instead, he swallowed hard and nearly choked. He took a big gulp of tea to wash the bite down the rest of the way, then gave a little cough as he finally completed the arduous task of eating.

"Sorry." Lorie sat back in her seat, shaking her head as she moved away. "I overstepped. I'm always doing that. Momaw used to always say, she'd say, 'Lorie, quit getting into other people's business if it don't concern you directly.'"

"It's okay," he said. He stood from the table and took his plate to the kitchen. He had eaten what he could of the tacos. The first few bites had been delicious, but he had too much on his mind at the moment to enjoy them now. Or maybe it was the company before him. He had more than his share of "woman problems" at the moment; he didn't need to add another to the agenda. "Thanks for supper."

She looked down at his half-eaten plate, then glanced to her own. She stood, leaving her food on the table. "Listen, I'm sorry. I mean, we don't know each other that well. But I really like you. I would really like to get to know you better, but—"

"Yes?"

"I'm not looking for anything serious, but I do want a man to be with me when he's with me."

And he wasn't.

"You're a good man," she continued. "And I'm glad to have you as a renter."

For a moment he thought she was going to say more, but she pressed her lips together and followed him to the door to his apartment.

# The Secrets We Keep

He should tell her that he was sorry. He did have too much going on at the moment to bring anyone else into his chaos. Not just with Bree and Rachel, but with the shooting, his life, his career, whatever came next. He needed to make that decision based on his own needs and not what he thought others needed from him. He'd always been that way, taking care of those around him. But maybe the police counselor was right, maybe it was time that he took care of himself.

But he couldn't say that he was sorry, because he wasn't sorry. Not yet, but he had a feeling one day soon he would be.

"Lorie, I—"

She shook her head and placed one finger over his lips. "Maybe in another life."

# Chapter Seventeen

"Here it is." Judith Preston held up a piece of paper in front of Rachel's face, too close to her eyes for her to read even one word of it.

She took the bill of sale from the woman and scanned it. The signature looked correct. But maybe if Judith or her cousin Richard had taken the journal from Nathan's motel room, they would know how to sign his name.

Rachel wouldn't put it past them to do something like that. But it didn't quite make sense. How would they have known about the journal in the first place? How would they have known to lure Nathan down to the creek, where the two of them had stood just the day before?

Speaking of . . .

Meeting him yesterday at the creek had been a mistake. There were simply too many memories there. Too many memories of what could never be again. They had made their choices. There was no going back. She was married. He was *Englisch*.

She should have never asked him to meet her there. She should have never pressed him for more details. It was too hard on her heart. Her head had ached all through the night as she tossed and turned in her bed. She had given Nathan her last few Tylenols, so she had suffered without relief. Not that she believed the tiny pills

## The Secrets We Keep

could have helped her in any way. Her head was hurting because her heart was breaking. Her heart was breaking, yet she couldn't do anything about it but go on.

That morning she had forced herself out of bed and downstairs, doing her best to act like nothing was wrong. Maybe Nathan was right. Maybe she shouldn't worry so much about Albie's death. He was dead. Nothing was going to change that. But the thought of someone getting away with his murder was more than she could stomach.

She was still adjusting to having both girls home during the day. Kate was obviously envious of the time her sister spent at school. She also wanted her mother to herself as much as possible. Rachel had a feeling it had something to do with Albie's death. And she was certain Kate could pick up on the stresses that were currently filling her mother's life. Like Nathan Fisher being back in town.

She was just pulling it all together, and now this.

Rachel handed the paper back to the smug-faced woman and coolly eyed her. She remembered what Nathan had said. "Okay, you'll have your pick of the puppies."

It made her heart hurt to even think about letting one of the puppies go. They were the very last thing she had from Albie, and she wanted to hang on to any piece of him she could.

"Come back in eight weeks, and you can choose." The words almost choked her, but she managed to get them out. She started to turn away, hoping that the vile woman would take it as a dismissal and leave, but instead Judith grabbed her arm. She held up a piece of yellow nylon cord. "I want to choose now."

Of course she did. Rachel opened her mouth to protest the intrusion but knew from past experience that Judith would keep on hounding the family until she got what she wanted. That was the reason Albie had stopped doing business with her and she had had to use a fake name and her cousin as a front to get a puppy from him.

265

Amy Lillard

The best thing to do would be to allow her this concession, let her pick out the puppy she wanted; then when the time came, it would be done.

"Follow me," Rachel said dully and made her way toward the barn. She didn't wait on the woman to comply.

She was dimly aware of her girls following behind. She didn't want them around Judith. The woman was as slimy as they came, but Rachel didn't want to start a war by making them go back into the house. The pair ran in and out of the barn with the same regularity as they did their own rooms. She shouldn't make a big deal out of this and blow it out of proportion.

"What are we doing?" Kate asked as she skipped behind Rachel.

"We're letting Judith pick out a puppy."

"Why?" Another skip.

"Because your uncle sold one to her . . . before he . . . died." It was so hard to say the words to her four-year-old. But with Kate she had learned to explain up front and be done with it. That was the easiest route.

"But I thought—"

"Not now, Kate." She managed to cover up the rest of the girl's words. Kate forgot nothing. And seemed to overhear everything. Rachel would have to be more careful about discussing anything important or that she didn't want repeated around the *maedel*.

Amelie walked like the little lady she was while Kate skipped behind them and into the barn, where Susie had moved the puppies after she had given birth.

The last thing Rachel wanted was to allow this woman into the barn, to look at the dogs, to even be in the presence of her children. But she would get this over and done with, and with any luck she wouldn't have to deal with Judith Preston again until it came time to pick up her puppy.

## The Secrets We Keep

Judith's smile gleamed wickedly in the dim light of the barn.

"This way," Rachel said, gesturing toward the last stall.

Judith barged past her. "I know where they are." She ducked into the stall as Rachel reluctantly followed behind. The way her day was going, the woman would still be there come supper. Rachel said a small prayer that Judith would pick her dog quickly and be on her way.

She hovered outside the stall, one girl on either side of her, as Judith squatted down in the hay and started examining the pups.

*How long is this going to take?* she thought to herself as the woman picked them up one by one, checking the gender, their eye color, and what permanent spots they had been born with. Then she started all over again.

Heaven help her. There were only six puppies. How long did something like this take?

Judith stood, her face hardening into a mask of accusation. "She's not here."

"What?" Rachel asked. She had been so involved in her grumbling thoughts that she hadn't realized the woman had spoken until the words had already floated away on the stale air.

"My puppy. The one I picked out the other day. It's not here."

"Of course it is," Rachel said. Her voice held a scoffing note, but she didn't care. She was tired of dealing with everything she was dealing with, and Judith was one of those dealings that she could bring to a close.

"There were six puppies here yesterday, and now there are five."

Rachel started shaking her head before the other woman even finished speaking. How could that be? It couldn't. The woman was overlooking one of the dogs. Rachel counted under her breath. One . . . two . . . three . . . four . . . five . . . wait. One . . .

She counted twice, then again. Five puppies squirmed and whined and rooted around in the hay. Only five.

267

"It has to be around here somewhere," Rachel said. But what she really wanted to demand was, what was wrong with the five that were there? Why couldn't Judith pick one of these?

"I want that dog." Judith's voice turned demanding. "I have a bill of sale that states that I get pick of the litter, and that is my pick. Now where is it?"

Rachel immediately started looking around the barn, hating herself for jumping into action. So much for telling Judith to take what was offered. But the puppy wasn't in any of the other stalls, or the tack room or any of the nooks and crannies the barn had to offer.

"Maybe she was starting to move them," she weakly offered to the fuming woman.

"Find it." Judith crossed her arms as if to say *I'll wait*.

Rachel turned away and headed out of the barn, wondering where the dog might have found to move her pups, if that was indeed what she had been doing. Rachel didn't know that theory to be a fact. For all she knew, the tiny puppy had grown wings and flown to the moon.

All right, now she was just being silly, but she was starting to feel a bit panicked. Where could the puppy be?

She checked the floor of the spring buggy that used to belong to Albie, the space behind the stack of hay her father had built next to the barn door, and under the front porch. She even looked in the shed where her father kept extra tools. No puppy.

"Mamm." Amelie's quiet words stopped Rachel in her tracks. Despite the glares she was receiving from Judith Preston and the fact that the woman was stuck to Rachel's heels like discarded gum, she couldn't ignore her child.

"*Jah*?"

Amelie looked from Judith to her sister, then turned her attention back to her mother once again. She crooked a finger for Rachel

# The Secrets We Keep

to come closer, her gaze still a bit distrustful as she kept it locked on the stranger.

Rachel bent down low so she could hear what her daughter had to say.

"Really?" Judith snorted. "My dog is missing, and you two want to play secret time."

Rachel ignored her.

"Amelie," Kate said, stomping her foot as if to gain her sister's attention.

Rachel ignored her too and waited for her eldest to speak.

"I think I heard something this morning. Upstairs. In our room."

"Really?" Rachel asked, pulling away and gazing hopefully into Amelie's eyes.

Her daughter nodded.

Rachel was so very aware of Judith's hard glare as she looked back over to where Kate stood. Rachel pushed to her feet and approached her daughter, wrapping her fingers firmly around one arm and pulling her a little away from the rest as she squatted down next to her.

"Kate . . ." she started. "Is there a puppy in your room?"

Kate shook her head, but Rachel noticed that her lip trembled when she did so.

"Kate, Jesus doesn't like it when we tell lies."

"Mamm, I—"

"Kate."

"I just wanted it to be safe." She dropped her head and spoke to the tops of her bare feet.

"What makes you think it wouldn't have been safe in the barn with its mother?"

Her daughter shrugged but didn't look up. Even with her chin tucked into her chest, Rachel could see the protrusion of her bottom lip.

269

# Amy Lillard

"We'll talk about this later," she told her youngest, then turned back to Amelie. "Can you wait here with your sister?"

Amelie nodded.

"Where are you going?" Judith demanded.

"I'll be right back," Rachel told them.

"I'm not letting you out of my sight." She started behind Rachel toward the house.

"No," Rachel said, holding up one hand to stop Judith's progress. "You'll stay here. I'll be back."

Thankfully, Judith didn't push the issue as Rachel made her way inside. She hated leaving her daughters outside with the hateful woman, but she couldn't have them all traipsing into the house, now could she? And Rachel had the feeling that if she didn't leave Amelie there with the woman, Judith Preston might wander all over the farm doing heaven only knew what until Rachel returned.

As quickly as possible, she made her way up the stairs and into the room that Kate shared with Amelie. The minute she stepped foot inside, she could hear it, the whining and scratching.

Rachel made her way over to the bed and dropped to her knees, pulling an old shoebox from the space. She opened the lid, and there inside was the missing pup. It was so small and cute and happy to see her as it chewed on her finger.

"Are you hungry, little fella?" she asked, lifting it from the box. "Little girl," she corrected. The pup was a female, she realized as she held it, her fingers wrapped about its middle.

It was the same puppy Kate had been wagging around since they were born. Her favorite, she claimed. Well, it looked like she would have to get another favorite. Unfortunately, this puppy was going to go live with the Prestons in a few weeks.

"Here you go," she called brightly as she made her way across the porch and over to where the fuming Judith Preston waited.

270

# The Secrets We Keep

Rachel could almost feel the animosity crackling in the air. Between Kate and Amelie. Between Judith and everyone else.

"You were trying to hide her from me," Judith accused. "Because obviously you wanted it for yourself."

Rachel shook her head but didn't dignify the accusation with a response. How did one explain the innocence of a child to a person who felt everyone was out to get them? It just wasn't possible.

"Would you like to tie your string around her neck now?" She didn't know what was so special about this puppy that it was the one Judith had to have, or even why it was the one Kate loved so much, but if the older woman wanted it and she had a bill of sale . . . well, Kate would have to find another dog to love.

Judith harrumphed but did as Rachel suggested, loosely tying the string around the pup's neck. It was tight enough that it wouldn't come off easily but could be removed as the puppy grew. Rachel would have to remind herself to check it weekly. She wouldn't want the puppy to be hurt because Judith Preston was a mistrusting soul.

"I don't know what you all are playing at," the woman started after she had finished attaching the string, "but I will be back every week to check on my dog until it is weaned and ready to come home."

"That's really not necessary," Rachel started.

"Oh, but it is," Judith said. "And if I come back here and she's missing, I will sue the pants off every one of you!"

She thrust the puppy back into Rachel's arms, then she turned in a huff and stomped toward her car.

Rachel stood at the edge of the drive flanked by her daughters and watched the woman angrily drive away. What energy it must take to be that hateful all the time. Just a few more weeks and she wouldn't have to deal with her again.

Once Judith had disappeared from view, Rachel turned toward Kate.

271

# Amy Lillard

"Are you mad at me?" her daughter asked. "Why are you mad at me?"

Rachel handed the puppy to Amelie. "Take her back into the barn, please."

Amelie nodded and headed inside the structure, the puppy cradled in her thin arms.

Rachel led Kate over to the porch and sat on the steps with her youngest.

"Katie," she started. She never used that nickname with her, and yet it seemed like the thing to do, to soften everything that was to come next. "Why did you lie about the puppy?"

"I didn't lie," Kate stubbornly replied.

"But you knew where the puppy was and yet you didn't tell me."

"You didn't ask."

"Kate." How to combat that truth. Lord, times like this she could use a helping hand. Her husband back. So why did Nate Fisher's handsome face pop into her thoughts? Another time, another place, a different life, maybe he would have been Kate's father. But it was this time, this place, this life, and she was on her own.

"How can she sue the pants off us? We all wear dresses."

Now was not the time to give in to her cuteness. "Your uncle sold that puppy to the lady who was just here. And when it comes time for the puppies to go to new homes—"

"But I don't want the puppies to go to new homes," Kate protested. "What's wrong with our home?"

It would do no good to explain that the hundreds of dollars the sale of the puppies would bring would help the household. A four-year-old's mind just didn't work like that. "Albie wanted the puppies to go to new homes. That's why he let Susie get puppies in her belly. So other people could have a dog like her."

272

# The Secrets We Keep

"I love them." Tears started welling again. Rachel might have expected this from Amelie, her more sensitive child. Amelie had been upset with the idea since she found out that Susie was having pups. It took getting the puppies into the world before it became real to Kate.

"We can keep one," Rachel said, hoping she didn't regret the decision. She wasn't looking forward to selling the dogs and losing that part of her brother, but she knew they needed the income from the sale and the flip side would be feeding five more dogs than they currently were. Just not possible.

"But I want that one," Kate cried.

"The one you had in your room?"

Kate nodded.

"I'm sorry, *liebschdi*, but that one is already spoken for."

"But it's the only one like that." Kate had started to sob.

Amelie came out of the barn and stopped in front of them. She dropped to the ground and sat cross-legged with her elbows braced on her knees and her chin propped in her palms.

"They're all unique," Rachel said, trying to decipher her daughter's love for the one particular dog. The same one that Judith Preston demanded. What was so special about the pooch that two people had to have it?

"He's the only one," Kate tearfully explained.

"The only one what?" Rachel looked up and met Amelie's gaze.

Her oldest daughter shrugged.

"He's the only one with a smooth belly."

"Their bellies are going to change. Remember? They are born white with black spots. Then as they grow they'll get more color, and they'll all have spots on their stomachs. Even this one."

"No." Kate hiccupped, and her despair was breaking Rachel's heart. If only she could figure out what made the dog so special to her daughter, then maybe she could ease that misery. "It's not the same."

"Show me," Rachel demanded. She needed to end this before her father got home and put a stop to it himself. She knew from past experience that her father didn't suffer foolishness. And Samuel Gingerich would definitely consider this to be foolishness.

She stood and reached out a hand to Kate. Then she pulled Amelie to her feet, and together the three of them made their way back to the barn.

It took only a moment for their eyes to adjust to the light, and they were quiet as they approached the dogs. Amelie held back as Kate barged into the stall and grabbed the little dog with the yellow string.

"Be gentle, Kate," Rachel warned. Kate was still learning about the fragileness of life and puppies.

Her daughter plopped down into the hay and turned the puppy onto its back, cradling it in the vee made by her crossed legs. "His belly," Kate said, smoothing a tiny hand over the puppy's stomach. "I like his smooth belly."

Rachel almost burst out laughing. "It's a girl puppy, *liebschdi*," she explained.

"I like her smooth belly," Kate corrected, and Rachel decided now was not the time for a gender lesson. "She's the only one with a smooth belly. I like to rub it."

Rachel knelt down next to her in the hay. One by one she picked up the dogs and gently turned them over onto their backs before returning them to their mother. All five left there were male dogs. Kate held the only female of the bunch.

"Well, if you want to keep one," Rachel started, "you'll have to take one of these without a smooth belly."

"But—"

## The Secrets We Keep

Rachel shook her head. "I'm sorry, baby girl, but that's all we have. You can take it or leave it." She didn't mean to be stern about the whole thing. But honestly, so much drama over one little dog. Judith had the bill of sale, and Albie had apparently taken the money, though Rachel wasn't sure if that amount was included in the wad of cash she had found in his bag or not. It didn't matter, though. Albie was gone and the girl puppy was sold. Kate was going to have to get over it. Sooner or later.

"I can still keep one of the others?" Kate asked.

"We can," Rachel said, including Amelie in the transaction. "But only one." One more mouth to feed and care for was enough.

But the altercation with Judith just proved that Albie had been thinking about money, thinking about leaving. He had written it in his journal, and Judith bore witness, whether she meant to or not. Why would someone who was planning on killing themselves take the time out to sell a puppy? It just didn't make sense.

Kate didn't look entirely satisfied with the transaction, but she relented. "Okay." She heaved a big sigh. "Can we name her Jennifer?"

Rachel laughed. "We're going to have to talk that one over."

# Chapter Eighteen

"I've got it."

Nate had stopped right there in the middle of Walmart to answer his phone when he recognized the number belonging to Shane Johnson. The other man had spoken without preamble.

"The autopsy report. It came in this morning."

"And?" Nate stopped and took a deep breath to combat the hard pounding of his heart. This was what they had been waiting for.

"I think you should come into the office. You can read it there, and then we can head out together and talk to the family."

Nate nodded and set the box of toothpaste on the nearest shelf. He hadn't brought enough toiletries with him for an extended stay, and it seemed that daily he was running out of one thing or another. But if the report was in, he might not need anything else. He might be on the road back home as early as tomorrow morning.

"I'll be there in ten," he told Shane, then left the store as quickly as possible.

His reception at the front desk was a little different this time. The tiny but fierce deputy stationed at the circular desk that

# The Secrets We Keep

guarded the rest of the offices nodded at him. "Third door on the left," she told him as he buzzed by. Shane was expecting him.

He rapped once on the smooth wood, then let himself in.

As chief deputy, Shane had a large-enough office, but perhaps only half what the sheriff boasted. There were pictures on the pale-blue walls, Shane with various celebrities who had come through for one reason or another, as well as framed diplomas and top certifications.

"That was quick." Shane stood as he entered the room.

Nate nodded. "This is the reason I'm still here," he told Shane as they shook hands.

Shane waited until Nate had settled himself in the chair in front of him before pushing the file folder across the desk. "It's all there," he said, sitting back in his chair. The leather creaked with the movement. "Not exactly what you were hoping for."

Nate hesitated only a moment before picking up the file and thumbing through it. He scanned the words, looking for whatever proof was needed for Rachel to be satisfied. "It says here that—"

"He died from asphyxiation," Shane offered. "A collapsed larynx."

"But what about the skull fracture?"

*I've never seen a skull fracture commit suicide.*

Shane shook his head. "I don't know how he got it, and apparently it's quite possible that someone else helped him hang himself. Or maybe when the old man cut him down. But with no evidence to support any theory of two people in the barn that night, it remains just that, a theory. Weakly supported by the possibility of previous injury."

Which meant they had nothing. "I don't think Albie killed himself. He was planning on leaving. Not dying."

"Regardless," Shane said. "Without evidence . . ."

"What about the barn? There was nothing?"

277

# Amy Lillard

"We didn't even know it was a possible crime scene until days later. Any evidence that might have been found was lost a long time ago. There's nothing to link Chance Longacre or any of his friends to this. Unless there's something in the journal pages that you would like to share."

"No. And for the record. I don't believe Chance is guilty of any wrongdoing," Nate started.

One of Shane's brows rose, and he sat up a little straighter in his seat. "Would you care to explain that?"

Nate gave him a sad smile. "No." He let the file drop back onto the desk with a disheartened slap. "When are you planning on telling the family?" Assuming that he hadn't already. But Nate had a feeling that Shane wanted to run it by him first.

"I was hoping that you might help us out with that."

"This is out of my jurisdiction," Nate replied. Even so, he hated the thought of being the one to tell Rachel the awful truth about her brother's death. Not who had killed him or the certainty that he had committed an unthinkable sin, but that they would never know the whole truth.

Either way, her brother wasn't coming back.

"You relate well with the family. It would be better accepted coming from you."

"I doubt that." The last thing he would be at the Gingerich-Hostetlers was well received. Not after—

"I did a little investigating of my own," Shane started. "A kill in the line of duty . . ."

"I didn't come here to talk about that." Nate felt the walls closing in around him.

"It's a terrible thing. Not that I've had to bear that burden. But I know some who have. And about half of those never carried a gun

# The Secrets We Keep

again." He looked pointedly at Nate, who obviously wasn't carrying a firearm.

"I'm out of my jurisdiction."

"Keep telling yourself that," Shane said. "Maybe eventually you'll believe it. Or maybe you'll come to realize that there are other things out there for guys like us."

Guys like us.

He could only assume he meant the good guys. The cowboys. The ones in the white hats.

Rachel's daughter Kate filled his thoughts. She would be missing her uncle. Nate should go talk to the family. As hard as it would be, Shane was right: It would be better coming from him. And after that . . . he was turning in his good-guy badge. Forever.

He picked the file back up. "You're driving," was all he said.

\* \* \*

The sound of a car engine close by brought Rachel to her feet. She hopped up from her place at the table, where she had been snapping the first of the green beans from her garden while Miri played in the sand Rachel kept for her. It always made a huge mess, but her sister derived such joy from the activity that she couldn't fuss about cleanup. Right now Miri needed as much joy as she could muster.

All day a feeling of dread and anxiousness had plagued her. Something in the air. Like a storm brewing. A storm she couldn't see. So she had kept herself busy while she waited for the other shoe to drop. Whatever that shoe might be.

She peeked out the window just as Nathan and the other detective got out of one of the black sheriff's cars. Nathan had a file in one hand and a grim look on his face. Whatever had brought them out, it wasn't good news.

Amy Lillard

Rachel glanced back at Miri and the sand she had spread over half the kitchen. She didn't have time to clean that up now. Instead she ran her hands down her front, wishing she could put on a clean apron, but there was no time for that either. She tugged on each side of her prayer covering and straightened her shoulders. It was the autopsy report. Had to be. But was she ready for this?

With more confidence than she actually felt, she marched toward the door and opened it. The men had just reached the porch and drew back with her sudden movement.

"I saw you through the window," she explained.

"Can we come in?" Nathan asked. "We have the results of Albie's autopsy."

"Oh." She stopped. Her breath stopped. It was one thing to think it and another to hear it said out loud. This was it. She had to tell herself to move again. Breathe again. "*Jah*," she finally said, and stepped aside for them to enter.

Nathan had been in the house too many times to count, but she wondered if the other man had ever seen the inside of an Amish home. He looked around, and she could almost see him gauging the life they lived and how different it was from his. What she couldn't tell was whether he considered himself superior or felt pity for the poor Amish. People usually held one feeling or the other.

"I'm sorry. Miri has been playing." She gestured toward the sand spread across the table as far as her sister could reach. It was also on the floor, but neither man seemed to give it a second glance.

"It's fine," Nathan said, shooting her a melancholy smile. It was the same one he'd given her when he told her he was leaving to play baseball, the same one he'd flashed when he had come back for Mattie's funeral only to flit away again like an elusive dream.

280

# The Secrets We Keep

That was what he had become for her: an unrealized fantasy. "We can sit on the other end." He gestured toward the far side of the table, and Rachel nodded. What had she expected? That he would refuse to tell her the results because of some sand on the floor? She knew him better than that. Or perhaps that was what she had been hoping, because judging by the grim line of both of their mouths, the news wasn't what she wanted to hear.

"Can I get you some coffee? Or some cake? I'm teaching Amelie to bake this summer, and—"

"Sit down, Rachel," Nathan quietly commanded.

She did as he bade, perching on the chair at the end of the table. Her *dat*'s chair.

"Is your father around?"

As if in response, Miri laughed and clapped her hands. If her behavior was concerning to the other detective, he didn't show it.

"He's over at the other house."

Nathan seemed to think about it a moment. "Do you want me to drive over and get him?"

Rachel shook her head. She didn't think she could wait that long to hear the news. Even if it wasn't something she wanted to be the truth. Or maybe because it wasn't. Better to get it over with as soon as possible.

"Okay." Nathan nodded to Shane, and the two men sat on either side of her. Nathan opened the file that contained the written results of her brother's autopsy.

"They didn't do it," she said softly, tears filling her eyes. Her brother's body would be brought back and placed outside the cemetery, right where he had been before. She had done all of this for naught.

"It's not that simple," Nathan started. "Here's what we know: Albie had injuries to his face. An apparent broken nose, but the

281

skin and other tissues were too far gone for them to see much else concerning any injuries he might have sustained before . . . the hanging."

Injuries sustained. Was the boy she had fallen in love with hidden inside the man he had become? Nathan of the old times would have never said anything like *injuries sustained*. It just went to prove how much time had passed. How much had changed. How it would never go back to where it had been.

"It was even impossible to tell if the broken nose happened before or after."

She opened her mouth to protest, but Nathan shook his head to silence her. "We don't know for certain, since the body was moved. The broken nose could have happened when your father . . . took him down."

He was being as gentle about things as he could, but the words were horrifying to her. She had left the barn with Kate before her father completed the task. She had no idea how he had treated the body after she left. But surely . . .

"Your brother had a skull fracture," Nathan continued. "This is unusual to see in someone who turns around and hangs themselves, and the coroner was fairly certain that the injury was sustained before the hanging."

"What exactly does that mean?" Rachel asked.

"It means they don't know any more than you do."

They all turned as her father came into the house. The screen door slammed behind him. He pulled off his work gloves and looked from one man to the other, then his gaze fell to his eldest daughter.

Miri laughed as if it all were some big joke.

Rachel pushed to her feet and ran nervous hands down the sides of her skirts. "I'm not sure—" She hadn't known what she

## The Secrets We Keep

was going to say, but she was saved the task of having to make up something when her father turned and pinned Nathan with his hard gaze.

"Nathan Fisher, you are shunned and not welcome in my home."

Rachel wanted to protest, but she couldn't. It was the truth. Nathan was under the *Bann*, and her father had the right to ask him to leave.

It was a long moment before Nathan pushed to his feet. The chair scraped loudly against the floor as he ran it back into place under the table.

He looked at her for a moment more, then nodded. "Rachel," he said. Her name on his lips came out a bit rusty but held the finality of goodbye. Then without another word, he let himself out of the house.

She wanted to run after him. She wanted to tell him a million things that she had never told him and a million more that she had said so often over the years they were together. But she stayed in place as if glued there by her father's anger.

The other cop cleared his throat. "What it means," he started, as if he needed to impart the news so he too could make an escape, "is that your brother died from asphyxiation. From hanging. Yes, he sustained a traumatic head injury, which would make it seem that perhaps there was a third party involved, but without evidence, no other charges can be filed."

"So as far as you're concerned, he committed suicide." She could barely say the word. It was all for nothing. She had caused family upheaval, kept Nathan in town when she knew he wanted to leave. She had upset her father, her children, her neighbors, and her sister. All so they could bury her brother right back where he had already been laid to rest in shame.

The man stood, picked up the file, and nodded. "I'm sorry. But yes, as far as we are concerned, his death was at his own hands."

* * *

Nate pushed out of the house and took a couple of deep breaths to still the anger rising in him. He had no call to be angry. Samuel Gingerich was well within his rights to ask Nate to leave, but Nate had hoped that time had taken the edge off some of the bad feelings. Well, he'd been wrong about that one. It was difficult when the years had mellowed him. He expected everyone to be as forgiving. After all, he had forgiven himself. But that was not the case here.

He propped his hands on his hips and sucked in another deep breath. He shouldn't have come here. But the idea of seeing Rachel one more time before he left town had been too enticing to let go.

"Hi."

He whirled around as Rachel's young daughter, Kate, came out of the barn, carrying a tiny white puppy with black ears and a black splotch surrounding one eye.

"What have you got there?" he asked. Just what he needed to dispel the hate and bad feelings swirling around inside him. The utter cuteness of a recently born puppy.

"She's my favorite," Kate said proudly, stroking the pup with one hand as she cradled it in the other. "Though Mamm says she won't stay this color. None of them will."

Blue heelers, Nate thought. Like the one lounging under the shade of the barn eaves. "Does she have a name?"

She shook her head. "Not yet. Mamm's going to sell the rest of them. Amelie and I get to choose one to keep, but I can still have a favorite that's not the same as hers."

"Of course you can," he said, restraining his smile.

"Do you want to see the rest of them?"

# The Secrets We Keep

"Are they in the barn?"

She gave him a *duh* look and motioned for him to follow her.

It was something of a cheap shot to use a little girl as the means to get into the big red building, but he had been wanting to see where Albie had killed himself ever since he found out about the head injury.

He just couldn't let that go. How did a kid with a skull fracture hang himself? *Why* would a kid with a skull fracture kill himself?

He had read the coroner's report. It was complicated and had a lot of two-inch-long medical words, but he understood enough to know that the head injury would have killed Albie sooner rather than later. It might not have been his actual cause of death, but if he hadn't been hung, then it would have been . . . eventually. Nate couldn't say *hung himself*. He didn't believe it. Not for a minute. And it had nothing to do with Rachel and her beliefs about the bullying teens. This was about sheer medical evidence. Too bad all the other evidence had been compromised.

Nate stepped into the dim barn and blinked a couple of times so that his eyes could adjust. It looked the way it always had, even back twelve years ago. There were changes, of course—not big ones. A few different diesel-powered machines, but everything else looked to be the same.

"They're down this way," Kate said, taking his hand and leading him toward the back stalls of the barn.

His eyes had adjusted now, and he could see the large beam in the middle of the barn. That had to be where Albie had been hanging. He could have thrown the rope over the beam, climbed into the loft, and jumped.

But why?

That was the question of the hour, and yet it had no viable answer. None believable, at any rate.

285

Nate turned his attention back to the mini Rachel who tugged on his hand. "Are you coming?"

"Yes."

He allowed her to lead him to where the mama dog had set up a place for them in the last stall. If Nate was remembering right, it had been used for storage before, in the time when he'd snuck in here to be out of the cold while he waited for Rachel.

There were six puppies in all, squirming and grunting and rooting around while their mother nudged them back into place and licked a few to show her love. She eyed Kate with sad eyes, as if she knew that soon her puppies would be hers no more.

"I think you should put her down now," Nate said gently.

"That's what Mamm always says." Kate shot him a look.

"You have a smart *mamm*," he replied. "You remember to listen to her."

She seemed to think about it a minute. Nate was about to pull out the ol' white-hat cowboy good-guy card when she finally nodded. "Okay. But I want to come out later and see them. I got to make sure that she's my favorite-favorite."

"Gotcha." He hid his smile as she placed the pup back with its mama and littermates.

The mama immediately sniffed her to make sure she was all right, then gave her a few firm licks to clean her or mark her or just to let her know she was loved, Nate wasn't sure which.

"Okay, let's go," he said, backing from the stall, then making his way out toward the doors. He couldn't help but stop once more and gaze up at the beam. Yeah, that had to be the one. But it was really too far away from the loft edge for Albie to have been able to stand in the hay and tie the rope to the beam. But there were no others in a good position for that either.

# The Secrets We Keep

He shook his head. It didn't matter. There was no evidence to say that another might have helped him hang himself. But if what he was seeing was true . . .

One of the machines caught his eye. He recognized the big yellow casing on the diesel engine used to run the air compressor. In turn, the air was used to power tools. Many Amish in the area had permission to use pneumatic tools to craft furniture and other items as well as streamline building. The same process was used over at the Amish-run sawmill. What he didn't recognize was the large air compressor sitting next to the engine. Things changed, but it wasn't the newness that captured his attention; it was the large dark stain down one side of the machine. Oil and dirt from a fuel overpour? Or something else altogether?

"The door's this way," Kate said as he veered off toward that side of the barn.

"I'll be right there," he told her absently. He retrieved his cell phone from his pocket and thumbed on the flashlight app.

He felt the tension leave his shoulders as he saw the thickness of the stain. Fuel mixed with hay dust and dirt. That was all it was. And a drip of red paint that probably had come from using the machine to power a sprayer to paint the outside of the barn. Though he hadn't realized that he was so keyed up about it until the feeling had passed. What had he expected? That he would find some evidence that Albie had been injured here and then strung up to make it look like a suicide?

As the thought came to him, he realized that was exactly what he was looking for. Because that was the only explanation for what had happened to him that fit with his injuries and the stories surrounding his death and the facts of the case. The only thing missing: evidence.

# Amy Lillard

He straightened up, realizing that if he could, he would take a sample of the paint smear and send it to the lab for testing. But he couldn't, and even if it ended up being something more sinister than paint, it proved nothing more than what it was. That wouldn't point a finger at how it got there. But if it wasn't just paint, then perhaps that would give another plausible explanation. A scuffle in the barn. Albie falls, hits his head, and the perpetrator panics, decides to string him up and make the whole thing look like a suicide.

Who?

But he was all out of suspects.

"Are you coming?" Kate insisted, hovering by the barn door, waiting for him to come with her, to step out into the bright Mississippi sunshine. It was such a difference in atmosphere that he almost shivered just thinking about it.

"Yeah." He straightened and followed her out the door.

"There you are." Shane shook his head as Nate came out of the barn. "It's time to go."

Nate glanced over to the porch where Samuel stood, waiting impatiently for the two of them to get off his property. "Outstay your welcome, did you?"

Shane made a face somewhere between a grimace and an eye roll. "Just get in the car."

"Bye," Kate said from beside him. She moved toward the porch and sat down on the steps. He couldn't say he wasn't a little thankful that she had perched between them and her grandfather. The man looked mad enough to tear them limb from limb. Forget *turn the other cheek*; he wanted them gone.

"Bye, Kate."

She beamed. "You remember my name."

"Of course I do," he said, so very aware of Samuel Gingerich watching his every move. "Because it rhymes with mine. Nate."

## The Secrets We Keep

"Funny." Kate giggled.

"Time to go, Fish." Shane slapped the top of the car.

Nate gave Samuel one final look. "I'm sorry for your loss."

The expression on Samuel's face was thunderous, but Nate knew he had hit a nerve. Samuel didn't want him to be kind to him. He wanted him gone. He wanted Nate to leave his family, his daughter, alone. He was staunch in his beliefs. Nate had broken the rules, and there was only one way to come back from that. A ritual of confession and forgiveness that Nate had never felt compelled to complete.

He let himself into the car, and Shane started the engine. "Finally," Nate said as he put the car into gear.

"What would you have to do to get back in with the church?" Shane asked as they drove along. He hadn't said a word as they pulled away, Kate waving and Samuel scowling. Somewhere inside the house, Nate knew that Rachel was watching as they left. He could feel her gaze on him as sure as her touch had been so many years ago.

"It's not something I'm willing to do," Nate said, stretching his legs and doing his best to settle himself down. He wished he had never come out here with Shane, but he hadn't been able to resist the chance to see Rachel one last time and to see this through.

One last time.

That was it. The last time he would ever see her. He didn't think he would ever stop loving her. Ever stop wanting her. Ever stop wishing things could have been different, but that was what made life such a bitch.

"No, I mean, we hear about shunning and such, but out here we don't understand what that really means, you know?"

He nodded and started to collect his thoughts. "What most *Englisch* don't understand about shunning is that it's not a punishment. The Amish shun to bring that person back round."

Shane thought about it a moment. "Kinda like tough love. *Here's what you're missing.*"

"Right. But for those of us who leave and don't come back, there's no time of forgiveness. Of acknowledging that we want to get back what we had before."

"For argument's sake, let's say you want to go back and pick up your life where you left off."

"Not happening." The words seemed to shoot from him of their own accord. There was no way he could return to a Plain lifestyle. His own religious doubts aside, simply too much time had passed. He wasn't the same kid who had left with big dreams of playing baseball and saving his sister's life.

"Humor me here. I'm trying to understand," Shane said.

"For argument's sake, if I wanted to rejoin the church, I would have to talk to the elders first. Tell them my intentions. They would talk to the church board, but that would be a formality. Then I would go in front of the church and confess all my sins. The church would vote, and I would have to serve a time of being accepted back. I would still be shunned until I proved that I was sincere about returning." Especially since he had been gone so long.

Shane whistled low under his breath. "That's something else."

"Are you just trying to distract me from what just happened?"

"I think I'm trying to distract myself." He pulled his car into Lorie's drive. There was just enough room for him to fit right behind Nate's truck. "Thanks for going with me," Shane said. "If I had known all that, I wouldn't have asked you."

"No bother. Even knowing all that, I went." For her. Always for Rachel.

Nate started to get out of the car.

"Are you out of here tomorrow?" Shane asked.

## The Secrets We Keep

That was something Nate hadn't been allowing himself to think about. Tomorrow. After today he had no reason to remain in Cedar Creek. No reason to not return to Tulsa.

"Yeah," he said. But the word barely made it past the lump in his throat.

Shane stuck out a hand. "It was good seeing you again."

Nate shook it and gave his friend a melancholy smile. "You too." Then he got out of the car and went inside the tiny apartment to get his things together.

# Chapter Nineteen

That evening Nate lay on his bed stewing. At least that was what his sister Sarah would have called it. He kept turning over the day's events in his head, replaying them, aligning them with the facts and cutting them with his emotions until he felt like he had some control over the day.

And then Shane's questions about shunning. It had Nate thinking about what it would really be like to come back, bend the knee and confess the transgressions of the last twelve years. Starting with but not limited to walking away from the only woman he had ever truly loved, breaking her heart, and moving on without a backward glance.

But that had been because if he had looked back, he would have stayed. And that would have been disastrous for them both. Leaving the Amish was no small feat, but spending four years with freedoms and conveniences and rules that didn't involve God at every turn and then coming back—that was next to impossible.

So he stewed.

How would he feel telling everyone he had ever known growing up that he had killed a man, a boy really, for pulling a toy on him?

# The Secrets We Keep

It wasn't that simple, he told himself. There was much more to the incident than he was allowing himself to factor in, but those facts were still the facts.

How did a person kill another and go on? Because the review board said it was a "clean kill"? How could any kill be clean? The whole of it was messy.

When he'd gotten back to the apartment, he had only wanted to be alone. He had too much in his head. Emotions, memories, regrets.

Lorie must have been watching for his return. She was at his door within a couple of minutes of him letting himself back in, telling him she had enchiladas in the oven and homemade salsa from a recipe she had picked up the last time she had gone to Mexico sitting on the counter. He had turned her down. She looked disappointed, play-pouted a little to show she didn't like his decision, but didn't press the matter. Truthfully, he had the feeling that she was offering a bit more than supper, and though it would give him a distraction that he desperately needed, he walked away. Just one more tie to Mississippi he didn't need.

Instead he had gone to the sandwich shop across from the motel. He'd had to drive across town to get there, but it was an excuse to look at Cedar Creek and Pontotoc one more time before he left tomorrow.

He hadn't told Lorie he was heading out. He had paid her for a full week, and he wouldn't ask for a refund. Nor would he tell her he was leaving until the morning.

He blew out a breath and stared at the ceiling. More than ever, he felt like he was in limbo. One more night here, and then tomorrow he would go back to Oklahoma. Then he would start to piece together a new life. It wasn't like he hadn't started over before. But, frankly, it was getting tiresome, defining himself again and again.

293

He wished just once he knew who he was and it would stick. Amish farmer, baseball player, deputy sheriff.

Rachel's daughter Kate popped into his thoughts, her pudgy hands propped on her tiny hips as she surveyed the puppies with a critical eye. She wanted to make sure that the one pup was her favorite-favorite.

Oh, to be so sure of everything that easily. It wasn't that he missed those days; he missed the surety of life. The things that just were. Get up in the morning. Milk the cow, feed the chickens, put the horses out in the pasture. Then as time passed, everything got more and more complicated, even in the simplicity that others saw in the Amish world. Farming was hard work even with the use of diesel-fueled equipment in the barn. The women had it even harder. No indoor plumbing. No ease of running to the store for everything they needed. They grew huge family gardens on top of food to sell, like corn and tomatoes. They were always working, taking care of children, canning, sewing, gardening. It never stopped.

But that was no longer his world.

He should call Bree and tell her he was leaving in the morning. There was truly nothing keeping him here now. Now that the autopsy results were back, he needed to be going home. No, there was nothing keeping him here except time and a nagging feeling that he was missing something.

At first, he had chalked it up to that limbo status again, but now he knew it was something else, though he wasn't sure what. It was that same feeling you got when you couldn't remember if the stove was turned off or the iron still heating. A nagging feeling that made him trawl back through the day's events—hell, the events of the last two weeks—to see what he had forgotten. That imperative something that seemed as significant as life and death.

# The Secrets We Keep

Possibly it was the clue he had found that day. Potential clue, he should say. Blood or paint? Would it have made a difference? Maybe. If it was blood, Albie's blood, and they could somehow get a confession from whoever he had encountered in the barn that night?

Nate jackknifed on the bed, sitting straight up as the pieces all clicked into place.

Two weeks ago. Forgiveness. Acceptance. A quick burial and puppies.

It all fit.

He pulled on his boots and settled his hat gingerly onto his head. Then, for the first time in a long time, he threaded his holster through his belt and press checked his gun to make sure it was loaded.

Dark was just settling around the farm when he pulled into the drive at the Gingerich homestead. He cut the truck's engine, wondering once again, as he had several times on the trip out, if he should have called Shane for backup. But if his hunches were correct, what good would it do to send an old man to jail? Nate just needed to know the truth for himself.

"Nathan." Rachel came out onto the porch, breathless and worried. Her father had told him to leave once today. Then her gaze fell to the firearm on his hip. She shook her head. "What are you doing here?"

"I need to talk to your *dat*," he said. His words sounded stiff and unyielding, but his heart pounded in his chest. Even as he knew the truth. He didn't want it to be the truth. Yet he still needed Samuel to tell him.

"I thought I told you to get out of here, Nathan Fisher." Samuel came out onto the porch to stand next to his daughter. Her two girls followed close behind.

295

"Mamm?" Only Kate spoke, but Nate could see Amelie peek her head around her mother on the other side.

"Samuel. Let's do this like men." He gave a pointed nod toward the females clustered around the older man.

"Go back in the house, Rachel, and take them with you."

There was a small moment when Nate thought she might protest, argue and hold her ground, but she was a mother first, and she would protect her children before anything else.

She turned to go back into the house as Samuel started down the porch steps.

"Let's talk in the barn," Nate invited.

Samuel's steps stuttered. He paused. "Why?"

"I want to ask you a couple of questions about the night Albie died."

It would have been the perfect time for him to protest, to declare they should stay outside even as darkness was about to fall. But he didn't. Maybe Samuel was as tired of the deception as everyone else around him was of not knowing.

Samuel slid open the door and stepped inside. He turned on a battery-operated lantern situated close to the door. "What's this all about?" His demand was halfhearted and tired.

"I think you know."

"Then why are you asking me?" He shook his head. "Speak your piece, Nathan."

"I know you didn't mean to do it. How could you? He was your son. But what did he tell you beforehand? Before you pushed him and knocked him into the air compressor? And why in God's name did you string him up like a side of beef?"

"It is an abomination." Samuel's voice trembled. "A boy can't—" He stopped and shook his head. Then tears filled his eyes. "He was going to leave. He was all packed and ready. I came out here to check

296

# The Secrets We Keep

on Susie and found him getting his things together. Maybe he had been planning it for a while. He already had a bag packed."

Nate nodded but didn't say anything. He didn't want to stop the flow now that the truth was finally coming out.

"Those boys had already roughed him up. I thought it was because he was Amish, different, you know. Not that—" He broke off once more, then seemed to collect his thoughts. "It was an accident. He told me that . . . that . . ." Samuel didn't seem to be able to go on.

"That he was gay," Nate supplied, hoping to jump-start the story once more. He could only imagine how hard it was for a devout man like Samuel Gingerich to admit to having what he considered to be a deviant son.

"*Jah*," he whispered. "I told him he could go away for a while, get counseling, but he said he didn't want to be sent away. That he would rather leave on his own terms than have to go through all that."

"You pushed him," Nate said.

"I shook him. I thought I would get some sense into him somehow. But when I let him go, he lost his footing. I didn't mean for him to hit his head. There was so much blood everywhere. I couldn't leave him like that."

"And you couldn't tell the truth."

"It's an abomination."

"So is suicide," Nate reminded him.

"I would rather have that on his standing than—" He shook his head once more and squeaked out a choked cough.

"So you hanged him. Not knowing that he was still alive."

That was when Samuel Gingerich hit his knees. Tears streamed down his face as he clasped his hands together and looked to heaven. "I didn't know. I swear I didn't. I wouldn't have otherwise. I loved him. He was my son."

Nate had nothing to say to that. He was sick to his stomach. So much deception. So much hate. So many unnecessary deaths and lies. This was just another to add to the tally.

Samuel lowered his head and sobbed, the sound heart wrenching and raw. Nate had no doubt that Samuel had had the best intentions in his heart. But good intentions or not, there wasn't a way around the truth.

Nate waited several minutes for Samuel to collect himself.

The other man sniffed and wiped his face on his sleeve. "What are you going to do?" he finally asked.

What *was* he going to do?

So far, he was the only one who had figured out that Samuel was the "murderer," but what good would it do for a man to go to prison for accidentally killing his son in the name of saving his reputation in the community? It wasn't like Samuel was a danger to anyone else around him.

Had anyone asked Nate that same question three months ago, he would have told them unequivocally: Send him to jail. A law had been broken, and a price had to be paid. But that was before he himself had gotten away with legal murder. Now the black and the white weren't so defined and the shades of gray had begun creeping in.

Just another reason it was time to give up his badge.

"I'm not going to do anything, Samuel. If you can live with what you've done, I can too." But he was talking about Samuel's transgressions and not his own. He had a great deal to work out with himself. And one thing was certain: He couldn't do it and try to uphold laws that seemed made to be bent, if not broken.

Samuel pushed to his feet but didn't respond, other than to wipe his nose once more. He eyed Nate warily, as if he were a snake that had just promised not to strike. But Nate was nothing if not serious. This wasn't for him to judge.

# The Secrets We Keep

The barn door slid open, and Shane stepped inside. Two uniformed officers followed behind him, chased by the red and blue swirling lights of a sheriff's patrol car. Outside, night had fallen.

One deputy had his gun pulled and pointed toward the ground, while the other carried handcuffs at the ready.

Samuel looked back to Nate, distrust lighting his features.

"Not my circus," Nate said with a shake of his head.

Shane took a moment to acknowledge his friend. "What are you doing out here?"

He shrugged. "Just saying my goodbyes."

Shane seemed to buy the reason and turned back to the older man. "Samuel Gingerich, I'm placing you under arrest for abuse of a corpse."

One of the uniforms grabbed Samuel's hand and urged it behind his back. Samuel didn't say a word as the man continued to handcuff him, then read him his Miranda rights.

The party moved out of the barn into the twirling color of lights. Nate followed behind, not saying anything at all. Neither did Samuel, and Nate wondered briefly if he would eventually confess to what he had done or if he would continue to keep it to himself. Either way, Nate had a feeling his time in jail would be minimal. No record. No priors. Sure, he had moved a body, more than once, but the intent hadn't been malicious. The DA had more important things to prosecute. He hoped so, at least. For Rachel's sake.

"Nathan?" She rushed over to him, grabbing his arm. "Are they arresting Dat? Why are they arresting my *dat*? What did you do?" She started to hit him in the chest, but he captured her wrist and used his hold to pull her close.

"Shhh . . ." He cradled her to him, holding her still as she began to cry.

"I don't understand," she said as they loaded her father into the back of one of the police cars. "I don't understand."

Shane shot Nate a look, but he nodded. He had this. Shane had to do what Shane had to do. Nate would comfort Rachel as best he could. And then . . .

And then nothing. It was over. Time to go home.

As the last of the lights disappeared, Nate felt Rachel go slack in his arms.

"Where are the girls?" he asked her quietly.

She hiccupped lightly and pushed away from him. "Upstairs," she whispered. "Asleep, I hope."

Through all this?

"Their bedrooms are in the back of the house," Rachel explained. Which meant the lights wouldn't have been shining in their windows. "And Kate . . ." She gave a gloomy laugh. "Kate can sleep through anything."

Even her *dawdi* being arrested.

"Mamm?" Amelie had come out onto the porch. "What's going on?"

Rachel turned toward her elder daughter. "It's okay, *liebschdi*. Go back to bed. Everything's fine." But they both knew it wasn't.

At first, Nate thought Amelie might protest.

And as she stood there in the moonlight, there was something familiar about the tilt of her head or the lilt of her chin, he wasn't sure which. Was it because she just looked so much like her mother? Then she nodded. The moment was broken as she turned to go back inside as her *mamm* had told her to do.

"Why did you do that, Nathan? Why did you bring the police out here?"

# The Secrets We Keep

"I didn't, Rachel. The charge against him has always been on the table. He moved your brother's body without notifying the police of his death. That one's not on me."

She pressed the back of her hand to her mouth. He could almost see her thoughts swirling around inside her head. How long would her father be gone? What was she going to do without him?

Her *dat* might be a son of a bitch, might have always been, but she depended on him now more than ever. Crops needed to be tended, animals cared for. She wouldn't be able to do it all without him.

*Not my problem,* he told himself. The community would rally around her. They would be there for Rachel and her girls. Nate couldn't stay. He wouldn't be welcome. It was not on him to be there.

"He'll have an arraignment tomorrow or the next day. They'll probably set his bail then. If you can get the money together, they'll release him until the pretrial hearing." He shook his head. There was a lot to the process for someone who was experienced in such matters. It would be overwhelming to a grief-stricken Amish woman who had never dealt with the courts and the police in her life. "A public defender will be assigned to the case," he tried again. "He or she will be able to help you. But your father will be gone for a couple of weeks at least. After that . . ." He had no answer for her.

"Go," she coldly told him.

He hadn't noticed the change in her while he had been trying to explain her father's situation. The shift in her demeanor was sudden enough that it took him off guard. "I'm sorry?"

"Go," she said again. "Get off my property. Dat was right about you, Nathan Fisher. You are nothing but trouble."

301

# Chapter Twenty

Her words echoed around in his head all during his sleepless night. *Nothing but trouble.*

He supposed to the conservative people of his past, he was just that. A black sheep, a rebel. A bad example for all who came after him.

Never in his life had he wanted that stigma.

He had left the Amish to save his sister. He had come back to bury her. Became a cop to do good. Returned once more to see his father buried. The unwelcome had been bigger than he could have ever imagined. But he was one of the good guys, wasn't he? White hat, shiny badge?

It all meant nothing now.

He got up the next morning with sand in his eyes and his throat clogged with remorse. Time to go home.

He grabbed his things and walked out to the porch, where Lorie waited.

"I was hoping you might stay a little longer," she said for a greeting.

He shot her a smile, as encouraging as he could muster. "You'll find a new renter soon."

She snagged his gaze, hers turning hot as she stared at him. "I wasn't worried about the apartment."

## The Secrets We Keep

"I'm glad I got to meet you, Lorie Atwood."

She smiled and lifted her coffee cup to him in salute. "You too, Nate Fisher. And speaking of—" She stood and fetched a travel mug from the table next to her white wooden chair. "A coffee for the road."

"Thank you." He shifted his meager belongings into one hand and accepted the mug from her.

"I didn't add anything to it. I figured you liked it black."

"You figured right," he said with a nod.

She grinned at her correct choice. "Yeah, all you macho cowboys like it the same."

To her he was a macho cowboy. That almost made it worth it to stay around for a while. But he knew he would just be prolonging the inevitable. It was time to go home and face whatever was next.

Besides, as strange as it sounded, he missed his cat.

Nate nodded once more to Lorie, allowed the longing for what might have been to wash over him, then turned toward his truck.

He tossed his things into the back seat and opened the driver's side door. He settled in, aware that Lorie stood on the porch, watching his every move. She was sexy and breezy in her summertime dress, blond hair pulled back in one of those clippy things women used. But looking at her made him wonder what Rachel was doing at that moment. Lorie had everything together. A job at the bank, a house that was paid for, and the tiniest apartment in Pontotoc for rent. For Rachel, the struggle had just begun.

He started the engine and gave the woman in front of him a small wave. Then he picked up his phone and texted the woman waiting at the other end. Bree.

*Be home this evening. How about dinner?*

\* \* \*

It was three days before he got up the nerve to get himself back to the sheriff's office. He couldn't say it was good to be home. Tulsa didn't feel like home any longer.

He had arrived back to his apartment just in time to take Bree to a late supper. She stared at him all through the meal until he felt like some bacterial specimen under a microscope.

"What?" he'd asked her.

She shook her head. "Nothing."

But they both knew he had changed. Something inside him had shifted, and it would never go back in place again.

When they returned to their apartment building, he expected her to invite him in. He needed the distraction her luscious curves could provide, but at the same time he couldn't stomach using her to forget another.

Instead of a nightcap, she had given him the bag of cat food she had bought and sent him on his way with a sad smile.

He had spent the rest of the night on the couch with Satchel curled up in his lap as a reaired baseball game played on the television.

Everything was the same. And it was all different.

It took three days for him to accept the truth of it. Accept it, come to terms with it. Even though he had no idea what was next, he knew this was the first step into the unknown.

So he'd gotten into his truck this morning and driven downtown.

Travis was coming out of the Faulkner Building as Nate was going in.

"I didn't know you were back," his scarecrow of a friend stated.

# The Secrets We Keep

"Yeah," was all Nate could manage. He was back, but he wasn't. *You don't have to go home, but you can't stay here.*

"Going in to see the captain?"

Nate nodded.

Travis studied him for a moment, then gave a small dip of his chin. "Keep in touch, okay?"

Nate didn't have to ask how his friend knew. He was a detective, and as much as Nate was trying to hide his true feelings on the matter, he was sure the pain and confusion he felt showed in his eyes.

Nate reached out a hand to shake. Travis took it and pulled him into a tight hug. He slapped Nate on the back a couple of times, then released him. "They're losing a good one."

"Stay safe," Nate told him.

Travis gave a quick nod, then moved away.

Nate pushed inside and made his way to the detective's offices. Captain Gary Holland was seated at his desk, talking on the phone, when Nate walked in. Nate waited patiently for the man to conclude the call.

When the captain hung up the receiver, Nate laid his firearm and his badge on the desk.

"Can we talk about this?"

Nate shook his head. "There's nothing to talk about."

"It was a clean shooting."

"Maybe," Nate conceded, "but I still took a life." He had been told his entire life that it was a sin to kill, and he had put those lessons on hold when he'd signed on to be a deputy. Now they were back in his face, haunting his dreams and pushing him to start again.

The captain stared at the badge for a moment more before reaching out and picking up the weapon. He shoved it into his desk drawer. "You know if you ever want to come back . . ."

305

"I appreciate that," Nate said. "But I'm done with law enforcement."

"What are you going to do?"

That remained to be seen, but he wanted something that didn't require him to wear a gun. He didn't want that responsibility any longer. It weighed too heavy on his heart. "I don't know," he truthfully stated. "Something else."

He took a few more minutes to straighten out his resignation, then made his way back out to his truck. He should be feeling free. He should be feeling like the world was his oyster, just waiting for him to come and conquer it. Instead he felt old and sad. Adrift.

Nate climbed back into his pickup truck and headed for home. He had just pulled into the apartment complex when his phone rang.

The number wasn't familiar. It was a 662 number. Mississippi.

He hit the green circle to accept the call, a little surprised to hear Shane's voice on the other end of the line.

"We have another death in Cedar Creek," he said without greeting. "In the Amish community," he clarified. "A possible homicide."

*Not my problem,* Nate wanted to say, but he choked on those words. "Who?" he asked instead.

"Jacob Yoder."

"The bishop?"

"Yep."

"That's too bad," Nate said, wondering why Shane was calling him. "I hate to hear that."

"What's too bad is that no one Amish is willing to speak to us."

"That sounds about right."

"I need an assist."

# The Secrets We Keep

"From me? I just resigned my commission."

"Perfect," Shane said. "You're free to get your ass here and do some real investigative work."

"No." The word shot from his mouth like a bullet from a gun. "I'm out of the cop business."

"I need you, Nate. Without you, we might not be able to get the information to solve this case."

"I'm excommunicated. No one's going to talk to me." It was the bald truth.

"They will if you make a play to get back in."

Nate's heart gave a hard thump in his chest. It was deceitful and not how he operated, but for some strange reason, the thought of going back to Mississippi filled him with hope. For his family, his mother . . . Rachel. If only to see her one more time. Beg for her forgiveness.

"Okay," he said. "I'll be there in a couple of days. But we're going to do this my way."

"Whatever you need. It's yours. Just get back here as soon as you can."

## THE END

# Acknowledgments

This is always the hardest part. Especially when you work on a book as long as I've been working on this one. Many hands are helping, but names get forgotten or go unnoted. I hate that. But I'm going to do my best to remember all those who helped bring Nate Fisher to life.

First, I need to thank my agent, Nicole Resciniti, for pushing me to write Nate even when I wasn't sure I was up for a book that wasn't filled with rainbows and kittens. It's difficult to switch gears, and your support and reassurance mean the world to me.

Thank you to Faith at Crooked Lane for giving Nate a chance. And many thanks to Thai for all the edits and corrections. I know the manuscript needed a hand, so thank you for lending it to me. And thanks to Rebecca and the rest of the Art Department team for providing me with this kick-a$$ cover!

The next shout-outs go to Pat Heatherly from the Browning Funeral Home and to Kim Bedford, the Pontotoc County coroner. Your information on autopsy turnaround time was invaluable. Any mistakes are mine and mine alone.

To the Boondock Grill that sadly closed during the COVID epidemic: May you forever be immortalized here in the pages of

# Acknowledgments

this book. You still hold my heart for the best—absolute best— fried green tomatoes. I still dream about them. As I'm sure my bestie, Stacey Barbalace, still dreams about the caramel pie.

And speaking of Stacey . . . thank you so much for being there for me when we are standing in Richardson, Texas (just for the record, neither one of us lives in Texas), and I say something like, "Let's run over to Pontotoc, Mississippi. I've always wanted to check out the Amish community there." And you don't bat an eye before filling up the car.

Mississippi. Mississippi will always be my home even though I've lived more years in Oklahoma than I did there. I was born there and raised there and will always claim my southern citizenship. Thank you for being a great state to be from. And thank you for the perfect backdrop for Nate Fisher.

And mostly I have to thank my real-life Nate Fisher, my husband, Rob. Who has taught me so much about being a cop by just coming home every night. It's not all glamour and glitzy shoot-'em-ups like TV. It's real and gritty and uncomfortable. There are consequences for actions, and those consequences can be harsh. Thank you for sparking this idea. For loaning me your expertise and knowledge. Again, any mistakes are mine, since I had the best directing me. And for those times when you couldn't stop to direct me, thank you for not totally hitting the roof when I googled things that may or may not (ahem, most probably *will*) land me on the FBI watch list. You are the best. Simply the best.

And to you, dear reader . . . thank you for reading. Cheers!